A Dangerous Talent

BY CHARLOTTE AND AARON ELKINS

THOMAS & MERCER

PROLOGUE

August 7, 2010, Ghost Ranch, Abiquiu, New Mexico

"I assure you, I am not dead," Henry Merriam declared with considerable heat.

He listened to the response with growing incredulity. "Am I...?" He held the telephone out from his face, the better to shout directly into it. "Yes, I'm *quite* certain!"

Loudly enough for Barb, sorting mail at her post behind the reception desk, to overhear. She smiled. It was good to hear him sounding like his old self, feisty and animated. Mr. Merriam had been coming to the summer and fall education programs at Ghost Ranch for almost forty years now, predating all the employees, herself included, and all but one of the faculty. In Barb's nineteen years there he had signed up for just about everything on the schedule, from "New Mexico Railroad History" to "Playing the Hammered Dulcimer."

This week it was "Joyful Basketry," although he'd been anything but joyful since he'd had to place his wife, Ruth, in an Alzheimer's facility three years earlier. Since then his annual two-week stays here had been more on the order of lonely respites from the awfulness of everyday life, rather than of the joyful learning forays they'd once been. He'd gone from being one of the most engaging of the Ranch regulars, a bright, clear-eyed, courtly old gentleman, someone she looked forward to seeing every summer, to a walking ghost, just another depressed, lonely, stooped old guy who was there because he didn't know what else to do with himself.

So seeing him come to life like this on the telephone did her heart good. With no phones in the rooms, and cell reception around the ranch dicey at best, Barb was often privy to private conversations when attendees came in to use the pay phone on the wall. Indeed, she had heard more than a few extraordinary declarations.

But *"I am not dead"*? That took the cake.

"I believe I know what was and wasn't sold in my own gallery," he was saying, "and I can assure you that never once…I don't care what the catalog says, I…" He glanced at Barb and rolled his eyes. "I…of *course* it's important to me, what do you think? If you can't…all right then, I'll drive down there myself if I have to and straighten this out. How would that be? Yes, tomorrow, why not?…Very well, two thirty. Yes, yes, I know where to come."

Shaking his head, he replaced the phone. "Who would believe it?"

"Problem, Mr. Merriam?" Barb asked with a smile. "Anything I can help with?"

"Oh, nothing much, Barb. Just a little confusion. Is the coffee fresh?"

"It depends on what you mean by fresh, but help yourself if you want to take a chance," she said. "I couldn't help overhearing. Did you used to own an art gallery? I always thought you'd been a professor."

"Yes, I was," he said, taking a cardboard cup from the stack beside the pot and pouring it half full. "But before that, many years ago—*eons* ago, in a previous life—I did have a gallery in Albuquerque, yes." He paused, remembering. "The Galerie Xanadu," he added quietly.

"And?" Barb prompted as he absently stirred in Coffeemate.

He returned with a sigh to the present. "And this morning I get an e-mail from an old friend in the business—well, the son of an old friend, but he's in the business too—and he was considering purchasing a painting for a client in Dubai, and in looking at its history, he saw that it had passed through my gallery in the 1970s. So he wanted to know if I remembered enough about it to have an opinion on it. Well, I remembered nothing about it, so as you can imagine, that got me thoroughly riled up."

Barb was a bit confused. "Well, after all it was forty years ago," she said gently. "Nobody can be expected to—"

He scowled at her. "Kindly do not patronize me, young woman. I do not mean that I don't remember having it. On the contrary, I *do* remember *not* having it. Quite clearly."

She wasn't getting any less confused. "Umm…"

"In other words," he said more kindly, "I am certain that it never passed through my hands. I would not have forgotten it. Not *this* painting."

"So you mean…well, I'm not sure what you mean."

"I mean—" He grimaced. "You know, this coffee really is dreadful."

"I warned you."

He took another sip anyway. "I mean that I never had the painting, that's all, and I don't like somebody saying that I did. So I called to complain." He smiled a little. "Upon which I was told that I couldn't be me, because I'd been dead for some considerable time now. And—well, you heard the rest of it."

"Ah, I see. So you have to go to Albuquerque tomorrow to straighten it out?"

"No, just to Santa Fe. But it means I'll have to miss my afternoon workshop—it's the one on decorative oak handles, too." He sighed. "I've been looking forward to that."

"Oh, I bet Ms. Mayfarth could be convinced to fill you in on what you missed."

"Do you think so?" he said, brightening.

"I'm sure of it. I'll speak to her myself. Mr. Merriam? When you told them you weren't dead..."

He looked at her over the rim of his cup, white eyebrows raised inquiringly.

"Did they believe you?" she asked.

That got the first smile out of him that she'd seen in three years. "If not, they're certainly going to be surprised when I walk in the door tomorrow, aren't they?"

– • –

How strange it all was. In the old days, when Ruthie was still herself, he used to covet the opportunities to drive somewhere on his own, without an unending stream of directions, instructions, and alerts from the passenger seat. Now he was always on his own when he drove, and he hated it. What wouldn't he give to have her sitting beside him, informing him that the sign they'd just passed had said fifty-*five* miles an hour, not fifty-*seven*? Or that there was an old pickup truck in the upcoming roadside rest stop that she didn't like the look of, and couldn't he see that it might very well pull recklessly out in front of him?

As if responding to her, he took a harder look at the pickup. He was driving south on Highway 84, in the deserty country between Ghost Ranch and Abiquiu, one of the most remote and unfrequented stretches of road in America. It was a route he traveled twice a year, from the airport in Albuquerque, through Santa Fe, and up to Ghost Ranch, and then back again, and if he'd ever seen an automobile in this primitive stop in the middle of nowhere before—it was just barren old pavement with weeds coming up through the cracks, and a few rotting picnic tables—it didn't come to mind.

He slowed a bit, suddenly cautious, even a little nervous. If Ruthie had really been with him, he wouldn't have been driving at all—not at eighty-five years old, not after that second heart attack and the coronary bypass. But Dr. Bernstein had told him that he didn't have to quit altogether; he just had had to keep to moderate speeds and, on longer trips, take frequent breaks to get up and move about a little.

He considered pulling in at the rest stop himself and walking around his rented compact a few times, but the fact was, he didn't like the look of that pickup either. A hulking, old Ford 250, he thought—his brother-in-law, Walter, had once had one that he used for hauling firewood. This one was crudely painted with orange and blue flames, and with a kid wearing a turned-around baseball cap sitting behind the wheel. When he got closer he saw that the kid, a thin cigarillo jiggling in the corner of his mouth, was talking on a cell phone. At one point their eyes met and the kid gave him what Henry took to be a mocking, smart-alecky smile.

Henry didn't like that either and stepped a little harder on the gas pedal, taking the speedometer up to fifty-nine. He was glad to see the last of the truck when he rounded a curve and a red-rock escarpment blocked it out behind him. He was approaching the segment of the road that he liked least, a curving, constricted stretch of a mile or so, with a vertical wall of cliff not only pushing uncomfortably in on the left, but limiting vision as well, and on the right a sheer hundred-foot drop down to the winding Chama River, glinting lazily in the sunlight. He slowed again, back down all the way to forty. Every time he'd come this way, for thirty-three years now, he'd been telling himself he would get in touch with the state transportation department and recommend a reduced-speed sign. But of course he never had, and the area remained signless. Probably not enough people drove through here to give it any kind of priority, but then why would they? With nothing much other than Ghost Ranch itself between here and the Colorado—

Coming around one of the many curves, he saw another pickup coming toward him, a quarter of a mile down the road. No, not a pickup—the cab of a semi, a big one. He began to get edgy again. That thing was *wide*, and there wasn't much room to spare along here. He glanced nervously to his right, looking for a place to pull off, but there was nothing, only the cliff edge, alarmingly close. He slowed some more, and as he did he was surprised to see the oncoming vehicle drift over the center line to the wrong side of the road, heading right for him.

He pressed the horn, a long, loud warning. The truck responded, not by changing lanes, but with a shrill, angry blast of its air horn. It seemed to Henry, in fact, to be increasing its speed, and they were not much more than a hundred yards apart. What in the world was wrong with the driver? Was he drunk? Was this some kind of insane game? He considered braking, but it was too late for that. The truck was bearing down on him like a locked-in missile; it would sweep the Toyota off the road and over the edge as if it were a hay wagon. There was nothing else for him to do but to get out of its way and swing over to the wrong side himself.

He turned the wheel to the left and was stunned to run into the side of *another* truck—no, it was the pickup that he had seen at the rest stop. My God, where had it come from? He'd never seen it come up behind him. Instinctively, he continued to try to wrestle the steering wheel to the left, but the little compact was no match for the heavier, bigger pickup, which held its own, keeping perfect pace with him and nudging him toward the edge. His eyes were even with the truck's side door panel: a circle of flames surrounding a picture of a girl in a bikini—"Bimbi."

It swerved closer, grinding against the Toyota, nudging it toward the edge.

"Stop! What are you doing?" he screamed, with his heart hammering in his throat, in his temples. "Are you crazy?" The oncoming truck was fifty yards away now, with no chance of it stopping before colliding with him, and no way for it to shift lanes, not with the other pickup blocking it. Despite his struggling to hold the wheel, another sharp thrust from the pickup forced him still closer to the edge. It was hard to...he had to...

His mind jittered, recoiled, shrank away from him. He couldn't think...

"Ai!" A terrible band, like a belt pulled suddenly tight, squeezed his chest, crushed his ribs, collapsed his lungs. Trucks, road, river, all disappeared behind a film of red. He was aware of the tires leaving the road but continuing to spin, and he waited, straining, for the fall, but he never felt it. It seemed to him as if the car hung suspended, transfixed in space and time. The film of red turned black.

Ruthie, he thought.

CHAPTER 1

October 5, 2010, Seattle, Washington

The view from the fourteenth-story condominium in Seattle's tony Belltown neighborhood was enough to knock anybody's eye out: Puget Sound sparkling in the thin Northwestern sunlight, toylike green and white ferries gliding by each other on their way to and from Bainbridge Island, the distant Olympics with their glacier-topped peaks.

Alix London, sitting beside the window, was aware of none of this grand spectacle. Her eyes, her complete attention, every fiber of her being, were riveted on a four-inch-square segment of oil-painted canvas depicting the base of a garden wall. This was the one part of the ninety-five-year-old painting that had begun flaking and scaling. With a soft brush, she had just gingerly saturated the area with a mixture of beeswax and damar resin. Now, with infinite care, tongue peeping between her teeth, she was using a warmed palette knife to gently flatten each individual flake and re-adhere it to the canvas.

It was the trickiest part of the entire cleaning and restoring process, and far and away the most nerve-racking. This was, after all, not the usual sort of painting she was employed to work on—some muddy, "school-of" picture picked up at an "antiques" store under the Alaskan Way viaduct—but a well-documented painting from the White Period of the half-mad, alcoholic Impressionist painter Maurice Utrillo. Alix knew for a fact that Katryn, the condo's owner, had paid $185,000 for it at a Christie's auction.

With sweat running down her temples, she pressed the last tiny flake into place and let out a pent-up breath. Removing the strapped-on binocular magnifiers, she blinked a few times to clear the perspiration from her eyes and had a good look.

Perfect. Beautiful. Whew. She sat back, much relieved. The rest, compared to this, was going to be a snap. She had only to—

The telephone beside her burred. She picked it up, still studying the rustic village scene. "Hello?"

"Good morning, my dear," a sunny, English-accented voice purred, "a very good day to you. You're well, I hope?"

"I'm fine, Geoff," she said curtly. Pointedly, she did not inquire as to whether or not he was also well.

But he was used to this kind of reception from his daughter, and, as usual, he barreled right through it. "The latest issue of *Art News* should have been in the mail today. I was wondering if you'd yet had a chance to read it."

"No, Geoff, not yet." Why she couldn't bring herself to tell her father that she couldn't afford a subscription to *Art News* at $39.95 a year—not when she could walk over to the Seattle Art Museum's library and read it for free—was an ongoing mystery to her. Particularly inasmuch as her financial straits were the direct result of his screwing up her life so spectacularly.

"Well, prepare yourself for a shock, my dear. They didn't put me in the show—now what do you think of that?"

"The show?" Her mind was still on the Utrillo.

"Moreover, in my opinion, it was by no means an oversight. Helen excluded me on purpose. She never did care for me, you know." She heard the slightest of chuckles. "I can't think why."

"Uh...Helen?"

"Helen Hall-Duncan? Senior curator at the Bruce Museum? Greenwich, Connecticut?"

"Ummm..."

"Hello? Is anybody home there?"

"Sorry, Geoff. I was thinking about something else."

"The Bruce Museum," he repeated patiently. "We went there, you and I, when you were a nipper of nine. I took you to a charming show full of doggie paintings. You loved it. You remember."

No, she didn't remember, but then, Geoffrey London had dragged his little girl to so many museums that they were a blur. "Sort of," she said. She considered telling him she was busy and hanging up, but now she was curious. "So what did this Hall-Duncan do that ticked you off so much?"

"'Ticked off'? I? Not at all. I merely express righteous indignation—to which I am most assuredly entitled, as you will soon agree. You do recall that they have opened a new exhibit—*Fakes and Forgeries: The Art of Deception*?"

She did remember that he'd mentioned something about it a week or so before. "Uh-huh. And the problem is?" No, damn it, she realized, she'd missed one little flake of paint—no, an incipient flake. More of tiny blister, really, but it had to be dealt with before it did flake off. She was reluctant to flood the spot with any more of the resin solution, but maybe if she just re-warmed the knife—

"The problem *is*," he said, "they have none of my work! Nothing! I am not even mentioned. Can you believe it? My Constables were every bit as good as Keating's, were they not? My Rouaults were far better than Hebborn's. Yet their work is generously displayed, and I—I am not even *mentioned*? It's outrageous, positively criminal."

Alix closed her eyes and took a deep breath. How many people in this world, she wondered, had fathers who went around grousing—Geoff London had a twinkly, jovial way of doing it, but it was still grousing—because they didn't get their due respect as world-class forgers? And how in the world could he have retained all of his old verve after what had happened to him?

She shook her head, remembering how she'd assumed that, having been convicted of forgery, theft, and interstate fraud, he would emerge from his eight-year prison term a broken man, a shriveled shell of his former self. He had, after all, been a much-respected conservator and restorer on the New York art scene—for four years a senior curator at the Met, no less—and much in demand socially. His delightfully silky, English-accented voice, his sparkling, kindly brown eyes, his ruddy charm (an article in *The New Yorker* had once referred to him as "cuddly," one of the few times she'd seen him express real irritation), and his obvious pleasure in socializing had made him a sought-after guest at the cocktail parties, salons, and soirées of Manhattan's Upper East Side.

But when he got out of prison, or so she'd thought, he'd be just one more ex-con. He'd still be in demand, all right, but it would be by an army of wronged, extremely peeved art collectors with lawsuits under their arms.

"Do you want to know what I think is behind it?" Geoff was still at it. "It's simple, unadorned spite, no more, no less. Petty jealousy—"

She shook her head and sighed. Clearly, she'd underestimated him. Now, almost a year out of the federal medium-security facility at Lompoc, California, lawsuits settled, he'd apparently had the same idea she'd had about a new life out West and—was he trying to ruin her life again?—had shown up in Seattle himself, where he had used what little money he had left to buy a failing trading company somewhere in the city's grimy, freeway-slashed industrial section. Venezia, its name was, and it specialized in supplying hotels and restaurants with schlock-art imports, or so he said. What exactly he did there she didn't know and she didn't want to know, but it didn't strike her as a good sign that his employees all seemed to be old pals from his art-forging days. Ex-cons, mostly, just like him, although few ex-cons could manage Geoff London's effervescent, unfailingly upbeat personality and—she had to admit it—his essential likability.

"Yeah, well, you did annoy quite a few people in the art world, you know."

"Didn't I, though," he said quietly, and she knew he had that puckish, irresistible, inarguably charming smile on his face. She smiled herself, imagining it, and for a moment she wished she could see it in person. She had loved her father, loved him dearly. But now...

Time to change the subject. "Speaking of the art world," she said, unable to stop herself from showing off a little for him, "I have a meeting with a collector tonight. At a donor's reception at the museum. If all goes well, this could be the entrée I've been hoping for."

"Oh, yes? More cleaning, is it?" He had never put it in so many words, but she knew that he thought the cleaning of paintings was beneath her abilities.

"No, not cleaning. Advising. Consulting. She wants some help—some expert advice on a purchase—and somewhere or other she's heard that I'm the one for the job."

"Well, it's about time people started recognizing your eye," he said with fatherly pride. "You're a natural, my dear. I like to flatter myself by thinking it's in the genes."

He just might be right about that, she thought. She'd been living and breathing art as long as she could remember. As a teenager, she'd spent many an enchanted after-school hour (before she'd discovered boys) in the workrooms of the Met watching and eagerly learning from her father. That much, at any rate, she owed him.

"And what does this mysterious collector of yours collect?" he asked. "Not more Victorian shaving mugs, I trust."

That was as close to sarcasm as he ever came. He was referring to her previous consulting job. Little did he know that Victorian shaving mugs were a step up from the one before, which she'd gone out of her way not to mention to him. She'd been advising a client on aquarium furniture, the little ceramic knickknacks— overflowing treasure chests, and deep-sea divers that bubbled, and mermaids—that people put in their aquariums. Who knew there was even a name for them? Or that people actually collected them? She'd taken it on mainly because the client was a high-level Microsoft executive, and she was hopeful that he'd give her referrals to other dot-comers for something a little more along her line. She'd done a good job for him too, spending hours on the Internet and in libraries to get up to speed on the subject, although now she wondered how many of her valuable brain cells were filled up with the junk.

"No. Not quite," she said with a certain amount of pride of her own. "It's Georgia O'Keeffe she's interested in."

Indeed, he was impressed. "Oh, I say. Now there's an artist one can get one's teeth into. You'll tell me if you can use any help, won't you? Tiny is very much an O'Keeffe expert. He might well be able to give you a few words of advice."

Tiny (six-four, three-hundred-plus pounds) was one of Geoff's ex-con employees and almost as charming, in his own slow, good-natured way, as Geoff. He could have been a superb mixed-media artist—watercolors and pastels—in his own right. Unfortunately, he had liked creating Homers and Whistlers more. Which was why he was now an ex-con. When Alix had been a child he had been her "Uncle Beniamino," and although not really a relative, he had been the favorite by far of all her "uncles." But a lot of water had flowed under the bridge since then, and she was no longer a child.

"Thanks, Geoff, I'll keep him in mind. I've got to go now. Still need to do a little more work on this Utrillo."

"Utrillo, is it? Do you know, I remember knocking off a Utrillo in a day and a half that was as good as anything Utrillo ever did—better, if we're going to be honest. I could do an O'Keeffe too, when you come right down to it. Perhaps not in a day and a half, but give me the subject, and of course the period, and—"

"Bye, Geoff."

— • —

What to wear for the reception.

She chose the timeless, elegantly simple, basic black skirt-suit from Prada, with a slender chain-link necklace to set it off; the Givenchy lapelled jacket with its ivory-and-black floral jacquard weave and its subtly padded shoulders; and the gleaming Salvatore Ferragamo three-inch black slingbacks to add a little pizzazz.

The perfect getup for an occasion that was part business meeting, part glitzy cocktail reception.

Picking the outfit had taken all of two minutes. It was, in fact, the *only* outfit she had for part-business-part-glitzy-cocktail receptions. Or for business meetings in general. Or for cocktail receptions, glitzy or otherwise. Or for just about anything else that involved being seen in public. Alix's wardrobe might've been classic, but extensive it was not. It wasn't new either. Almost everything in it was from consignment sales at Le Frock Vintage Clothing, the secondhand shop in Capitol Hill's low-rent zone, practically under the I-5 freeway.

There had been a time, she thought dreamily, when her clothes had come straight from the designer showrooms. How long ago it seemed now, almost as if it had been someone else's life. How easily it had all come to her, how much she took it simply as her due to grow up on Manhattan's posh Upper East Side, to have a family box at the Metropolitan Opera, to spend the family summers in Rhode Island's elite and exclusive beach community of Watch Hill ("straight out of *The Great Gatsby*," her father liked to say, to the extreme annoyance of Alix's mother), to move effortlessly among the rich and the influential. But all that had come to a crashing end with Geoff's indictment. The family money had vanished down the bottomless rat hole of lawyer's fees and settlements, quickly becoming a distant memory. What a rude shock that had been. The only bright spot, if you could call it that, was that her mother's death two years earlier had spared her the scandal.

Alix had been in her senior year at Harvard at the time, and although the sixty thousand dollars left in her college fund had been untouched by the lawyers, she'd dropped out anyway and arranged to have the money, every cent of it, put aside for Geoff, the only provision being that he was not to know who or where it was from.

(His gratitude was not something she wanted weighing her down.) Instead, he was to be told it was the residue of his one-time assets. Quitting school had hurt, but he was still her father, and he would be almost seventy by the time he got out of Lompoc, disgraced and impoverished. The sixty thousand and its interest would at least give him something to help him last out his remaining years. It had, too; he'd used it to jump-start his new business.

She'd thought back then that perhaps she'd be able to return to Harvard at some point, but life, and the need to earn a living, had gotten in the way. The only—

She jerked her head. Enough. Water under the bridge, she told herself for the second time in two hours. It was the future she needed to be concerned with now.

And yet she couldn't stop thinking about Geoff. He hadn't had the nerve to actually appear on her doorstep yet, but he called regularly, blithely ignoring the chilly receptions he got and the obvious fact that she never called back. Clearly, it was going to take some kind of a scene, a face-to-face meeting, for him to get the message. It was a prospect that filled her with dread.

So, by his lights, apparently, he was doing fine—or, at least he did a very good imitation of someone who was. *Her* "career," on the other hand, and her life, for that matter, left a lot to be desired. But Alix, like her father, was not merely a survivor, but a survivor who persisted in looking on the bright side. Well, most of the time. Look at the way things were working out now for her, for example. Here she was, living in this absolutely fabulous Seattle condo. Signor Santullo, the wonderful old man she'd apprenticed with in Europe, had set it up for her from Rome, before she'd even left to return to the States: a year's stay in the place while Katryn was off in France, in Provence, in return for cleaning and restoring six paintings from her formidable Post-Impressionist collection. Was that lucky, or what? The work, hardly full-time, even allowed her to take on other jobs for her few expenses. And only today a wonderful new opportunity had presented itself—

She drew herself up. A final check in the full-length mirror, a brief touch at a stray tendril at her temple, a tug at her waistband to make sure it was straight, and it was time to go.

On with the show.

CHAPTER 2

The Seattle Art Museum, or SAM, as the locals called it, was one of Alix's regular haunts. Not being a donor, she had never been to a donor reception before, but she was a member (at the least expensive level), and with the building only a short walk from the condo, she was there a few times a week, either to use its library or to prowl happily through its collections. Yet in all this time there was one space, the main atrium, into which she would never have set foot if hadn't been necessary to go through it in order to reach the exhibits. Even then, she usually sailed through at warp speed, looking neither right nor left, and especially not up.

The reason for this was that to pass through it one had to walk under what was inarguably the most sensational installation in the museum. "Inopportune: Stage One," it was called, and although she didn't altogether understand the meaning, she thought it highly fitting. "Inopportune: Stage One" was a stomach-churning cascade of nine tumbling white Ford Tauruses—real, full-size Tauruses—suspended from the ceiling by scarily slender steel rods that didn't really seem up to the job, in her opinion. The cars "took off" from the Brotman Forum on one side of the atrium and "landed" in the South Hall on the other side. In between, they leapt and twisted and plunged across the ceiling, radiating sprays of colored lights that made them look as if they were exploding. Indeed, she had read that they were meant to suggest the progress of a single automobile in the process of being blown up, caught in nine separate cinematic frames. She had also read that their Chinese creator, Cai Guo-Qiang, had stated that the grim theme he had in mind was car bombings and terrorism, and how we all go placidly on with our lives despite them.

However, it wasn't the theme that had kept her from lingering in the atrium; art was a pretty eclectic business these days, and she was willing to allow room for tastes other than her own. No, it was simply the idea of standing any longer than she absolutely had to underneath a bunch of one-ton automobiles precariously dangling forty feet above her head, in a region of the country well known for its earthquakes. Alix wasn't a particularly fearful person, but the idea of earthquakes had her spooked. She was from New York State, and other than the rare, watered-down hurricane that came up from the south, the only climatic phenomena to worry about were the nor'easters that blew out of New England in the winter—the difference being that, unlike an earthquake, if you simply stayed indoors, a nor'easter wasn't going to kill you.

But now she was faced with a dilemma. On the one side was her unease about the cars; on the other was the fact that the buffet tables were set up directly underneath them. Also the fact that the buffet looked terrific. Also the fact that she was suddenly starving. Not to mention the additional little detail that her food budget for the week was in tatters—she'd been a little down in the dumps on Monday and had splurged on a Dungeness crab lunch.

As a result, dinner at home tonight would mean canned lentil soup and a grilled cheese sandwich.

So if she wanted some of those wonderful-looking salmon-stuffed endive leaves, or the cream-cheese-filled pea pods, or the teriyaki chicken satay, or—especially—the *brie en croute* (she could smell it from here!), she was just going to have to risk it. Either that or stay hungry.

The *brie en croute* won out. What the hell, you can't live forever, she told herself, and if nothing else came out of the evening, at least she'd have had something good to eat. She strode boldly up to the tables to begin filling a plate with two each of the delectable cheese puffs, vegetable spring rolls, and what she was fairly sure were spinach tartlets. As she was reaching for a napkin, someone spoke—bellowed—in her ear.

"I understand you're Alix London." A hand was stuck out toward her. "Well, hello, I'm Chris LeMay."

Alix turned to see a big, rawboned woman in her late thirties, with a dramatic black-and-yellow-striped shawl artfully draped over a turtlenecked black sweater, and her legs in flowing black slacks. Alix had seen her earlier, greeting friends or associates with gusto, slapping one man on the back so zestily that the olive he'd just popped in his mouth popped back out. Alix had noticed her not only because of the energy she radiated, but because she was the tallest woman in the room, a strapping six-two, and that was in flat heels. It hadn't occurred to her that this jovial, hearty, imposing person might be the Christine LeMay she was looking for because, on the Eastern art scene, collectors simply didn't look like that. They ran instead to painfully (some said fashionably) thin, languorous size fours, any two of whom could have fit into Chris's sixteen-plus with room to spare.

At five-nine, and wearing three-inch heels, Alix wasn't used to looking up at other women, but unless she wanted to climb up on the table, with Chris there was no way around it.

She set down the plate and shook the proffered hand, expecting to wince, but Chris took it easy on her. "I'm so glad to meet you, Chris. And thank you for getting me an invitation to this."

Chris brushed the thanks aside.

"Yum, what are those? Whatever they are, they look good." Her voice had an unusually throaty, husky quality—a honking quality if you wanted to be unkind—but it was oddly pleasant to listen to, as if there was a laugh bottled up inside just waiting for an excuse to come bubbling out. "Let me get a plate and load up, and then let's find someplace else to talk—" Chris's eyes rolled up toward the hanging cars, "—before we have an earthquake."

Alix grinned. She already liked the woman. "I'm glad to hear you say that. I thought it was just me. I'm from New York. I'm not used to the idea of earthquakes."

"If you ever find someone who's used to the idea of earthquakes, I'd like to meet him," Chris said, piling on the hors d'oeuvres. "Oh, look, is that champagne?" She had spotted a waiter sliding sideways between clumps of people, his tray of tulip glasses held aloft. With Alix trailing after her, she made directly for him and snared glasses for both of them. "Let's get ourselves one of those," she said, gesturing with her chin toward some small tables set along one wall. "I think they might be out of the range of falling vehicles."

They threaded their way through a noisy and still swelling crowd of mostly well-dressed people, many of whom obviously knew Chris and greeted her, but the last empty table was snatched up just before they reached it.

"Oh well, looks like we're going to have to juggle," Chris said. "Life is a bitch, ain't that the truth?" They found a marble windowsill to do duty as a sort of table, and Chris used a toothpick to spear a tartlet, popped it in her mouth with an eye-roll of pleasure, took a swallow of champagne, and looked directly at Alix. "So. You're Geoffrey London's daughter, right?"

Alix's throat went dry. Practically the first words out of this woman's mouth, and they were about—what else?—her father. Was he forever going to be an albatross around her neck, wherever she went, however remote from Manhattan? In this age of Google, of the instant and pervasive availability of information, the answer was probably yes.

"Yes, I am," she said, trying to show nothing, although she felt her lips compress and her jaw muscles harden.

But showing nothing was not her strong suit, and Chris was startled by the abrupt change. "Hey, did I say something wrong? I was only trying to...I just wanted to say...look, I'm not exactly famous for my diplomatic skills, and as usual I've started with my foot in my mouth. Whew." She paused for a breath. "Okay, let me start again. What I was trying to say was that you have some unusual baggage, yeah, but don't let that get in your way. You're in the Wild West now, kiddo, in Seattle, and it's not the way it is back east. Family names, family history—pooh, they don't count for much out here. What matters is what you can do, not who your father is or isn't." She laughed. "A good thing too, or with my screwed-up family, I'd be walking around this thing with a tray on my shoulder."

Alix felt her cheeks flush. "Thank you, Chris, I really appreciate that. I apologize for taking it the wrong way for a minute there. I...I guess I'm a little..."

"Oh, look," Chris said, "there's a free table, in the far corner, there. Let's snag it before someone else gets it. I'll run interference, you go straight for it."

With Chris's formidable body getting in the way of others with the same idea, they got there before anyone else. "Cheers," Chris said, lifting her glass as they settled into their seats.

"Cheers," Alix echoed, clinking glasses. But she set the glass down as soon as she'd taken the obligatory sip. "Look, Chris, I'm really sorry I was so—"

Chris waved a dismissive hand. "Oh, come on, there's no need to apologize."

"I appreciate that, but…it's weird." She shook her head. "It's been almost nine years since Geoff wrecked my life—his too—and I've come a long way on my own, and you'd think I could just shrug it off by now. A few people have said I ought to change my name, but that's something I don't want to do, you know? I'm kind of attached to it."

"Absolutely, and anyway, in the long run I don't think it would have done you any good, not since you're staying in the same line of work. We live in a new age, kiddo, and sooner or later you'd be hyperlinked, or field-searched, or whatever, and it would come out. Besides," she said with a sudden flash of warmth, "you're not the one who has anything to live down, he is."

She paused to elegantly down a cream-cheese-filled peapod, then inelegantly licked cheese off her fingertips. "You know, to be honest, I think I'm a little envious of you, having a father like that. If nothing else, at least he's interesting. My father was a building contractor." She jerked her head exasperatedly. "Oh, that's baloney. Why do I do that? My father was a plasterer, that's all, and not a very good one either, especially when he was off the wagon, which was ninety percent of the time." Another roll of the eyes, but not with pleasure. "See, you're not the only one with a reprobate father in the family closet."

Alix smiled. "Well, Geoff's interesting, all right. I can't argue with that."

"Believe me, I can understand how hard it must have been on you—it was all over the news. You would have had to be living on Mars not to hear about it. I mean, 'Prominent Metropolitan Museum Expert Accused of—'" She flinched. "Oops, there I go again. See what I mean? Mmff." She zipped her mouth shut with an imaginary zipper.

"No, really, it's okay," Alix said, laughing, "but on the other hand, I wouldn't mind changing the subject. How did you find me? Was it my ad in the Gallery Directory?"

"Uh-uh. One of my patrons—I own this little wine bar—is Christopher Norgren?" It was said in a way that implied Alix was supposed to know the name. Alix shook her head no.

"The Baroque and Renaissance guy here at the museum?"

Another shake of the head. "I don't know him."

"Well, he knows you, or at least he knows who you are. He said you were first-rate, that you'd studied for years with Fabrizio Santullo in Rome. Even I know you can't do any better than Santullo. And when I called him, he gave you a terrific recommendation."

"You actually spoke to Fabrizio?"

"Oh, yes, for a good ten minutes. He couldn't say enough good things about you. Your natural skills, your knowledge of techniques and media, your understanding of styles and modes—all extraordinary."

"Did he really say all those things?" Alix asked, pleased. "He was one pretty demanding taskmaster, not exactly lavish with his praise."

"Oh, the man's a pussycat. He also told me, by the way, in a tone of something like awe, that you have the best connoisseur's eye he's ever come across. I have no idea what the hell that means, exactly, but how could I not hire the person with the greatest connoisseur's eye Fabrizio Santullo ever saw?"

"Oh, 'connoisseur's eye' is just a term some people use for—"

"Never mind, explain it to me another time. What do you say we get down to business? First off, I'm delighted you're going to be working with me, Alix."

I am? thought Alix. *Does that mean I'm hired?* She hoped she was doing a good job covering up the excitement that ballooned in her chest, better than she'd done hiding her reaction at the mention of her father.

"I'd really like to get going on this as soon as we can," Chris went on. "Would it be imposing too much on you to ask if you can clear your schedule for a quick trip to Santa Fe this weekend? If not, I suppose we could—"

Alix almost laughed. What schedule would that be? Well, there was the work she was doing for Katryn, but taking a weekend break from it would probably be a good thing. Still, she pretended to mentally check her calendar a moment, all the while savoring the thought that she'd actually done it—she'd been hired. She was on her way. "No, I believe I can make it," she said, as if on sober reflection. "This weekend would be fine."

"And what are your fees?"

"My fees," Alix said and cleared her throat. "Well, my fees… of course, it depends on the, um—"

Chris saved her. "I'd be taking up two or three entire days of your time, and I realize that's unusual, so I was thinking…well, would a thousand dollars a day be acceptable? Plus all expenses, of course."

Alix had been gearing up her nerve to ask for five hundred dollars a day, which would have been fairly low for the field, but then she was hardly an experienced consultant with a lengthy list of client testimonials at her disposal. "Oh, no, that would be too generous, Chris. I'm just getting started. Five hundred would be fine."

"No, a thousand dollars is what I allowed for, and a thousand it'll be."

"Well...say seven-fifty. That's more than generous."

"Absolutely not. Eight-fifty, no less. After all—"

They both sputtered into laughter at the same time. "I don't think this is the way they teach you how to bargain in negotiating classes," Alix said.

"The hell with it, screw the negotiations. A thousand a day, take it or leave it."

Alix surrendered with a smile. "I'll take it."

Chris leaned forward, elbows on the table. "Now that that's settled, let me fill you in on what's going on. I have this friend, Liz Coane, who owns an art gallery in Santa Fe. Unlike me, who didn't know a Picasso from a pizza pie five years ago, Liz has always been into art. Well, we used to work at the same tech company, Sytex, and she was always talking about how, if she ever got enough money together, she was going to open a gallery in Santa Fe or Taos or someplace like that and become a big kahuna in the art scene down there. She also planned to buy herself a string of boy toys to comfort her in her old age. Rent them, I guess I mean," she said with her wild-goose honk of a laugh.

"And did she?"

"Did she ever. When Sytex went public and our options matured, that's just what we made—a lot of money. I mean, a *lot*. And three months later Liz opened the Blue Coyote Gallery, right on Canyon Road, which is where all the too-too trendy Santa Fe galleries are, as I'm sure you know."

"Oh, I know, all right. I'm really looking forward to seeing it for myself."

"And she really has become a big kahuna," Chris said a little wonderingly. "She's the power behind this New Directions in Art Conference they have in Taos every year now. Draws artists and dealers from all over. Very highly regarded."

"Impressive. How about the boy toys?"

"Oh, yeah, she's working hard at that too. Every time I see her, she's got some new young 'artist' hanging around her. They're always the same type, too. They all look like James Dean wannabes—you know, dark, sulky, edgy, a little dangerous..."

"Not my type," Alix said, although she had yet to figure out what her type was.

"Mine neither!" Chris said with conviction. "I like grown-ups. I also prefer them more civilized. Some of the sleazy types Liz hangs out with…But what the heck, live and let live. What do I know about men?"

She appeared to give this question a few moments' wry consideration, then gave it up with a shrug and continued. "Anyway, a couple of years ago when I suddenly had all this money, but I had yet to come up with a purpose in life, I opened a little wine bar in Belltown with the idea in mind that it would be a discreet, arty kind of place for grown-ups—you know, one where the music is actually music, and you don't have to yell to be heard over it, and you can have a nice, quiet conversation over a good glass of wine. It's called Sangiovese. That's the name of a—"

"Red wine variety from Tuscany," Alix said, and regretted it as soon as it popped out. She didn't even know why she'd said it; probably only to remind Chris that she was not unworldly, but it had come across, even to her own ears, as boastful and know-it-all.

If it bothered Chris, she didn't show it. "Right. Of course. I forgot you spent all that time in Italy. In any case, have you heard of the place?"

"I think I have," Alix said. "Wasn't there an article about it in the *Weekly* a little while back? One of those places where aspiring artists would kill to get their works on the walls?"

"Well, I do have rotating exhibits, yes, and I try to put some interesting things up, and I guess that the artists I've had up there so far have been pretty pleased with the sales they generated. The customers seem to like them too."

"You know, I live in Belltown myself, not that far away, and I keep meaning to stop in, but..." But with the prices she'd heard about, she couldn't see blowing the cost of a couple of dinners on one glass of wine and some finger food. "Well, you know," she finished lamely.

"I'd love to have you come by, Alix. Believe me, I'm not kidding myself that I actually know good art from bad. I'm really looking forward to learning from you."

"I'm sure you know more than you think. If you didn't, your shows wouldn't be so popular."

"Well, I've been lucky," Chris said, "but I do know enough to know that this Cody Mack Burley character, Liz's latest protégé—for want of a better term—isn't the kind of painter I want in a show of mine. She talked me into giving him one on the basis of three e-mailed pictures of his work that looked pretty interesting. I said yes—she's an old buddy, after all, and so I guess the poor guy worked his tail off and did some fifteen pieces, and Liz sent them to me. Well, they weren't anything like the e-mailed ones, and I just didn't like them. At all," she added for emphasis.

"Not very well done?" Alix asked.

"Well, no, I don't really know how well done they were or weren't, but they were, well, ugly. You know, ugly on purpose—weird, twisted women, sort of turned inside-out, with their insides showing." She shivered. "Yech."

"So you didn't show them?"

"No, I packed them right back up—didn't even look at them all—and sent them back the same day; I didn't even want them around. Liz didn't say much about it—after all, what could she say? It was my place we were talking about—but I knew I'd hurt her feelings, and I was looking for some way to make it up to her. And then I remembered that the Blue Coyote sold the occasional Georgia O'Keeffe, and as it happened, I'd been thinking about buying somebody like that to put my collection—I mean my own collection, my private collection—on its feet. So I asked her to keep an eye out for me, and when something came on the market that she thought I'd like, to let me know. And…well, here we are. She called me last week to tell me that one was available, sent me some nice photos, and was I interested?"

"And of course you were," Alix said.

"Well, sure." For a moment she looked uncertain. "Um… shouldn't I be?"

"Absolutely. Your friend Liz might not be seeing this Cody Mack person clearly," she said, "but she's certainly not steering you wrong on Georgia O'Keeffe. If it's American Modernism you're interested in, almost any work of hers would be a fantastic addition to your collection—to anyone's collection. You couldn't get it off the ground with anyone better."

"Really." Chris brightened. Her face smoothed. "See? I'm already glad I hired you."

"Do you know where she's gotten this particular one from? Who the seller is?"

"No, Liz can't tell me. It's some kind of family heirloom—they've had it for decades—but now they've had some financial problems and they need the money. But they don't want the word to get around."

Alix's antennae popped up and vibrated. This was but a minor variation on the time-honored theme used by crooked art dealers for at least two centuries: *An old Italian family, a noble family whose name you would recognize, has owned this painting for many years. Alas, they have come upon evil times, and with heavy hearts, they must now let it go. Their name, however, must remain secret. The disgrace. You understand.*

Chris detected the change in Alix's expression. Her brow contracted again. "Is that a problem?"

"Not necessarily," Alix said, truthfully enough. She didn't see any reason to worry Chris now, but she didn't like the sound of this. O'Keeffe's works had begotten their share of forgers, and the more that was known—and reasonably verifiable—about this particular painting, the happier Alix was going to be. At the same time, there was certainly nothing necessarily problematic about hiding the name of the seller. It happened fairly often, particularly at auctions. But it was something to keep in mind, especially if other doubts arose. "How much is she asking for it?" she said.

"Two point nine million. I—" Abruptly, she broke off with a snort, which was probably Chris's version of a giggle. "I can't believe I just said that. Did you hear the way I tossed it off?" She mimicked an elegant yawn, tapping her fingertips against her mouth. "Two point nine mil, ho-hum, no big deal."

"It is a lot of money," Alix agreed.

"You're telling me. Believe me, I'm having a hell of a time getting used to having that kind of dough to throw around."

"Well, everybody's got problems. I'm sure you're doing your best."

Chris grinned. "You better believe it. Anyway, I talked with the curator of modern here at the museum, and she looked at the photos, and she said that from the looks of it, the price was in the ballpark—on the low side, in fact. So I paid it."

"You paid it? You've already bought it? Then what good am I—"

"Well, no, not exactly paid, but I did buy it. I put down a pretty hefty deposit, too. But there's an escape clause in the contract. I have ten days to come to Santa Fe and look at it. If I then decide I don't want it, the purchase is canceled."

"And when is the ten days up?"

"Next Wednesday. That's why I'm kind of in a hurry to get there. Anyway, after I put down the deposit I started thinking, *What do I know? I need somebody who knows what she's doing, an expert.* Which is you."

"Do you mean your friend Liz doesn't know I'm coming?"

"Well, no, how could she? Until today I didn't know it myself. But I'll call her before the weekend. Don't worry about it; she'll be expecting you." Again, that look of uncertainty on Chris's face. "Did I make a mistake? Am I paying too much? Dammit, I knew I should have checked with you first, but you see, I didn't know you yet, and I was so excited, and I was afraid somebody else would come along and offer her more, and—did I do something dumb?"

"Well, it does sound like a pretty good price for an O'Keeffe, but of course it depends on what it looks like in the flesh. But if Liz is an old friend, I can't see her gouging you on it."

"I have the photos," Chris said, reaching for her bag, but Alix stopped her.

"No. Don't want to see them."

"You don't?" Chris's hand was still in the bag.

"Nope, the fewer preconceived notions the better. I'll wait until the real thing." She smiled. "Part of this 'connoisseur's eye' thing."

"Whatever you say. As you can plainly see, I have no idea what I'm doing, and I'm a little nervous about it all."

Alix began to say something reassuring, but Chris perked up on her own. "Now, I don't know about you," she said, zipping the bag shut, "but I could use one more chicken satay—well, maybe two—this is turning into dinner, isn't it? But then it always does. I have no self-discipline whatever—and then let's go say hello to Tony Whitehead, the museum director over there. And after that I want to introduce you to a few of my fellow babe-in-the-woods collectors that I think would be real interested in meeting you, and vice-versa. Okay?"

"Okay is the understatement of the year," Alix said, grinning. "I really appreciate it, Chris."

Following Chris through the crowd, Alix wasn't able to wipe the smile off her face. There was a tremendous, exhilarating sense of a corner having been turned.

Life was good.

— • —

By the time she got back to the condo, she was hungry again, and after slipping into the baggy, comfortable sweats that she slept in these days, she padded into the kitchen, opened the can of lentil soup, poured some into a mug, and stuck it in the microwave.

While it heated, she went to look at the answering machine in the living room and felt a little gray cloud of gloom settle over her at seeing it sitting there unblinking. She frowned, puzzled, her hand on the phone. Why the gloom? From whom had she expected a call? Who did she even know, aside from Chris, whose call she would have welcomed? Who did she even know, period?

Her buoyant mood punctured, she returned to the kitchen, where she stood at the counter and slowly drank the soup from the mug. Was she lonely? Was that what her problem was? It made sense. Once, eons ago (actually, it had been nine years ago, just after Geoff's conviction), she'd briefly been married. It had been a disaster that, coupled with her father's disgrace, had just about flattened her. She'd crawled into her shell for months, feeling oh so sorry for herself, and avoiding people, even friends. Then, living in Italy, there had been a language barrier for the year or so it took her to become fluent. And somewhere along the line, she'd turned into a loner without really thinking about it. At twenty-nine.

She'd been in Seattle almost eight months now. When was the last time she'd had a date or what passed nowadays for a date? When was the last time she'd sat with a friend for a gossip over a glass of wine at someplace like Chris's wine bar? How many people did she know that she could honestly call friends? Answers: a) two months ago, b) never, c) none.

At ten o'clock, subdued and even melancholy—how strange, how unreasonable one's moods could be—she went to bed.

— • —

For a change, she'd remembered to set the Mr. Coffee before going to sleep, so she awoke to the welcoming smell of it, refreshed and back in good spirits. It was foggy outside—she couldn't see more than halfway across Puget Sound—but who cared? Today was a new day, with plenty to do. Last night's blahs, so unlike her, had been nothing more than the inevitable adrenaline crash following the exciting events of the day; she realized that now.

She went and poured herself a cup of the coffee and brought it back to bed. There, sitting with a pillow propped behind her, she sipped the fragrant black brew and gave herself over to reliving the delicious events of the previous evening and the prospects that lay ahead. She would spend the morning at SAM's library boning up on O'Keeffe and bringing herself up to date on Santa Fe's art scene. She'd have lunch in the museum cafeteria to save time, then go back up to the library—

The telephone was in her hand before she'd quite realized that she'd heard it ring. "Hello?"

The jolly, chuckly voice exploded in her ear. "Good morning, my love—"

She winced. Her father. When was she going to remember to get caller ID, so that she could head him off?

"Hello, Geoff," she mumbled, sagging back against the pillow.

"My dear, I'm calling to ask how things went last night with your O'Keeffe collector. Did they go well?"

"They went fine." She could feel the irritation building up, tightening the muscles at the back of her neck. How did he always manage to call her at just the right time—the wrong time—to put a damper on her spirits?

"You got the job?"

"Yes."

"O'Keeffe?"

"Yes. Look, Geoff, I have to—"

"I was telling Tiny about it, my dear, and he has a few words of caution for you. He's standing right here. Tiny—"

"No, I'd rather not speak with him."

A momentary pause. "Of course not, if you don't want to."

She heard Tiny's slow, hurt voice in the background: "She don't wanna talk to me?"

Her heart wrenched. It was the first time she'd heard "Uncle Beniamino's" voice in well over a decade. A big—well, huge—lovable lug of a guy who seemed—well, was—not terrifically brain-endowed, he was an extraordinary craftsman who could imitate just about anything. For her fourteenth birthday he had made for her a beautiful oval wall mirror set in a painted wooden panel decorated with wonderfully done cherubs cavorting among the clouds. The whole thing looked like something from the background of a sixteenth-century Florentine portrait. Considering his huge hands with their sausage fingers, it had been amazing. It had been the one possession she'd kept when she'd sold everything, clothes and all, and gone to Italy to study with Santullo.

"No, I don't," she said through clenched teeth. "I have to go, Geoff." She hung up.

She was seething. How like Geoff to manage to make her feel guilty about Tiny. What did she owe Tiny? So he'd been nice to her when she was a kid, big deal. He was a crook and a cheat, just as Geoff was a crook and a cheat and a parasitic leech. All those times he'd been to their apartment in Manhattan, along with her father's other "friends"? They'd probably been planning the next time they were going to rip off some defenseless, widowed old lady who'd been left her husband's collection and was in over her head.

And yet she did feel guilty, damn it. Why should *she* feel guilty? Why didn't her father feel guilty? Besides, if he was so interested, so tenderly concerned with her welfare, how come he'd waited until this morning to ask how her meeting had gone? She'd finally shared something of herself with him yesterday—the biggest thing in her life right now—and despite all that "interest," he hadn't even bothered to call, not until this morning. What stopped him from calling last night? If he cared so much, why hadn't there been a message from him waiting on the answering—

Wait a minute, this is ridiculous. I'm mad at him when he calls me, and I'm mad at him because he doesn't call me? What kind of sense does that make? It's almost as if...as if—

When the unwelcome thought finally cracked through the stone wall she'd put up to keep it out, she couldn't believe it, she refused to believe it. And yet, deep inside, she knew it was so.

The voice she'd longed to hear on the answering machine last night, the voice anxiously wanting to know how things had gone with Chris, how things were going with her life in general—it had been her father's. But why would she...how would she...

With the wall breached, other thoughts, unwelcome and unsolicited, thoughts that had been lying in wait a long time, poured through in a rush. Why, really, had she dropped out of Harvard? Had giving the money to Geoff truly made it impossible for her to continue? With her top-notch grades, couldn't she have approached the school for a scholarship or even a loan, and finished up and then gone on to a graduate degree? She'd be an associate professor at some good university by now, someone with a steady income and a nice social life. Instead, she was a broke, pitiful, almost-thirty-year-old living in someone else's condo and scrabbling like mad to break into a tough, dicey profession. If you could call "art advising" a profession.

Was Geoff honestly to blame for that? Would he even have accepted that money if he'd known it was her college fund? Well, she already knew the answer to that; she'd known from the beginning. Why else would she have gone to the trouble of making sure he didn't know?

There'd been plenty of other crossroads and decision points along the way that had brought her to where she was now, and Geoff hadn't had a thing to do with any of them. They were all hers. On the other hand, it had sure as hell been Geoff's doing—Geoff's greed and selfishness—that had derailed her life in the first place. If he hadn't—

She jerked her head. Why was she going through all this right now? She'd had nine long years to think it through, to work it out. Instead, she'd just licked her wounds and blamed her father for them. Was she on her way to becoming one of those sad-sack forty- or fifty-year-olds who go around laying all their faults and failures at the feet of their unloving, or overloving, or underloving parents?

She shook her head again and sighed. One thing was for sure—she had some long overdue head-straightening to do.

CHAPTER 3

The man was tall, lean, good-looking, evenly tanned. In his midthirties. A little sharklike, but that might simply be because of those wraparound aviator sunglasses and the casually arrogant way he lounged in his chair. He had caught Liz Coane's attention the minute he'd walked in, and she'd been watching him ever since—discreetly, of course, out of the corner of her eye so he wouldn't notice. He was rich, too, but not show-off rich, just comfortable-with-himself rich. Liz, with her keen and knowledgeable eye for fashion, could tell that just from his clothes. His shoes were buttery Gucci loafers—seven hundred dollars a pair—and his sport coat was a beautiful, soft, mocha-colored cashmere, straight out of Brioni's fall catalog, that had to have set him back a cool three thousand. But he wore them in an unfussy way, with a plain, open-collared white shirt and a pair of faded denims (designer jeans, to be sure, but genuinely faded, the old-fashioned way, not from being acid-washed but from long wear). His short, dark hair had not been cut in a corner barbershop. You couldn't get a crisply mowed, beautifully layered Caesar cut in any corner barbershop she'd ever heard of. Two hundred bucks, minimum.

He definitely wasn't her type, this guy—too smooth, too polished. She liked them with rougher edges. But he was definitely... interesting. He practically smelled of money aching to be made. And if there was one thing Liz Coane was in dire need of at the moment, even more than usual, it was money.

He sat several tables away with Doris Goudge of all people, the empty-headed old lady who had the kitschy Avanti Gallery on Gallisteo Street, and they were deep in a discussion about art. Not that she was close enough to hear what they were talking about, but what else could it be? This was Santacafé, after all, and it was Friday afternoon, and it was damn near an immutable law that if any serious art-related business was happening on a sunny Friday afternoon in Santa Fe, the tree-shaded, adobe-walled dining patio of Santacafé was where it was going down.

Every table was occupied, and at each one were two or three people—dealers, collectors, artists both established and trying to break in—all with their heads together, doing art business: selling, buying, promoting, conning. Hell, if you were just some poor schmuck tourist who'd read about the food and the genteel, 150-year-old ambience of the place and wandered in for a decent lunch on a Friday afternoon, you were out of luck. Because the business of art came first in Santa Fe. It was the lifeblood of the city. As American cities went, Santa Fe was tiny—508th in population, according to the last census—but it comprised the third largest art market in the country. Third! Only in New York and LA did more art-related money change hands.

Everybody in the restaurant knew everybody else, of course, or almost everybody else, but Liz hadn't seen the guy with the shades before. She could make a pretty good guess as to who he was, though, and she was eager to find out if she was right. She took another sip of her margarita and put it down. "Cody Mack, do you happen to know who that is?" she asked her table companion. "Over there, talking to Doris?"

Still chewing at his chicken enchilada, Cody Mack turned around in his chair.

Liz rolled her eyes. "For Christ's sake, don't be so obvious."

"No, I don't know who he is," Cody Mack said. And then, mumpishly: "What do you care, anyway?"

Oh God, do I see a snit coming on? Liz thought. *Is Boy Wonder actually jealous?*

The Boy Wonder in question was Cody Mack Burley, Liz's latest protégé in a rather too-long line of boy wonders and protégés—or rather, Liz's latest soon-to-be *ex*-protégé. Barely so-so as an artist, but vigorous if not overly sensitive or imaginative in the sack, he and Liz had been an item for six months now, and inasmuch as six months was about par for the course, he was about to be dumped. The truth of it was, he'd already been dumped; he just didn't know it because she hadn't gotten around to facing the final, inevitable, boring scene when he would learn to his astonishment that even a gorgeous body, a honeyed, suggestive Mississippi accent, and a goatlike randiness could outwear their welcome if they didn't go with brains, or talent, or personality, or character. In Cody Mack's case, even one of them would have helped.

Perceptiveness was another trait that he was missing. Liz had had something going with his replacement for over two weeks now, and Cody Mack had yet to notice a thing. Even what should have been the telling fact that Gregor Gorzynski, the brooding, intellectual, heartstoppingly handsome young Polish artist was having an opening at the Blue Coyote tonight had failed to penetrate Cody Mack's bland self-regard. Of course Gregor wasn't really much of an artist either; in fact, you had to stretch things to call him an artist at all. A self-proclaimed "post-minimalist constructionist," he worked exclusively in toothpicks, M&M's, string, noodles, and superglue. As far as Liz was concerned, the stuff belonged in a garbage can, but then garbage sold quite well these days, so who was she to criticize?

"Don't worry about it," she told Cody Mack, "he's not my type. And don't," she couldn't help adding, "chew with your goddamn mouth open." This is what came, she thought wearily, of going around with twenty-four-year-olds. When was she going to learn? (At least Gregor was all of twenty-seven.)

Cody Mack put on his sulking face. "I wasn't chewin' with my mouth open."

Yes, you were, Liz thought tiredly, *but the hell with it.*

He continued to scowl at her. How was it she'd never noticed before how much he looked like those pictures of glowering, dumb Neanderthals when he sulked. That heavy brow, that mean, fleshy mouth—

"And don't think I don't know that margarita you got there is a double."

"What the hell business is it of yours what I—" she began, then clamped her mouth shut and glanced around. Nobody was looking at them. Good. There was a scene in the offing, all right, but this wasn't the place to have it. *This is your last free lunch on me, buddy boy,* she thought. *Your final meal. I'm moving on to greener pastures.* What had possessed her to take up with him in the first place? Whoever heard of an artist named Cody Mack, for Christ's sake? Whoever heard of an artist from Mississippi?

At the other table, she saw that the stranger had gotten up and gone inside. "Stay here," she told Cody Mack. "I'll be right back."

"Well, what am I supposed to—"

"Just sit there and wait. And shut up. And close your mouth when you chew."

Cody Mack reddened and flung down his fork. "Hey, I don't take orders from you. You're not my f—"

"Oh, stuff it, will you? For Christ's sake."

She worked her way around the original old Spanish well, now restored and prettily roofed, that was the patio's centerpiece, and through the crowd, exchanging nods and smiles and seemingly delighted hellos with people at almost every step. When she reached Doris's table she sat down.

Doris glanced up from her apple tart dessert. "Oh, hello, Liz. Sorry, I've got company. He just went outside to take a call on his cell phone. All this thick adobe interferes with the reception."

"I know, Doris. I'll only stay a minute. I just wanted to ask you who your friend was."

"He's not really my friend. I just met him yesterday. He stopped by the shop. He's a dealer from Boston. Name's Roland de Beauvais. He goes by Rollie, though," she added with an unattractive simper.

"Roland de Beauvais," repeated Liz. "Ooh-la-la. Is he French?"

"No, just French ancestry. He's very, very Boston." *Bahston*, she said, to emphasize the point. "He's only been here a day or two." While she spoke, Doris noisily and energetically stuffed her face with tart. Liz had to look away. *Jesus, am I the only one in Santa Fe who chews with her mouth closed?* "Gary Selway sent him over to me, but I'm not sure I can help him."

"Yes, I'd heard there was a back-East dealer checking things out. What's he looking for?"

"American Moderns."

"American Moderns?" Liz repeated, her eyebrows going up. This was better than she'd hoped. "I'm getting a Chadwick on consignment this week, and I'm pretty sure I can get my hands on a couple more. Marsden Hartley too. Maybe even—" She hesitated, not wanting to lay it on too thick. On the other hand, this was Doris Goudge she was talking to. Subtlety would be a mistake. "And maybe even a Georgia O'Keeffe or two," she finished.

"Well, that's certainly more than I can do," Doris said resignedly, then looked up with a mildly avid gleam in her eye. "Would you like me to refer him to you?"

"Does he understand what stuff like that costs?"

"Oh, yes. He's quite knowledgeable. Plus, I get the impression that money is not a problem."

"Well then, you bet I'd like you to refer him to me." It was *exactly* what she'd like. She smiled her most winning, grateful smile. Now that Doris had finished the tart it was possible to look at her again.

Doris hesitated. "Er, standard arrangement? Five percent on anything he buys from you?"

Liz's eyes narrowed. "I don't do the standard arrangement, Doris," she said coldly. "Two percent."

"But…but everybody does—"

"But I don't. Now, of course I can contact him directly myself, although I prefer not doing that. But if that's what you—"

"No, no," Doris said hurriedly. "Two percent is fine. I mean, if that's your usual commission."

Liz smiled. "Thank you, Doris," she said warmly. "I appreciate that."

"I'll see what I can do. Liz—" She paused, troubled, seemingly of two minds, then decided to go ahead. "I should mention, though…well, I'd be careful around him. I think…well, I think he might be...bent, you know? I wouldn't want you to wind up in any trouble."

"Bent! Why would you say that?" This was getting more appealing by the minute.

Doris shrugged. "It's nothing he said or did, it's just a feeling." She looked over her shoulder to make sure he wasn't on his way back. "There's something...sharp about him."

Liz leaned forward, frowning. "Sharp?"

"In the sense of *unethical*. I don't think he gives much of a hoot where the paintings come from or how they got here."

"He actually said that?"

"No, it's more what he didn't say. Never a word about wanting to see provenances, never a word about catalog or sales records... you know. It just seemed odd to me." Again she hunched her shoulders. "But it's more than that. I don't know, he just seems a little *off* to me. Too smooth, maybe. Slick, sure of himself. You'll see. Anyway, I thought I ought to warn you. Of course, you're probably a better judge of character than I am."

You got that right, sweetie, Liz thought, *and the more I hear about this particular character the better I like him.* Rollie de Beauvais sounded like somebody she could do business with. "Thanks, Doris, I'll watch my ass. And I really appreciate this. I'd better get back to my table now."

At the table she found Cody gone, having left behind a plate of congealing enchilada sauce and the unpaid bill, turned over so she could read the message on the back, scrawled in capitals: SCREW YOU.

Charming.

— • —

The tall man in the Brioni jacket and the Gucci loafers was not really out on the street taking a phone call. There had been a call, all right, but he had muttered a quick "Call you back in a minute" into the phone and flipped it shut as he entered the building. Then, instead of continuing through to Washington Avenue, he had stopped beside the bar, where he could look back at the patio unobserved, through the glass panes of a French door. The female bartender had approached but had been turned away with a smile and a shake of the head. He had taken off his aviator sunglasses, revealing eyes of a clear, piercing blue—surprising eyes, considering his dark hair. At the moment, those eyes were fixed on the table he had just left, at which he surreptitiously scrutinized Liz Coane with as much interest as she had surreptitiously (so she thought) been scrutinizing him.

The woman made an interesting study: at forty-two (he knew her age; he knew quite a lot about her), she was developing a blowsy look—incipient jowls, vanishing jawline, brown roots visible in her too-blonde, too-youngishly spiky hair. She dressed, however, as if she'd just stepped off a page in a glossy magazine devoted to the Santa Fe look. She wore beautifully tailored denim slacks that flared out below the knee. Elegant embroidery designs ran down the outsides of the pants legs and were duplicated on the short, cropped jacket—a sort of charro look, he thought, and it didn't look bad on her. A soft white silk blouse with a plunging neckline set off a heavy Navajo turquoise and silver necklace. The neckline, he thought, was a little much; she was getting a bit bosomy for that. All in all, though, he had to say that she was pretty well put together and had once probably been beautiful. She looked intelligent too. He liked that. He was pleased. This was going to be a good one.

He slipped on the sunglasses again and stepped out into the street, into the shade of the veranda that ran the length of the block. There he leaned his back against the restaurant's adobe wall and flipped open the cell phone. He pressed the speed-dial button. The telephone dutifully whirred out the number and rang it: 202-324-3447.

202 was the area code for Washington DC.

322-3447 was the number for 935 Pennsylvania Avenue, NW. The J. Edgar Hoover Building.

Headquarters of the Federal Bureau of Investigation.

— • —

His name was not Roland de Beauvais, he was not of French ancestry, and he was not a dealer in art. He was originally from Boston; that much was true, and that was about all that was true. His name was Ted Ellesworth, and he was a member of a small, elite unit of the FBI formally designated as the Art Crime Team, but generally known as the Art Squad, which consisted of thirteen special agents, three trial attorneys, and one operations specialist. Ted was a special agent, one of only two who specialized in undercover work. The person whose call he was returning was the invaluable Jamie Wozniak, the unit's operations specialist, who provided "investigative support," an all-purpose term that didn't come close to describing the computer skills, information-ferreting abilities, and cut-through-the-bureaucracy savvy that she brought to the squad.

He looked up and down the street. No one within earshot. Good. He was more than ready to ditch the laid-on Boston baked bean accent for a while. "Jamie, hi, what's up?"

"So how's it going?" she asked in response. "Connected with the subject yet?"

"Just about. Unless I'm mistaken, Ms. Coane is in the process of establishing contact with me, even as we speak. I'd be surprised if I don't hear from her tomorrow. Maybe even this afternoon."

"Gee, what took you so long? You've been there over a day."

"Must be the altitude. I'm dragging a little."

"Seriously, it's going smoothly?"

"Going perfectly."

Indeed, it was. Liz Coane was the focus of an investigation into a scam entailing the sale of extremely expensive art forgeries to Asian and Middle Eastern buyers. Since the Blue Coyote Gallery was the main conduit for the paintings, Liz was necessarily right at the heart of it. What was not known for certain, however, was whether she herself was criminally involved, or merely a dupe in the chain between forger and buyer. Ted suspected it was the former, and one of the things he was here in Santa Fe for, in the person of the elegant, slimy Roland de Beauvais, was to find out for sure, one way or another.

In this kind of operation, it was essential that the "subject" think she had made contact with him of her own volition. His first day in the city, he had stopped in at several galleries—not the Blue Coyote—to let word percolate through the art community that there was a new man in town, a player with money to spend and, not to put too fine a point on it, a man not overburdened with ethical concerns. On information from Jamie (how did she find out about these things?), he had arranged a lunch with Doris at *the* place to see and be seen on a Friday afternoon if you were anybody who was anybody in the Santa Fe art crowd. And it had worked beautifully. Liz Coane had obviously heard about him— the art world grapevine almost matched the speed of the prison grapevine—and he had barely reached his seat before he saw her checking him out.

"Tell me, though," he said, "why were you calling? Anything new?"

"Oh, yes indeedy," she said enthusiastically. "You remember Geoffrey London, don't you?"

"How could I forget? He was what started me in this very bizarre line of work. But that was before your time."

It was nine years ago, in fact. He had been an agent for less than a year then, operating out of the New York office, specializing in corporate fraud and white-collar crime. The Washington-based art squad had requested the help of an agent who was familiar with the New York art gallery scene. Ted was the closest thing they had, inasmuch as he had some considerable knowledge of art. His father had established Ellesworth Fine Art and Antiques on Boston's Newbury Street in 1962 and had owned it until 2004. Ted had worked there for three years while attending Boston University. These qualifications had been more than enough for the art squad, and they had snapped him up for a temporary undercover assignment. He'd had a relatively minor role in the London affair, but he'd loved the fascinating world it opened to him. When he'd learned of a vacancy on the squad two years later, he'd applied. And there he'd been ever since. Married to the job, as his mother sometimes grumbled about her handsome son's failure to find a permanent mate (or to look very hard for one).

"Okay, well, did you know he's been out of prison for a while now?"

"Nope."

"And that he has a daughter?"

"Nope."

"And that the daughter has been away studying 'restoration' in Europe with some of the best?"

"Ah, following in Daddy's footsteps, you think? Preparing for a life of crime?"

"The thought has crossed my mind," Jamie said. "And did you know that said daughter is on her way—by private jet, I might add—to Santa Fe?"

"Jamie," he said patiently, "if I didn't know there was a daughter in the first place, how could I know where she's heading?"

"What an old grouch you are. I'm just trying to enhance the narrative tension here, add a little spice to your life."

"Well, you've succeeded. I'm very tense."

"Excellent. Now, would you like to know the reason she is speeding to Santa Fe at this very moment?"

"I would, but could *you* kind of speed it up a little? I need to be getting back."

"Oh, all right. The reason she is speeding to Santa Fe at this very moment is that she is now an 'art consultant'—don't ask me what that means—and she is headed there to, quote-unquote, 'authenticate' a supposed Georgia O'Keeffe painting that has seemingly materialized out of nowhere—no provenance, no record, no—"

"Well, that's interesting, I guess, but I don't think—"

"Not as interesting as which gallery is involved with this. Care to hazard a guess?"

"Ah-ha. The Blue Coyote?"

"Bingo."

"Now you *have* gotten my interest," he said. "Who will she be working for? Liz Coane herself? Or is it a potential buyer that's brought her on?"

"That I don't know. There is a potential buyer, but I don't know who it is."

"You don't *know*? Jamie, I'm shocked."

"What can I say? I'm not perfect—yet. Don't worry about it, I'll find out, but at this point I would assume it's the buyer she's working for. Why would Ms. Coane want to pay to bring somebody out from Seattle, let alone in a private jet? Santa Fe has got to be crawling with art experts."

"Yes, but is it crawling with *bent* art experts?" Ted mused. "Is it possible that Liz has got a little something prearranged with her? You have to wonder: aside from the cost of bringing someone from Seattle, why would anyone in their right mind—dealer or buyer—go out of their way to hire Geoffrey London's daughter, of all people, unless there was something fishy going on?"

"Good question. Beats me. This is getting pretty deep."

"What's the daughter's name, Jamie? I assume she doesn't use London anymore."

"But she does. Her name's Alix London."

"Alix London," Ted echoed. "I'll make a note. And you see what else you can dig up."

CHAPTER 4

The day couldn't have started off better. Chris had her driver swing by Alix's condo so that the two of them could ride out to Boeing Field together, where Chris's gleaming, white private jet—well, her one-sixteenth fractional share Gulfstream 200—was waiting for them. For whatever reason, the two of them were feeling lighthearted and chatty, and the result was an uproarious, hilarious drive to the airport. The interior of the plane brought a soft "Wow" from Alix: all gleaming, polished mahogany and buttery black leather. But the minute they seated themselves everything changed. The pilot, Craig Something, came from the cockpit to introduce himself and welcome them aboard. Alix liked him on sight. He was tall, clean-cut, and sandy-haired, with a crisp, neat mustache to match, and soft brown eyes. If she wasn't mistaken, those eyes widened in surprise when he saw Chris and then almost immediately lit up—but Chris's reaction was as different as different could be. One look at him and she turned to stone.

"Oh no," she muttered, probably to herself, but it was obvious that Craig heard her and saw her rigid reaction. The bashful, appealingly eager smile he'd come in with froze in place, and in a monotone, looking mostly at the ceiling, he rattled off boilerplate information about emergency exits, life jackets, seat belts, restroom, and the coffee, snacks, and drinks that were there for them in the storage cabinet.

"What in the world was that about?" Alix asked as he returned to the cockpit. "Isn't he a good pilot?"

"He's a jerk," Chris muttered. "An idiot, a chump, a total nitwit."

"Oh, well, that's reassuring," Alix said. "For a minute there, I was worried about flying with him."

But Chris, so sociable and voluble until then, was no longer in the mood for joking. She quickly made it clear that she didn't welcome the opportunity to talk about whatever was bothering her, and for the duration of the flight she was about as communicative as an oyster.

Thus, the flight that Alix had been looking forward to—a leisurely, comfortable three hours to continue to get to know Chris better—was a total dud, both boring and tense. Interminable. When the wheels finally touched down on the tarmac at Santa Fe's little municipal airport, she breathed a sigh of relief, but things failed to improve even then.

Waiting for them in the terminal was a flushed, slack-faced Liz Coane (was she tipsy? It was barely two p.m.), who grandly announced that she had canceled the car and driver that Chris had arranged and was personally driving them to their hotel. And when Liz set eyes on the pilot, she yelped with surprise, threw her arms around him, and kissed him wetly on (and in) the mouth. The flabbergasted Craig reacted about the way he would have if he'd been tongued by a warthog: with an instinctive, grimacing recoil that arched him backward. Alix had the impression it was all he could do to keep from wiping the back of his hand across his lips.

But Liz was oblivious. "And you're going to need a ride into town, too, Craig." She looked fondly from Chris to Craig and back again and grinned happily. Yes, she'd had one or two, all right, Alix thought. "Imagine that, the three of us back together again, here in Santa Fe. This'll be great. The good old days all over again."

"Which good old days are those?" Craig said coldly. "And if that was a lift you were offering me, thanks but no thanks. I've got to take care of the plane and get the paperwork in." He turned his back on her and headed for the terminal.

Chris was more polite, but only marginally. "It wasn't necessary for you to meet us. The car I hired would have been perfectly satisfactory."

"Gee, doesn't anyone love me anymore?" Liz asked. "I thought I was doing everybody a favor."

"Well, it's not that we don't appreciate it, Liz," Chris said, defrosting just a little. "It was a nice thought." She sighed. "Okay, thanks, where are you parked?"

Alix almost spoke up. The idea of being driven by the not-strictly-sober Liz was not a happy one, but the atmosphere being what it was, she let it go. Anyway, Liz had made it from town to the airport; chances were good she could make it safely back again.

Liz's reaction to their less-than-joyous greeting had been delayed, but by the time they got to her car she had clearly come to the conclusion that her feelings had been hurt. The result was a drive, mercifully only twenty minutes long, that was as bad as the flight: Liz concentrated glumly on her driving and Chris stared fixedly out the window.

Alix simply sat quietly in the back seat, as far away as she could manage to get from the toxic stew of whatever history was behind the uncomfortable Chris-Craig-Liz relationships. Whatever had happened between them, whatever problems they had, she wasn't about to let herself be drawn in. She was there to do a job, for which she was being well paid, and that was exactly what she would do, and all she would do. If what had seemed until this morning to be a budding new friendship panned out, that would be wonderful. If not, that was okay too. She had more than enough baggage of her own without volunteering to deal with other people's.

Only at the end of the drive was there a slight thaw, when Liz reasonably affably said she was looking forward to seeing them at her gallery that evening for an interesting opening. It was the American debut of a brilliant young Polish artist, Gregor Gorzynski, who was going to stand the art world on its ear. "My protégé."

"Sure, that'd be nice," Chris said, warming yet a little more.

"Alix?" Liz asked.

"Absolutely, I'm looking forward to it. Will we be able to see the O'Keeffe then, or don't you have it at the gallery?"

"No, I've got it at the gallery, all right. I got it out of the vault for you this morning. Look, why don't you stop by before the reception—four thirty, say? I'll have it out for you in my office and you can feast your eyes. I'll put out some champagne too—the good stuff, not the crap I'll have out for the opening." She smiled at Chris. "We can toast old times."

That brought back the chill. "Liz, I think we'd better go in and register now."

Liz shrugged and grinned. "See you later, guys."

"I just hope she doesn't kill anybody on the way back," Chris said to Alix as they headed for reception. "She's a few sheets to the wind."

"I thought so too. Was she a boozer back in the old days?"

"If she was, she sure knew how to hide it better," Chris said, and then, a little more charitably: "I don't think she's very happy."

— • —

The Hacienda Encantada, although in the heart of Santa Fe, only a few blocks from the plaza, had eight lush, beautifully planted acres to itself, with lodgings both in the main building—a two-story, Hollywood-inspired "Indian Pueblo"—and in individual adobe casitas laid out along the curving paths that meandered through the grounds. Alix's spirits lifted. The place was beautiful, and so was what little she'd seen so far of Santa Fe, although the high desert air was chillier than she'd expected.

"It's nice to have you with us again, Ms. LeMay," said the smiling young woman behind the desk (Caitlin, according to her brass nameplate). "Let's see," she said, clicking away at her keyboard and checking the computer screen. "We have you in the Desert Canyon Suite here in the main building. Ms. London, we have you in the Roadrunner Casita, one of our nicest."

"But didn't I reserve adjoining suites?" Chris asked.

"Um…no…" Caitlin said doubtfully. "It says here—"

"Oh, it doesn't matter," Alix said. "A casita will be fine." Better than fine. The air was still pulsating with…something, and she was only too glad for the chance to get away on her own for a while. And Chris looked as if she could use a little decompression time herself.

"Well, all right," Chris said. "I guess it doesn't matter." She looked at her watch. "Two fifteen. Canyon Drive is less than ten minutes from here. Shall we meet here in the lobby at four fifteen? We can walk, if you're up to it."

"Absolutely. I could stand to stretch my legs." But on second thought, two hours of solitary decompression might be more than was good for either of them. "Wait, what do you say we meet at three instead? The Georgia O'Keeffe Museum should be right around the corner—"

"It is," said Caitlin. "Well, a couple of blocks."

"Great. What do you say we spend a little time there before we go look at your painting, Chris?"

"I'd like that, yes."

Caitlin plinked the bell on the desk, and in about two seconds a couple of bellmen materialized, one of them loading Chris's bags (she'd brought three) onto a cart, and the other, younger one taking Alix's single soft-sided suitcase outside and stowing it into the back of a pink golf cart with a fringed awning to match.

"Climb in, I'll drive you there. Easy to get lost if you haven't been here before."

He was a chubby, friendly, rosy-cheeked kid (Tommy, his nameplate said) who looked as if he'd be more at home riding a tractor on a farm in Indiana than a gussied-up golf cart in Santa Fe. Clearly, he enjoyed zipping around in the cart, but as soon as he noticed that she was shivering, he let up on the accelerator.

"It's the elevation. Everybody thinks we're, you know, warm, like Phoenix, but we're not. We're seven thousand feet here," he said with pride. "It can get a lot colder than this. Where are you from?"

"Me?" Not such an easy question, she thought, and took the simplest way out. "Seattle." As good an answer as any.

"They get a lot of rain there," Tommy said sagely.

"That they do," she agreed.

At the casita he hopped out. "I'm gonna get the fireplace going. Get you toasty in no time."

She followed him into the room, immediately liking the place: curving adobe walls, exposed viga-wood ceiling beams, an arched, kiva-type propane fireplace, Southwestern furnishings... Midway across the red tile floor, she stopped, her brow wrinkling. "Wait. Do you smell something?"

Kneeling at the fireplace, poised to turn the switch to light the gas, he lifted his pug nose and sniffed. "Like something died?"

"Like rotten eggs," she declared. "Let's get out of here. That smells like a propane leak. We need to go back to reception."

"Naw," he said, "can't be that." His hand was still extended toward the switch. "Propane don't have any smell. I know because—"

"Tommy, stop! Don't light that damn thing!" she yelled. "Let's go!"

He blinked and retracted his hand. "Yes ma'am. Um...you don't want me to put your bag in the room?"

Her answer was a vigorous, two-handed tug at his collar that jerked him to his feet. "Let's *go*! Now!"

Back in the cart on their return to reception, calmer now and wondering if she'd overreacted, she said, "I'm sure it's nothing, Tommy. It's just, while you're right, propane doesn't have any smell—that's exactly why they add an odorant to it, so you can tell when there's a leak. When I lived in Italy, they used these awful little propane tanks they called *bombalas*, which was a good name for them, because if you weren't careful—"

A millisecond before she heard the tremendous explosion, she felt a sudden blast of heat on the back of her neck. Before she could make sense of it, the sound came, a huge detonation—no, a rapid series of detonations, like a string of Chinese firecrackers, only deeper, bigger, immensely more powerful.

Stunned, Tommy stomped on the brake and they both spun around. They were in time to see the pieces—she recognized fragments of the wooden ceiling beams—on their way back down. The casita itself was a mass of sooty flames that spouted like geysers, windows broken out, door tumbling to the grass ten yards away, the roof, as far as they could tell, completely gone.

"Holy mackerel," Tommy said wanly. "If you didn't...if you hadn't...we coulda been...we woulda been..."

"Yes, killed," she said grimly. "Dead."

He nodded dumbly, staring at the flaming, steaming, hissing ruin. "As a frigging doornail," he said wonderingly.

– • –

Cognac in the middle of the afternoon was hardly an everyday event, but then neither was coming that close to being as dead as a frigging doornail. It was with deep pleasure that Alix took her second long swallow and felt the welcome heat of it slide soothingly down to her stomach.

"Nice to be alive," she said.

Chris, indulging in a gin and tonic, nodded approvingly. "See, I told you a drink would do you good. It's not doing me any harm either." She shook her head, lowering her voice another notch. "What a day, and it's not over yet."

Alix smiled, taking another sip. "Well, I've had enough excitement to last me for the rest of the day, thank you very much, so I hope we have a nice, extremely boring evening."

The hullabaloo after the explosion had been tumultuous but reassuring. Sirens, firemen, efficient, concerned staff response—even someone noticing her shivering and bringing a beautiful, warm serape that she was able to wrap three times around her shoulders—all helped to calm her nerves and bring her heartbeat back to normal. Add to that Chris's near-motherly solicitousness, and Alix willingly gave way to the luxury of being cosseted. After so many year of aloneness—largely self-inflicted, of course—it felt surprisingly good to let herself be taken care of.

She had been reassigned to a room in the main building ("There will be no charge for your stay, of course, madam"), her bag had been carried up to it, their drinks had been provided gratis, and Chris had let her talk herself out about it all. Now they sat in amiable silence in the Hacienda's otherwise empty Cottonwood Bar, sprawled in comfortable armchairs next to the fireplace—a real snapping, crackling, log-burning one, not propane, thank God—sipping their drinks and luxuriating in the pleasure of the world righting itself.

"Alix..." Chris said; it was the first time Alix had heard anything like hesitation or uncertainty in her voice. "...I owe you an apology. I was rotten company on the way over here today, and I wouldn't want you to think it had anything to do with you."

"I didn't think that, Chris."

"It's just that..." She was rotating her glass between her fingers and staring down at it. "It was just...oh, damn it, just that..."

Alix hesitated as well. It wasn't much more than an hour ago that she'd lectured herself about steering clear of other people's problems, but now things were different. She was alive when she might so nearly have been dead, and Chris was quickly beginning to seem like a friend, a real friend...

She took a breath and dived in. "Just that you and that pilot, Craig, had something going once upon a time," she said. "And Liz was in the middle of it somehow. Or maybe Craig and Liz had something, and you were in the middle of it. Some kind of triangle, anyway. Is that pretty close?"

Chris burst out laughing. "Was I that transparent?"

Alix smiled. "I'm afraid so. So which way was it?" She had another slug of brandy. "If you want to talk about it, that is."

"I do," Chris said. She swallowed the last of her drink and held up her glass to the bartender to signal that she wanted a refill. "Light on the gin this time," she called. "And could we get some chips or something?"

Chris settled back in her chair and turned to Alix. "You were right the first time. Craig and I were an item, but it was an odd situation. I was actually his boss for a while."

"That must have been a little uncomfortable." Alix gave the bartender a negative wave of her hand when he inquired with a lift of his eyebrows whether she wanted another drink.

"A little, but not as much as you might think. It was only for a couple of months. See, with the project management approach Sytex had, the lines of authority were always changing. Besides, it was a pretty laid back company, and they didn't care very much— at all, really—about personal relationships between employees, even bosses and subordinates, as long as you were professional at the office. Considering we were all working crazy hours, seven days a week, it made sense. Who had time for anyone outside the company? Oh, and I was also Liz's boss at the time, as it happens."

"The plot thickens," Alix observed.

"Just a little. Thank you," she said to the bartender, who had placed a fresh gin and tonic on the side table between their chairs, along with a sectioned tray of potato chips and nuts. Chris chomped on a handful of the nuts and took a swallow of her drink, chewing away and studying Alix over the rim of the glass. "You were studying in Europe, weren't you, during the tech bubble?"

Alix nodded. "Yes. Oh, I'd hear things about new tech companies, IPOs, stock options—the Italians were pretty big players, as well—but it'd go in one ear and out the other. I still don't even know what an IPO is. It just had no relevance to me. I bet it was exciting, though, to be in the middle of it."

"It was really something. Sytex was just one of a whole lot of start-ups then, but we all felt that we were part of something that was going to be big, and that made it tremendously exciting. It's impossible to describe the climate; everything was possible. Anyway, Craig and I weren't engaged or anything—we were all too busy to think about stopping long enough to get married— but everybody understood that we were together, or so I thought until one Saturday when the three of us and a few others were working on a big presentation over the weekend. I left at about five, but on the drive home I realized that Liz had some material I needed to review before a Monday morning meeting. So, okay, I walk into her office and—"

At the memory, the corners of her mouth turned down. "And I find the two of them…oh, Christ…I find them…screwing on the carpet, right on the floor, like a couple of goddamn animals in heat."

"Oh no."

"Oh yes," Chris muttered.

"What did you do?"

She laughed bleakly. "The same thing you would have done. I turned around and walked out. I was mortified."

"Of course. I meant—"

"I know what you meant," Chris said in a low monotone.

"Chris, there's no need for you to talk about it if you don't want to. I'm sorry if I—"

But Chris barreled grimly ahead. "Naturally, I was as mad as hell at both of them, but Liz came to me later that afternoon, as contrite as a little mouse: she hadn't meant for it to happen, they'd never done it before, but Craig had been giving her signs for weeks—an 'accidental' touch here, a little-too-long handshake there, lingering glances that were unmistakable—and in a weak moment—he was awfully attractive, after all—her hormones had taken over and she just plain gave in to him." Chris shrugged. "She was in tears, she felt horrible, she'd never have done anything like that to me if she'd been in her right mind, or if Craig hadn't been so persistent, and on and on. She begged me to forgive her."

"And?"

"And I forgave her." Another weary shrug. "We were old friends—I'd known her a lot longer than Craig—we'd done so many things together. Craig...Craig was a different story."

He had told her he was sorry, yes, and he'd seemed to mean it. But that was it. No defense, no denial of what Liz had said, no explanation other than that he'd made a bad mistake and it wouldn't happen again. He said that if Chris preferred not to be around him, he'd quit Sytex and move on. All she had to do was say the word.

"So I said it," Chris said softly. "I was terribly hurt; I couldn't believe he'd let me down that way. I never wanted to see him again. And I guess part of it was that I wanted to make him pay. I was really angry." She smiled. "Boy, did I make him pay. Eight months after he left, the company went public, Liz and I wound up making a fortune, and Craig was just one more unemployed techie. When the tech bubble burst a few months later, he was one more *unemployable* techie."

An image of Craig's open, likeable face flashed through Alix's mind. It was hard to picture him rolling around on the floor with the frowzy, silly woman who had met them at the airport. But of course, Liz wouldn't have been frowzy then. Still…

"Ouch," was all she said.

"Ouch is right. Liz and I came away with millions. Craig, after all the work he put in, came away with zilch. Truthfully, I feel kind of bad about that."

"Well, he's not exactly poverty-stricken. Being a pilot for ShareJet surely isn't minimum-wage."

"No." A pause, and once again Alix picked up a sense of hesitation. "He doesn't know it," she said, her eyes lowered, "but I'm responsible for him getting that job."

"How do you mean?" *This plot keeps thickening*, Alix thought.

"Well, I'd worked with one of the execs at ShareJet, and I knew that Craig had been an amateur pilot, but without enough flying hours to commercially fly people solo, so I convinced my pal to let him copilot while he worked on getting his commercial license. Of course, Craig never knew my fine hand was involved. Then, if they thought he was working out, they'd hire him for solo flights. He did, and they did. You look confused."

"I am, a little. If you never wanted to see him again, how come you use ShareJet and not some other company?"

"Because we used them at Sytex and I just stuck with them afterward. There's supposed to be an understanding that he's never to be my pilot. I don't know what went wrong; he never was before. Aren't you going to have any of these chips? They're delicious—thick-cut."

Alix shook her head. "My stomach's still a little fluttery. But about Craig—you mean today was the first time you'd seen him since...since the thing with Liz?"

She nodded. "You can imagine how I felt, with him suddenly walking in out of the blue, after so long. The last person in the world I ever wanted to see again. It just threw me for a loop. I just...oh, hell." She looked down at her glass and grimaced. "What a mess."

Why, you're still in love with him, Alix thought.

"I've been going over and over it all day," Chris said tiredly. "Did I blow it back then? Was I too quick to take Liz at her word, too unforgiving, too quick to dump Craig?"

"Could be," Alix said. "People have weak moments. People do make mistakes."

Chris thought about it, then shook her head. "No, this was more than a mistake. The lingering glances he was giving her, the 'accidental' touching...that went on for weeks."

"According to Liz."

Chris peered at her. "What are you saying?"

"I'm saying that's Liz's story. She's the one you heard it from, not Craig. Maybe it's not the whole story. Or maybe it was the other way around. Maybe she was chasing him."

"And that's supposed to make a difference—who was chasing whom?"

"Well, sure. Wasn't that your basis for keeping Liz as a friend and dumping Craig?"

"I didn't dump him," Chris began, then shrugged. "Well, yes, okay, I guess I did," she said uncertainly. She was silent for a moment. "To be honest, I think I did have my doubts about Liz. Even in those days, there was something about her that...But it's all moot, Alix. I gave him a chance to defend himself, to explain, to blame it on Liz if that's the way it was. Deep down I was praying that he would—but he didn't. Why not?"

"You're right, I am just speculating here, but couldn't it be because he was trying to do the gentlemanly thing? That he felt he should take responsibility for his actions? That shifting the blame to Liz wouldn't have been—I don't know—gallant?"

Chris laughed her seal-bark of a laugh. "Gallant! Now there's a word you don't hear very much these days." Slowly, she sobered. "But you know," she said wistfully, "I suppose he actually is the kind of guy to whom something like that would matter."

"There you are then."

"I am? Where? And how come, by the way, you're taking Craig's side in this and not Liz's?"

"I'm not taking anybody's—"

"Yes, you are."

"Okay, I suppose I am."

"Well, why?"

"Because—" But she didn't feel she could very well say that it was mostly because she liked Craig on sight and disliked and distrusted Liz from the moment she saw her. "Because I saw the way he looked at you when he first came out of the cockpit."

"How did he look at me?"

"Like he was excited to see you. Maybe a little nervous, a little uncertain, but eager and happy. For about one second, anyway. But during that second, let's just say I sure got the impression that if you wanted to be friends again, he wouldn't take much convincing."

Chris was genuinely surprised. "Are you kidding me? He just rattled off a canned speech—here's the exit, there's the toilet—and stumped back into the cockpit."

"True, but that was only after you started muttering and doing your clam imitation."

Chris frowned, considering. "Alix, is that really the way it was? It's not the way I remember it."

"That's the way it was, Chris."

"Oh God," Chris sighed and sagged back in her chair. "My brain is numb. I'm going to have to sleep on all this. But as for right this minute, I'd a lot rather go and look at my O'Keeffe than sit around stewing. Are you still in the mood for a walk?"

Alix was out of her chair before the question was finished. "Desperately," she said.

CHAPTER 5

"'Roland de Beauvais, Fine Art Acquisitions, Boston,'" Liz read aloud from the embossed, linen-textured card that Michael, one of her two assistants, had placed on her desk. Below that a telephone number. That was it. Expensive linen stock but simple black font, no logo. Understated but classy. She laid the card on her desk, unable to resist a smile of satisfaction. It hadn't taken long for the fish to jump for the bait. She'd figured he wouldn't show until tomorrow.

"I told him you had a show opening in less than an hour," Michael told her, "and an appointment before then, and he said if this was an inconvenient time, he could come back tomorrow."

"No, no, don't you let him get away. You go and bring him in right now," Liz said, putting down her half-empty champagne glass. She wasn't about to let him swim off and wind up on the end of someone else's line. Besides, the timing couldn't be better. She'd just this minute set up Chris's O'Keeffe on an easel, and it would be bound to impress the hell out of him. She shifted its position a little, moving it off to the side, so it wouldn't seem as if she were trying to impress him, but that it just happened to be there, an everyday sort of thing for the Blue Coyote. Ho-hum.

She neatened her desk, gulped the rest of the champagne, put the glass and bottle in the refrigerator, did a quick check in the mirror, dabbed unsuccessfully at a couple of stray, stubborn tendrils with a moistened finger, cleaned up her blurry lipstick line with the same finger, and managed to get back behind her desk just as her office door opened again, and in he came.

He was still wearing his shades, but he'd changed clothes. At the Santacafé it had been cashmere sport coat, white shirt, and jeans—casual and outdoorsy. Now, with evening coming on, it was still smart and casual, but just a touch more formal: blue blazer, mauve, open-throated silk dress shirt with French cuffs— the gold cuff links peeped out from his jacket sleeve—and gray slacks. The brown Guccis had been replaced by tasseled black Guccis. This, she thought, more or less licking her chops, was one very cool guy...one very *rich* guy.

"I won't take much of your time," he said. Unfortunately, what came out of his mouth was a bred-in-the-bone Boston Brahmin accent, effete, fussy, and oozing with self-regard. Christ, he sounded like Thurston Howell III, the millionaire character on *Gilligan's Island*. "I happened to be speaking with Ms. Goudge this afternoon, and she happened to mention that you might be able to help me find a picture or two that one of my clients would be interested in." He finished with a quick, flashing smile that could be interpreted a whole lot of ways.

This guy was not only cool and rich, Liz thought, but just as slick as he looked. The way he'd twice used "happened" in that little speech he'd just made—"I *happened* to be speaking with Ms. Goudge" and "she *happened* to mention"—laying an almost imperceptible emphasis on the word both times—it was meant to sound perfectly straightforward if Liz was inclined to take it that way, but to let her know, if her antennae were up and working, that he knew perfectly well that she had arranged with Doris to steer him to her, and it didn't bother him a bit.

Not everybody could bring off something like that, she thought admiringly. Here, after all, was a bent dealer who was pretending to be a straight arrow…but managing to send signals at the same time that he was *only* pretending, that he knew what was up and that he could play it whatever way she chose to go. Damn tricky work, and he'd done it like the pro he obviously was. She sensed—and her instinct for this sort of thing was rarely wrong—that they were going to be able to get along just fine, the annoying accent notwithstanding.

"Would you care for a glass of champagne, Mr. de Beauvais?" she asked. "I was about to open a bottle. I sometimes have a little before a show opening. After all, why should the guests have all the fun?"

"I would, yes," Ted said. "Rather." *I would, yaass. Raahthah.*

"I hope you like Moët and Chandon?"

"If Dom Perignon is unavailable," he said, and they both laughed.

— • —

She was somewhere between tipsy and totally snockered, he had determined, and that had made it easier to get down to business in a hurry. They had circled around each other for a few minutes to establish the rules of engagement. Ted had explained that he represented several extremely wealthy foreign clients, all of whom preferred that their names not be revealed. They were interested in American Modernists, he had told her, specifically in Marsden

Hartley, Arthur Dove, and Georgia O'Keeffe. Liz, taking her turn, had told him that she might, just might, know where to locate a few pictures that would suit their needs, and at attractive prices too. However, there might conceivably be a few "issues"—minor issues, inconsequential issues—with their provenances; that is, with the record of their creation and their ownership through the years, and with their guarantees of authenticity. Was that going to be a problem?

Problem? Not at all, Ted said; he had never been much of a believer in provenances or guarantees of authenticity anyway. Too easy to fake, and besides, a knowledgeable person didn't need paperwork to determine if a painting was what it was purported to be. One relied on one's experience and one's "aahtistic intwition"; didn't she agree? Oh, yes, Liz said earnestly, she agreed one hundred percent, couldn't agree more.

"Now that O'Keeffe on the easel there," Ted said. "Would it be too much to hope that it hasn't been spoken for?"

"O'Keeffe?" Liz said, her eyebrows going up. She looked over her shoulder. "Oh, that one. I'd forgotten it was there. Yes, isn't it wonderful, Mr. de Beauvais?"

"Rollie."

"Rollie. But I'm afraid it's been sold. It's only recently come to light, you know, so it's, um, unrecorded as of yet."

"How interesting."

"Yes, interesting." There was a not-uncomfortable silence while the several possible connotations of "interesting" hung in the air. "It's one of several, actually," she continued, "a suite; all from early in her Abiquiu period, but never sold at the time. Possibly, the entire suite was given away as a gift—some gift, huh? Maybe she didn't feel they were up to her standards. Although that's hard to believe. Isn't it beautiful?"

"Yes, very beautiful," Ted agreed, truthfully enough. "So... these others of which you speak—would they happen to be for sale as well?"

"I think I could arrange that, yes. Of course, I'm being quite choosy as to whom I'm letting in on this. Only my friends..." she lifted her lipstick-stained glass to him and smiled, "...and those I trust implicitly. Discretion here is a must. If word were to get around that a dozen new O'Keeffes were out there, I don't have to tell you what would happen to prices. Supply and demand. You understand."

"Of course I understand." He touched his glass to hers. "Your friends, and those you trust implicitly. I do hope you include me in at least one of those groups, if not now, then soon."

She swallowed the rest of her champagne and pursed her lips together. "We shall see what we shall see," she said with a secret little giggle, slurring the words a bit. She was edging closer to totally snockered.

"Liz, can you give me a ballpark idea—say I were interested in acquiring four, or perhaps five of them—what you would be asking?"

He could practically see the dollar signs dancing on her eyeballs, the way they do in comic strips. Her voice turned husky. "Well, that would depend." She reached for the bottle and poured them both some more champagne. "Now then," she said, with an openly conspiratorial smile, "what would you be offering?"

CHAPTER 6

Canyon Road. Eons ago, it had been a dusty Indian trail linking the pueblos of the Rio Grande and the Pecos. Later, each in their turn, came the armies of Spain, of Mexico, of the American Confederacy. Then, once the town had settled down, the road became an out-of-the-way burro trail into the low, piñon-studded hills, used by villagers on the hunt for firewood or game. In the eighteenth century modest adobes began to rise under the cottonwoods, to be followed two hundred years later by not-so-modest adobes.

Nowadays, where once the conquistador legions marched, darkly gleaming Mercedes and Porsches crept along at the pace of the old donkey carts, their richly purring engines barely above idle. To do otherwise would risk running down the ambling sightseers, camera straps slung over sunburnt necks, chattering away and unconscious of spilling into the roadway as they toured what has become one of Santa Fe's prime attractions.

With scores of high-end galleries, many of them in refurbished two-hundred-year-old adobes, and all of them with high-end artwork and high-end prices, Canyon Road's mile-long length was arguably the swankest Gallery Row in America (a distinction the Old Guard still held out for Manhattan's West Fifty-seventh Street), and—inarguably—the prettiest. Oh, it was possible to find something cheesy to buy on the Row, but if that's what you were looking for—a T-shirt with a picture of a coyote on it, a baby cactus in a thimble, a piece of gay cowboy erotica (yes, it existed)—you'd do better going downtown, to one of the storefronts on Palace Avenue or Old Santa Fe Trail.

On this particular pleasant October afternoon, the street was already blocked off from traffic for the famous Friday evening art walk, and those galleries with new exhibitions had put out their signs, but the crowds had yet to arrive. A few clumps of early birds were sauntering down the street, Alix London and Chris LeMay among them. They had walked briskly from the hotel and had arrived a full half hour before their four-thirty appointment at Liz's Blue Coyote Gallery, so they stopped at a couple of the openings and wandered through a few of the attractive courtyards that flanked many of the galleries, with their lush, aromatic plantings, bronze sculpture gardens, and tinkling Moorish fountains. If anything, it was all lovelier than Alix had anticipated.

Liz's gallery turned out to be in one of the more contemporary buildings, but the architecture blended handsomely with the centuries-old adobes nearby. Stepping into the main showroom, Alix liked the professional, unfussy way the art was displayed, but the variety—Western bronzes, contemporary European paintings, Japanese ceramics, Navajo sand paintings, nineteenth-century American trompe l'oeil—set off a tingle of unease. Nobody, let alone Liz Coane, could be truly knowledgeable about a range that broad. And Alix well knew that an eclectic selection like this was sometimes used by crooked dealers to mitigate potential inquiries into their roles in nefarious doings: How was I to know it was a fake? How was I to know it was stolen? How can you possibly expect me to be an expert in so many different art forms?

No, wait, she wasn't being fair. She'd disliked Liz from the first, and what Chris had told her in the Cottonwood Bar had only strengthened the feeling. It had predisposed her to be suspicious of Liz, her gallery, and the O'Keeffe. Enough of that, she told herself sharply; she was fully capable of evaluating the painting on its own merits, and that's what she would do.

One of the assistants, on learning they were there to see Liz, took them to a door near the rear of the gallery. A quick double-tap, and the door was flung open for them. The first thing that caught Alix's eye was what had to be Chris's O'Keeffe, propped on an easel at the side of the room. A few feet away, Liz was seated at her desk talking to a dark-haired man whose back was to them. There were two half-empty champagne glasses on the desk, one of them smeared with Liz's lipstick. *My God*, thought Alix, *the woman must live on booze.*

Liz, who'd been leaning comfortably back in her brown leather chair when the door opened, sat up abruptly and stared. "What are *you* doing here?"

"It's four thirty," Chris answered. "You were going to give us a look at the painting, remember? But obviously, we've caught you at a bad time—"

"You're kidding. Is it really four thirty already?" She stared confusedly, and a little blearily, at her watch. "Jesus, it is! I must have—I mean—jeez, I'm sorry..."

"It's my fault, I fear." The man gracefully unfolded himself from the chair. Alix's instantaneous reaction was *clotheshorse*. The look was elegantly casual—studiedly so. This was not somebody who simply threw together what he was going to wear; he planned for it, probably took an hour deciding on whether the cuff links should be gold or sterling silver. And the haircut, now that Alix got a look at it, wasn't something he'd gotten at the neighborhood Supercuts either. No, this was a guy who put in a lot of time making himself look good. A lot of money, too. For the second time in one day, Alix found herself disliking someone on sight, which was distinctly unusual for her. Maybe it was just her mood; coming within a few seconds of being blown to smithereens probably had some effect on how you tended to view the world for a while.

"I barged in on Ms. Coane without an appointment," he went on, smoothly apologetic (but not really). "I know I should have made arrangements to return tomorrow, but the opportunity—"

While he was speaking, Liz had gotten up as well. "No, it's my fault. The time just got away from me. This is Roland—"

"Rollie," the man corrected.

"—Rollie de Beauvais, a prominent art dealer from Boston. He was hoping I might be able to help him find some things for his clients. As a matter of fact, he was quite interested in your O'Keeffe, Chris, but unfortunately for him—"

"*Your* O'Keeffe?" de Beauvais said to Chris with a visible quickening of interest. "So you're the lucky lady who's going to get it. Congratulations, it's extraordinary."

"Yes," Chris said a little shyly, but with a touch of smugness she couldn't hide. "I'm in town to look it over. Oh, sorry, I'm Chris LeMay." She extended her hand. "From Seattle."

"Is that right?" de Beauvais said with what Alix thought was a particularly oily smile as he took Chris's hand. Chris, to Alix's disgust, practically melted.

– • –

Oh-ho, thought the FBI agent, *so you're the mysterious buyer. Which means your friend here has to be the London woman.* Talk about serendipity. Things were getting more interesting by the minute.

His quick, practiced eye took in Alix in seconds, and he didn't like what he saw. Well, he liked it in *that* sense—she was certainly attractive enough: light brown hair with auburn highlights, nicely cut to frame a pretty face; a trim, athletic figure; elegantly simple clothes, unfussy jewelry—but he didn't like *her*. It wasn't that she struck him as a bunco artist, which was what he'd expected, but quite the opposite. What she looked like was the girl next door—if next door was an eight-thousand-square-foot beachfront mansion in East Hampton. Arrogance, condescension, spoiledness, conceit…they all marked her as surely as if they'd been written on that smooth forehead. She'd grown up as a child of privilege—on Geoffrey London's ill-gotten money—and it showed in everything about her: her posture, her looks, her palpable self-satisfaction.

Assuming that she was in on whatever knavery was going on, he looked forward to bringing her down. He smiled at her, turning his smooth, seductive, well-honed Roland de Beauvais charm on to its fullest and (to Alix, anyway) most repellent. "And what about you? Who would you be?"

"Alix London," she said brusquely, barely giving him a glance. She turned her eyes toward the O'Keeffe.

Ted might be a professional, but he was also a male, and his masculine pride had just been punctured. A cold shoulder was something he didn't like and wasn't used to, either as Ted or as Rollie. In either case—either as a male or as a professional—he didn't give up as easily as that.

"I was thinking—" he said, directing his speech to Chris.

A young man appeared in the doorway, looking harried. "Liz, Gregor's here and he's not happy."

Liz blew out a boozy breath. "Dammit, now what's his problem?"

"He doesn't like the lighting—too soft, he says. He wants sharper shadows."

"Well, it's too late to do anything about that. He should have said something before."

"And he says his Wet Dream Number 3 is hung upside down."

Liz rolled her eyes. "Yeah, right, like anybody's gonna know the difference? Okay, okay, I'll deal with him. Sorry, Chris, looks like this really isn't a good time. My bad. How about after the opening? Eight o'clock? You could see the show, do the art walk in the meantime, or get something to eat or something."

"Fine," Chris said. "Very nice meeting you, Mr. de Beauvais. I hope you find what you're looking for."

"Thank you. Ah...I was thinking...if you ladies are at leisure and would care to join me for a drink and perhaps a bite to eat, I'd be delighted to have your company."

"Why, that would—" Chris began.

"We're busy," Alix said curtly. "See you later, Liz." And off she marched without a glance at Ted, giving Chris no choice but to follow.

CHAPTER 7

"Now what in the world was that all about?" a bewildered Chris asked, managing to catch up as Alix strode down the hallway toward the temporary exhibit room. "What did the poor guy do to you?"

"Oh, he didn't do anything to me," Alix grumbled. "He just… I just…I don't know, I just couldn't stand him. Brr."

"But why? I thought he was cool."

"That was pretty obvious," Alix said with a smile, then shrugged. "I don't know exactly what it was about him that got to me, Chris." They had stopped near the entrance to the room, standing to one side, out of the way of the people beginning to drift in. "Yes, I do. That smarmy manner, as if he thought we were going to drool all over him…conceited, arrogant, spoiled, self-centered…"

Chris was staring at her, laughing. "You got all that in about five seconds? The guy only said ten words."

Alix smiled. "It's that connoisseur's eye," she said, relaxing. "Chris, I'm sorry, I apologize for taking over like that. But to put it in a nutshell, he just reminded me too damn much of my ex-husband."

Chris stared at her. "You've been married?"

"Yes, why is that so surprising?"

"I don't know…I just thought…well, I don't know, you never mentioned it. I guess I just assumed…"

"Well, you assumed wrong. Yes, indeed, I've been married. For all of ten days I was Mrs. Paynton Whipple-Pruitt."

Chris's eyes opened wider. "Are we talking about *the* Whipple-Pruitts here?"

Alix nodded. "Of Boston, Watch Hill, and Palm Beach. Benefactors of the arts, regulars on the society pages, taste-makers and trendsetters all."

"Wow, no kidding." Chris drew Alix aside, into a workroom filled with mailing and packing material. "Mrs. Paynton Whipple-Pruitt," she repeated. "That's really…wait a minute, did I hear you right? Did you say ten days?"

"Almost eleven, actually."

"Oh, eleven. Well, that's different."

Alix could laugh about it now, but it'd been far from funny at the time. She'd been engaged to Paynton for two months when her father's infamous and stunningly unexpected downfall had turned her world upside down. The truth of the matter was that she'd already begun to have serious doubts about her fiancé. The longer she knew him the more clearly she saw that he was very much a chip off the old Whipple-Pruitt block: priggish, snobbish, and condescending. And snooty. And not very bright. Still, when he'd offered to go ahead with the wedding despite the unconcealed displeasure of his family, she'd gratefully accepted. More than gratefully—it had been as if she'd been about to go down with the Titanic and he'd come up with a seat for her on his own private, well-equipped lifeboat.

No doubt she should have realized things were less than promising when his family insisted she sign a prenuptial agreement allowing her nothing in the event that the marriage lasted less than a year. But still in a state of shock over her father's disgrace—and yes, to be honest, the financial calamity that had engulfed her—she'd plunged right in. It had taken her four days of wedded "bliss" for the truth to get past her defenses and sink in: the marriage was an unmitigated disaster.

The whole thing, it seemed, had been a misunderstanding. Poor Paynton's offer to go ahead with the wedding had been prompted by a misguided sense of noblesse oblige; he had offered, yes, certainly, but he had fully expected her to do the decent thing, considering the altered circumstances, and turn him down. When she hadn't, Paynton, now in his own state of shock, had taken what seemed to him the manly course: he'd girded his loins and gone through with it. Once this became clear to Alix, of course, it was impossible to continue. On the fifth day of their life as man and wife, they had formally separated. On the eleventh day they had filed for divorce. The collective sigh of relief from Paynton and his family could be heard all the way to western Connecticut.

But she wasn't about to go into all that with Chris. Maybe sometime, but not now. "And it was a long eleven days," was all she said.

"Aahh, I see. And Rollie de Beauvais reminds you of him. Although to tell you the truth," she said with a tiny smile, "I think I could last a lot longer than eleven days with a guy that looked like de Beauvais and had the Whipple-Pruitt money."

"Well, yes, but Paynton had this manner, this way of...of..."
She shook her head. "It's hard to explain. It was just—"

Chris gently held up her hand. "Alix, I'm sorry for being so
damn nosy. Look, sometime, if you ever do feel like talking about
it, you've got a sympathetic listener right here. Until then, let's
forget it. Okay?"

"Deal," Alix said gratefully. "Listen, I shouldn't have gotten up
on my high horse the way I did in there. If I didn't want to have
a drink with him, I should have just said so, I certainly shouldn't
have ruled it out for you too. Why don't we go back? If he's still
there, you can—"

"Uh-uh, not a chance. Now that I think about it, there was
maybe something a little *too* cool about him. Or too oily. Or too
something. Come on, let's go look at the opening. Maybe I'll
find something else I'd like to buy. It's always exciting to—" She
stopped, blinking, as they entered the room. "Whoops, no, I don't
think so. Sheesh."

Sheesh, indeed, Alix thought. "The brilliant young Gregor
Gorzynski's" creations were prime examples of what her father
contemptuously referred to as Euro art trash: absurdist, preten-
tious, pseudo-intellectual works, mostly by anarchistic young
males who were more interested in hooking a wealthy patron—
preferably a gullible, needy female of a certain age—than they
were in pursuing their "art." In the center of the room, Gorzynski
himself, in a scuffed leather jacket and artfully torn jeans, was vig-
orously and histrionically expostulating in heavily accented English on the subtle merits of his creations—oversized, unframed
canvases with ragged edges and irregular shapes, splattered with
long, swirling globs of glue, string, and what were clearly M&M's.
Scattered around were several sculptures (using the term loosely)
of two-by-fours jury-rigged together and decorated with string,

Cheerios, and frayed rope. Draped over the strings, Dali-like, were limp-looking but stiffened strands of transparent rice noodles.

"Frankly," Chris said, "I can't imagine ever wanting to have anything like this in my house, even if the prices weren't ridiculous. Or would my newly engaged art advisor care to advise me otherwise?"

"Your newly engaged art advisor would not," Alix whispered. "Your newly engaged art advisor will instead give you a simple rule that should serve you well through the years: it is not recommended to hang anything biodegradable on your walls."

"You mean M&M's are biodegradable?" Chris said, laughing. "Who knew?"

Beside them, a youngish, blond-bearded man and a woman were peering thoughtfully at a composition of string, glue, and M&M's on brightly painted blue particle board. "What I like," the woman was saying, "is the way he left the little M's right on them, as if to blur the distinction between reality and the thought of reality, as expressed in art."

"Yes," the man responded after an appreciative pause. "And you notice how he uses the field of blue as the one unifying element of rationality and order, so that not only the formal-structural aspects are brought out, but the symbolic implications as well?"

Chris and Alix looked at each other. "Do you think they really believe that bullshit," Chris whispered out of the side of her mouth, "or are they just showing off?"

Alix smiled. "It reminds me of something my father used to say. He said that the reason there's so much unintelligible drivel written and spoken about today's so-called art is that without it, how could you tell it from garbage?"

"Smart guy, your father," Chris said.

Whatever Alix was going to answer was cut off by Liz's strident voice, practically in her right ear. "Cul-lyde! Come on in, Cul-lyde. Look around, have a glass of champagne."

"No champagne for me, thank you," was the prissy reply. "I'm here simply to pick up a couple of catalogs. As you should know by now, I don't drink alcohol."

The speaker was a balding, waspish man, the first man Alix had seen in Santa Fe in a suit and tie, and not only a tie, but a zebra-striped bow tie—the pre-tied kind that fastened with a clasp, but a bow tie nonetheless.

"Suit yourself," Liz said. "Clyde, this is Chris LeMay, an old friend who's just getting started as a collector—she's the one who's purchasing that O'Keeffe you were helping me with—and this is her consultant, Alix London. Ladies, meet my esteemed friend and associate Clyde Moody. Clyde's the librarian at the Twentieth Century."

The Twentieth Century, of course, would be the renowned Southwest Museum of Twentieth-Century American Art, a couple of blocks from Santa Fe's central plaza.

"*Archivist*," Moody amended with some asperity. "And among the many and varied responsibilities of that position," he explained to Chris and Alix, "I am expected to keep copies of art exhibition catalogs from major New Mexican galleries, even when, in my humble opinion—" he cast a meaningful glance around the room, "—they have as much to do with art as *Garfield* has to do with the *Mona Lisa*."

This brought gales of bleary laughter from Liz, which in turn brought angry stares, and fingers to lips, and even a *Shh!* or two from visitors who had no idea that the loud woman with the coarse laugh was their host and the provider of the goodies they were scarfing down. Liz didn't notice any of it. She draped an arm over Moody's narrow shoulders despite his obvious discomfort with the familiarity. "This guy only sounds like a wet blanket, guys. Underneath that gruff exterior there lies—"

"Yes, I know," Moody said, trying without success to wriggle out from under her robust arm. "A heart of gold, pure and unalloyed. Elizabeth, if you please, all I'm here for is a catalog, so perhaps I could—"

"This guy," Liz said with an affectionate squeeze of a captive shoulder, "this guy might not look like much, but in that pointy little head of his is the brain of a giant. The man is a walking encyclopedia. I don't know what I'd do without him. It would amaze you what he can come up with from those musty old archives of his, just amaze you." She threw him coy, conspiratorial look. "Why, I could tell you stories—"

But Moody had managed to squirm free at last and was scuttling toward the door. "Bye, Cul-lyde," a laughing Liz called after him, then drifted off to stand adoringly next to Gorzynski, her arm entwined in his, and sharing in his glory.

"I'm ready to go if you are," Alix said. "I've seen all of the show I want to see."

"More than I want to see," Chris agreed. "Let's scram."

With nearly three hours to go before they were due back to look at the O'Keeffe, Chris suggested that they find a restaurant, but Alix demurred. For one thing the aftereffects of the explosion on her nervous system had killed whatever appetite she might have had. For another, she'd been hearing for years about Santa Fe's Canyon Road and its celebrated Friday art walk, and with only a brief taste of it on their stroll to the Blue Coyote, she was eager to experience more.

"Tell you what," Chris said, as they strolled out. "There's a restaurant up near the top, El Farol. Let's stroll up that way, taking in the sights. Then you can drop me off there for a bite, keep ambling to your heart's content, and swing by again at seven fifteen or so for a glass of wine, and then we'll head back here from there. How's that for a plan?"

"That's perfect, but I'm not going to want any wine. Coffee, maybe. At most."

– • –

On the brick patio at the front of the gallery they stopped for a moment to get their bearings. The sun was low in the sky, throwing long shadows from the cottonwoods onto the adobe-lined street, now filled with chatty, sauntering groups of varying sizes, moving down the street or entering and exiting the galleries. Alix was enchanted by it all: the exhilarating high desert air, the pretty, curving street (lane was more like it), the people, and the wonderful clarity of the light even at dusk.

With four gallery stops it took them over an hour to get up to El Farol. Eager to see still more, Alix left Chris at the restaurant and continued on her own as darkness came on and the streetlights lit up. As she was passing one of the contemporary galleries, she saw a middle-aged man and a pretty little girl of ten or eleven emerge from it, holding hands and prattling away. Both of them laughing merrily, they had eyes only for one another, the girl's filled with adoration, the man's with a pride and tenderness that took Alix's breath away.

Literally. It was as if a fist had closed around her heart and squeezed. She stood stock-still, submerged in a sudden wave of emotions. How many times had she and Geoff come out of galleries or museums holding hands and laughing like that? Looking into each others' faces with all that love?

The girl and her father passed her still form without seeing her. "That was *funny*, Daddy!" she heard the little girl say through her giggles. Geoff had had a wonderful ability to make Alix laugh too—the silly jokes, the riddles, the muddled-word fairytales. She could still remember how his hilarious take on Cinderella would double her up with laughter no matter how many times he wrote it down for her ("Center Alley worse jester pore ladle gull hoe lift wetter stop mutter an too heft-sea stars..."). Even now, she could feel the giggles building up deep down in her throat—but along with something tight and constricted, and bitter as well.

"You okay, miss?" an older gentleman asked. "Can I help you?"

"Oh...no, I'm fine, thank you. I was just...thinking." She began walking again, slowly, lost in a maze of memories, her thoughts conflicted and contradictory. Almost as if it had gotten there without her help, she found her cell phone in her hand. What would it be like to telephone him? Right now, this minute? A new thought occurred to her. The morning he'd called her after her meeting with Chris? The call during which she'd said she didn't want to speak with Tiny and she'd exasperatedly rung off? That was the last time he'd called. It had been three days, a long time for him. She'd been so absorbed in doing her O'Keeffe research and preparing for Santa Fe that she hadn't noticed. No, that wasn't true. She'd purposefully blocked thinking about him or about her own decision-making, promising herself she'd do some serious contemplating about everything later.

Had he at long last given up on her? Had he interpreted her rejection of Tiny as her way of finally telling him to bug off? To leave her alone? She didn't know what she wanted, but she didn't want that dismal exchange to be their last contact.

She moved out of the flow of foot traffic, sat on a low adobe wall, flipped open the phone, and began, with trembling fingers, to dial, then abruptly stopped. She couldn't call him; she didn't have his number. She didn't have his address either. To have recorded either of them would have been, to her way of thinking, like opening a door to him, an admission that, at some point in the future, they would have a real relationship again.

She continued to sit there awash in a muddle of contradictory feelings. Was she disappointed or relieved to be unable to call? She honestly didn't know. The whole thing had been a kind of emotional spasm, a seizure, a nostalgia attack brought on by seeing that father and daughter. But they were a block away now, out of sight and hearing. She could practically feel the coldness re-settle around her heart and was grateful for it. Those long-ago times had been wonderful—*he* had been wonderful, there could be no arguing with that. But once-upon-a-time childhood memories couldn't make up for his risking everything—his own hard-won reputation, his very freedom, Alix's welfare—to use his rare, God-given skills to become a crook, pure and simple—a swindler, a parasite.

No, maybe the time would come, or maybe not, when she could put all that behind her. But not yet. Not yet.

She got slowly to her feet and put away the phone with the feeling that she'd narrowly missed making a mistake. She also felt as if she'd been put slowly through a wringer. That glass of wine with Chris was starting to sound good after all.

CHAPTER 8

In the event, she had a glass of wine, a cup of coffee, and a couple of the fancy tapas that Chris enthusiastically recommended: chorizo sausage with fig aioli, and skewered Moroccan spiced pork. It was over their coffees that Alix was struck with a bizarre thought.

"Chris," she said slowly, "when we first walked into Liz's office, do you remember what she said?"

"Sure, she said she was surprised to see us."

"No, she said, 'What are you doing here?'"

Chris frowned, clearly puzzled as to what Alix was driving at. "Well, isn't that the same thing?"

"Not exactly. Who did she say it to?"

"What kind of a question is that? To us. Alix, what are you—"

Alix shook her head. "No. I just realized she was staring straight at me when she said it. 'What are *you* doing here?' Emphasis on the *you*."

"All right. And your point is?"

Alix toyed reflectively with her coffee cup for a few moments. "I think it was me she was surprised to see, not us."

Chris folded her arms and leaned back in her chair. "Alix, you have totally lost me."

"I'm just wondering," Alix said, "if she was surprised to see me because she assumed I'd be dead."

It took a moment to sink in, and then Chris stared at her. "You think the explosion…you think Liz…you think she tried to blow you up?" Her voice went up an octave on the last few words.

"No, I doubt that, but I'm wondering if she didn't try to poison me with a propane gas leak, but the leak was bigger than she expected and there was an explosion."

Chris's eyes were bugging out now. "Are you nuts? She tried to kill you? Why?"

"To keep me from looking at the painting?" Alix said. It came out as a question because the idea had started to seem silly to her too. "Because the painting is a forgery?"

"But that makes no sense. What would stop me from getting someone else? Would she kill him too? And the one after him? And how could Liz get into your casita to mess with the propane before you arrived? She drove us there, remember? She was with us right up until we checked in. And how would she even know which casita you were staying in? And why would she—"

"Okay, you're right," Alix said with a sigh. "I guess I'm getting a little paranoid."

"Well, who wouldn't be, after what happened to you today? But I really think you're barking up a nonexistent tree on this one. Liz might not be the most lovable person in the world, but a killer? Uh-uh."

Alix nodded. "You're right," she said again. "I think I need a good night's sleep. Forget what I said. Come on, let's go look at your painting."

By the time they got to the Blue Coyote, however, one of Liz's assistants was out in front of the darkened gallery, locking the door. "Oh, I'm sorry, we're just closing up."

"I understand. I'm Chris LeMay, and this is—"

"Oh, right. Liz is expecting you, but would you mind going around to the patio behind the building? There's a back door to her office there, and it's the way people go when they just want to see her. The outdoor lights stay on all the time, so you won't have any problem."

"Fine. Thank you."

"Um…" The young man hesitated. "If she doesn't answer right away, you might have to knock kind of loud. I'm pretty sure she's, uh, taking a nap, and she can be a pretty hard lady to wake up sometimes." He shrugged, as if in apology.

Chris and Alix looked at each other. They understood exactly what he was saying: Liz was schwacked.

Some clouds had built up under the moon, so the pathway lights were helpful. They followed the winding path around some handsome, half-life-size bronze animal sculptures set on plinths—a wild boar, a mountain goat, a crouching cougar—to the single door in the back of the building.

"It looks as if it's dark in there," a puzzled Alix said. "Why would she have the lights out?"

"As he said, taking a nap," Chris said, rattling the doorknob. "Liz!" she called, switching to foghorn level. "Are you in there?" For good measure she rattled the knob some more.

"Maybe," Alix said, "we should—"

The door burst open, slamming hard into Chris, who slammed hard into Alix, who went tumbling over backward, with Chris falling on top of her. With everything dark, and with flailing arms and legs all over the place, it was hard to tell which way was up, let alone what was going on. But it was impossible to miss the man—it was a man, all right, he was huge—who came hurtling through the doorway, only to trip over one of Chris's size elevens. Whatever it was he'd been carrying went sailing into a clump of miniature piñon pines a few yards away.

"Ouch!" said Chris.

"Damn!" said the man, who managed to keep to his feet but floundered into the bronze cougar headfirst, with a sound like a mallet hitting a good-sized bell. "Shit!" He sank to his knees with a groan, both hands pressed to his forehead.

"Hey!" Chris yelled at him, trying to get her own feet under her while Alix, still partially pinned by Chris's considerable bulk, struggled to move at all. By the time they'd gotten untangled from each other after falling one more time—it was like one of those old Laurel and Hardy shticks—the man had pulled himself together, staggered up, and gone lurching back toward Canyon Road, hands still held to his head, and quickly disappeared around the edge of the building.

"What the hell—" Chris began, but Alix was already at the grouping of piñons. "It's what I was afraid of," she said, sliding out the object she'd seen land there and leaning it against the bushes. With the moon just beginning to glide into an area of thinning clouds, there was no mistaking what it was.

"It's my O'Keeffe!" Chris exclaimed. "Oh, no, is it…is it…"

"I don't see any damage," Alix said, "but let's get it inside, in the light."

"My God," Chris mumbled angrily, as Alix gathered it carefully up, "he was stealing it—my painting. If we hadn't come along at just at that moment…"

She stopped, and from the expression on her face Alix could see that the same thought had belatedly struck both of them.

Liz. Where was Liz? What had happened to her? Why hadn't the commotion awakened her?

They ran into the office. "Liz, are you here? Where are you?" Chris called, while Alix fumbled along the wall for the light switch.

Once she'd found it and the bright ceiling fluorescents had flickered on, Chris's questions answered themselves. Along one wall, behind the now-empty easel, was a burgundy leather-covered couch. Liz was stretched out on it with her mouth open and her eyes closed. Her arms and legs were flung awkwardly and unnaturally about, like a puppet's, and her body was sharply twisted at the hips. On the floor behind her head lay a burgundy pillow from the couch.

"Liz?" whispered Chris, cautiously approaching. She knelt beside the couch, grasped Liz by the shoulders, and shook gently; then less gently. "Liz!"

Alix had never seen a dead body before, other than at a funeral, but there was no doubt in her mind about what she was looking at now. She put a hand on Chris's arm. "I don't think she's going to answer," she said quietly, reaching for her cell phone. "I think we need to call 911."

— • —

The next two hours went by in an exhausting blur. A fire department emergency vehicle arrived almost before Alix had hung up, and a police car with two uniformed cops showed up no more than a minute later. Then a crime scene van, then a private car from which a Detective Wilkin emerged, and then another car with a deputy medical examiner who hurried into the office to look at Liz's body.

Alix and Liz were separately questioned by the two officers, and then again, more extensively, by the detective, who used a tiny tape recorder to take down their statements. They were driven to the police building on Camino Estrada, where they were again separately questioned, even more extensively, by a Lieutenant Mendoza.

Mendoza was a resourceful interrogator, and under his expert, persistent probing Alix was able to dredge up from her memory a few details about the man who had crashed into them and run off: He was big, at least six-three, and big-boned. Reddish hair, short reddish beard. Or it could have been blond; the light hadn't been that good. And he was a pipe smoker, a heavy pipe smoker. Geoff had once been a heavy pipe smoker too, and she was familiar with the way the pipe tobacco saturated his clothing. Mendoza, interested, asked her if she recognized the kind of tobacco, but all she could tell him was that it wasn't the same blend her father smoked. She was finally allowed to leave a little after ten. Chris was being kept longer—because, Alix assumed, she could provide more background information about Liz.

Mendoza sent her back to the Hacienda in a car, but she asked instead to be dropped off at the central plaza, still fairly lively at this time of night. She thought that seeing ordinary people ambling around the square, eating at the restaurants, doing ordinary things, might settle her nerves a little, which it did, but only a little. She strolled around it twice and then walked the few blocks to the hotel. There she left a note for Chris to call her if she got back from police headquarters by midnight. At twelve thirty, with no word yet from Chris, she gave up and went to bed. She lay staring at the beamed ceiling for another hour, nerves buzzing away, before she finally drifted off into an on-again, off-again sleep.

– • –

Twenty miles south of Santa Fe, on the road to Albuquerque, in the old mining town of Los Cerrillos, Brandon Teal was also having trouble getting to sleep. He was sitting in the dark, rocking disconsolately back and forth, on the rickety porch of what had once been the offices of the Spanish Belle silver mine, but was now his home and workshop. Brandon Teal was a painter, and a good one, which made his current predicament—"predicament" was putting it mildly—all the more appalling. His head continued to throb despite the four aspirins, and the clumsily bandaged four-inch gash at his hairline continued to seep blood, but these were the least of his worries.

Questions for which he had no answers racketed around his skull like ball bearings in a can. Had they seen his face? Could they identify him? Who *were* they? Were the police already hunting for him? Should he go off somewhere else for a while, or would leaving suddenly only call attention to him? The same went for the beard: shave it off or not shave it off? Above all—and this one would *never* be answered—how could he have been stupid enough, and greedy enough, to get himself into this horrible mess?

He reached down beside him for what had been an unopened pint-bottle of Wild Turkey when he'd taken it out of the cabinet, but was now half empty. He gagged as it went down. Teal was no drinker, and all the alcohol was doing was making him sick and muddying his brain. What he needed—needed desperately—was someone to tell him what to do.

He stumbled into his studio, found one of the telephones, and clumsily punched in a number with deadened fingers that felt more like wood than flesh.

CHAPTER 9

Ted Ellesworth had been around long enough to know that police officers tended to be protective of their turf, especially when it was the FBI that was doing the trespassing. And, if truth be told, this was understandable; the Bureau could sometimes be just a wee bit overbearing and officious. But if Santa Fe Detective Lieutenant Eduardo Mendoza was annoyed by Ted's presence in his office the next morning, he didn't show it. The Santa Fe police department had been called by Washington earlier that morning (at Ted's request) and told that Special Agent Ellesworth was in town and would like to pay a courtesy call on the officer in charge of investigating the previous night's homicide at the Blue Coyote Gallery. Mendoza, who must have been up to his ears in details, had nevertheless cleared the hour from eight to nine a.m., his first hour back in the office, for Ted, and had received him with all good grace. Coffee was offered and accepted. Donuts were offered and turned down.

Once Ted had explained what he was doing in Santa Fe, and after they had amiably assured each other that neither had any intention of stepping on the other's toes, they got down to business. A horse-faced, long-nosed forty-year-old wearing a frayed University of New Mexico Lobos baseball cap, Mendoza had shown real interest on hearing that the FBI was in the middle of a fraud investigation involving Liz's gallery. Indeed, he had as many questions for Ted as Ted had for him, so it wasn't until almost eight thirty that they got to the murder. Ted had been forthcoming with information, and Mendoza proved to be the same.

"Okay, the two of them called 911 at 8:06," Mendoza was saying, "and according to them it couldn't have been more than three, four minutes after they ran into the big guy with the painting—or vice-versa, I guess I should say. They think he hurt his head when he took his tumble, so that might turn out to be a help in finding him. We contacted the hospital emergency room, but the only head injury they had all night was a fly fisherman who hooked his own ear."

"There's fly-fishing around here?"

"Sure, plenty."

"Well, could the women provide a description?"

"Yeah, a pretty good one, considering. They both agree he was male, they both agree he was big—six-three or six-four, two-hundred-plus pounds. Beefy, not fat. White. Short red hair. The London woman thinks he had a reddish beard too, but LeMay doesn't remember it. And they both remember he stank of tobacco. London's pretty sure it was pipe tobacco."

Ted nodded. "Not bad, but are you sure it's not all a fish story? I mean, do you think it's possible that they might have done it themselves and invented this guy to lead you off on a wild goose chase?"

"No way. We considered it, of course, and for more reasons than I have time to go into, it doesn't compute. No, their story holds up. And then our CSI guys got some fresh blood off the statue they said he smacked into, so that holds up too. And that should also provide us with some DNA, but, you know..." He shrugged.

"Right," Ted said. "It's not going to do you much good unless you have something to match it against. Any fingerprints?"

"The picture's full of them, but most of them are London's and a few of Coane's. Then some others that might be promising, pretty clear too, but, you know, same problem—"

"Not going to do much good unless you have something to match them against," they both said together.

"What about TOD?" Ted asked. *Time of death.*

"ME says she'd been dead no more than two hours when he got to her. That's all he's willing to say until he does the autopsy. That, and that the cause of death was suffocation, probably done with the pillow that was on the floor."

"So you're pretty sure this guy is your killer?"

Mendoza waggled his hand, palm-down—a maybe, maybe not motion. "That's the most probable scenario around here, yeah. Either she caught him stealing the picture and he killed her—"

"Or he had some other reason for killing her, and he took the picture to make it look like a robbery."

"You got it." Mendoza got up to pour himself more coffee from the pot on a side table and held the pot up. "Want some more?"

Ted covered his mug with hand. "No, thanks." The coffee had been a typical police-station brew, too strong to start with, and too long in the pot; one mug of it was plenty. "You said 'most probable scenario.' Does that mean you have some less probable ones?"

"More than I can count." Mendoza sighed as he dropped back into his chair. "Our victim here was not what you would call a well-liked lady. She changed men like other women change shoes, and apparently there are a lot of pissed-off guys out there, mostly so-called artists. And the other gallery owners weren't crazy about her either. She stiffed a lot of people over the years, one way or another. A lot of 'em have grudges. We already have a dozen people in town we want to talk to about it, and there'll probably be more before we're finished."

"Uh-huh. But if it was one of these others who killed her, where does the guy who was taking the painting fit in?"

Another shrug from Mendoza. "I don't know—crime of opportunity? He shows up for some reason or other, sees she's dead, sees the painting, figures what the hell, and takes off with it."

"And has the rotten luck to run smack into the two women," Ted said doubtfully. "Could be, I suppose."

"Yeah, I think it's a long shot too, but I don't want to rule it out. We've got some out-of-town possibilities too: this LeMay woman and a guy named…" He checked an open file folder on his desk. "Templeton, Craig Templeton. He piloted the plane that got her here. Him, LeMay, and Coane go back a long way, and they got themselves into some kind of a messy love triangle four or five years ago. Those things can get nasty."

"Tell me about it," said Ted with a smile.

"Now LeMay was pretty open about it with us. Haven't talked to Templeton yet. He's being interviewed right now, I think."

"Four or five years ago? For a crime of revenge or jealousy, that's an awfully long time to wait, wouldn't you say?"

"Yeah, I would. Ordinarily. But look at it this way: the two of them show up in Santa Fe at two o'clock in the afternoon—along with this Alix London—and by eight o'clock Coane is dead. Kind of a coincidence, wouldn't you say?"

"Yes, I guess I would," Ted said slowly. "And as for Alix London—look, I don't mean to be telling you your job, but if I were you I'd check her out pretty carefully too."

Mendoza frowned. "Yeah? Why?"

"The name 'London'—is it familiar to you?"

"You mean before yesterday? No, I don't think so. Why?"

"You don't remember Geoffrey London? This would have been in New York, eight or nine years ago—"

Mendoza held up his hand. "Oh, oh, yeah, I remember. This was that high-society art expert or whatever he was that turned out to be a big-time forger? He bilked some people out of a lot of—wait a minute, he's related to her? Uncle? Father?"

"Father."

"Ah. Well, look, Ted, that's interesting, but I don't believe in guilt by association."

"You don't? I do, or at least in suspicion by association. But there's more. I got a call from our op specialist this morning just before I came over. She did some digging, and it turns out that the power behind the scenes, the one who arranged it so that LeMay 'just happened' to settle on Alix London to be her consultant out of all the people she could have chosen, was…I'll give you one guess."

"Her father," Mendoza correctly mused. "Mm, so what are you thinking? That maybe the picture is a fake that her daddy made and Alix is here as his accomplice—to certify it *isn't* a fake?" His chair creaked as he leaned back in it. "You know, to tell the truth I was wondering if there was something a little hinky about her myself. One of the things she told us was that she thought Liz Coane might have tried to kill *her*."

"*Kill* her? That's crazy."

"Well, not altogether. The watchamacallit, the casita she was in at her hotel? Damn thing blew up this afternoon. I heard the explosion from here. Propane leak. Missed her by less than a minute."

"No kidding," Ted said thoughtfully. "But you don't really think—"

"I don't know," said Mendoza. "Ordinarily, I'd say she was just being a little paranoid about it, which'd be understandable, but with Coane herself getting killed a few hours later...well, I don't know. *Something's* going on."

Ted sat back and reflected for a moment. "Eduardo," he said, "the homicide case you're working on and the fraud case I'm working on—has it occurred to you that they might be different parts of the same story? That maybe Coane was killed because of her part in the scam she was involved in?"

Mendoza smiled. "Nope, not until half an hour ago, when you walked in and laid this forgery stuff on me. Now, I think: could be. We don't get too many homicides in Santa Fe, you know, and we don't have a whole lot of exploding casitas either. To get both of them on the same day, involving the same set of people, well..."

Ted nodded. "Right, you have to wonder. And who's the link between them? Alix London." A thought struck him, and after a moment he said thoughtfully: "The painting that the guy was taking from Coane's place. What was it?"

"It was a painting. What do you mean, what was it?"

"I mean do you know who painted it, or what it was of?"

Mendoza consulted his file again but came up empty this time. He rose, went to the door of his office, and opened it to talk to one of his detectives in the bullpen. "Hey, Jock, the painting from the Coane investigation—does it have some kind of a name or something?"

Ted heard paper shuffle for a few seconds, and then the answer floated back through the doorway. "Yeah, it's got a label on the back, Lieutenant. It says, '*Cliffs at Ghost Ranch, Georgia* O'Keeffe, 1964.'"

"I knew it!" Ted exclaimed. "That's the painting that was sitting on the easel in Coane's office when I was there in the afternoon. She told me the name of it. LeMay's supposed to be buying it, and London's the 'expert' she's brought along to evaluate it."

Mendoza nodded thoughtfully. "Interesting."

"You know," Ted said, "I'd love to look at it again, if that's all right."

"Sure." Mendoza raised his voice. "So Jock? Where is it now? We have it, don't we?"

"Of course we do, what do you think?" said the aggrieved Jock. "It's in the evidence room. We've got one of the two women coming in to verify it's the one they saw the guy running away with."

"Which one?" Ted asked Mendoza. "LeMay or London?" He was aware that he was treading on Mendoza's turf, but it was starting to look as if it was going to have to be shared turf after all. Still, he felt constrained to politely say to Mendoza's back: "I mean, if you don't mind telling me."

Mendoza shrugged and forwarded the question to Jock. "It's the good-looking one, London," the detective called. "Should be here any minute. Hooper's taking her in."

"Good. Oh, and tell Hooper she asked for an easel. Tell him to get the one out of the conference room."

"Will do."

"And tell him to let me know how it goes."

"Right."

"Okay, thanks, Eduardo," Ted said as Mendoza was closing the door. When the lieutenant had returned to his desk, he said with some urgency, "You know, I had a feeling she'd be in this up to her ears. Look, would it be all right with you if I just happen to show up in the viewing room when she's there?"

Mendoza hesitated. "Uh, no offense, Ted, but I'd just as soon handle this on my own. You know—"

"Of course!" Ted said. "I have no intention of getting involved in the homicide part of it, believe me. It's strictly the fraud case that I'm interested in."

"Well—"

"I just want to see what she has to say about the painting, that's all. It would help a lot. I'd really appreciate it."

"Yeah, okay, I can see that," Mendoza said. "Okay, let's head you over there. We can say we wanted you to identify it as the picture that was in Liz's office when you were there in the afternoon. Which is true, come to think of it."

"Great, thanks a million. Don't forget, though, she thinks I'm Roland de Beau—"

The telephone on Mendoza's desk buzzed, and the lieutenant picked it up. "Yeah? Yeah? No kidding, is that a fact? Okay, tell her thanks for the heads-up."

He put the phone down and looked with sudden seriousness at Ted. "That was one of my guys. London just asked him to call me. She says I need to know about this fishy character that she's pretty sure is right in the middle of this whole mess. She just saw him right here in the station."

Ted was puzzled. "Who?"

The laughter that Mendoza could no longer control came out in a snort. "You."

— • —

The first thing that had surprised Alix when she entered the detectives' bullpen area was the sight of Roland de Beauvais. Lieutenant Mendoza was standing in the open doorway of his office talking to one of the detectives, and seated at the lieutenant's desk, where she'd sat last night, was de Beauvais, in shirtsleeves, looking very much at home. The second, which happened as Mendoza was closing the door, was hearing de Beauvais say to him, "Okay, thanks, Eduardo."

That stopped her in her tracks. *Eduardo?* What was this slippery Boston art dealer or broker or whatever he was supposed to be, doing on such chummy terms with the chief of Santa Fe's homicide unit? But what really threw her for a loop was the *way* he'd said it. Not that archaic, drawled Brahmin-speak—"Ohkai, thahnks, Eduahhhdow," but the plain, straightforward, standard American version: "Okay, thanks, Eduardo."

What kind of double-dealing was this guy up to? What was with the phony Boston accent he'd been using? Or maybe *this* was the phony accent, although that seemed a lot less likely. Either way, he was going around pretending to be something he wasn't.

An overweight, tired-looking man in a rumpled white shirt, loosened tie, and open collar rose from one of the desks. "Hey there, Miss London, thanks for coming in. I'm Detective Hooper. I'll take you to the property room."

"Thank you, Detective. Um...the man in there with the lieutenant? Would you happen to know who he is?"

"No ma'am, didn't see him." He scratched at his five-o'clock-shadowed jaw and waited patiently. She wondered if he'd been up all night.

She hesitated, then went ahead. "Well, I do, and I think there's something the lieutenant needs to know. Could you call him—"

"You mean right now, this minute?"

"I think you'd better, yes. Would you tell him that the man he's talking to isn't quite what he seems?" She lowered her voice a notch. "In fact..."

— • —

Once the detective had somewhat reluctantly relayed her message, Alix was happy to forget about Roland de Beauvais. The ball was in Mendoza's court, and he could do with it what he wanted. She'd done her civic duty, and now she looked forward to her time with the O'Keeffe. She'd had barely a glance at it the afternoon before, and she'd been itching ever since for a closer look. She certainly hadn't anticipated doing it in a police station, but that was as good a place as any for doing her job.

Hooper signed in with the property clerk and used a wall-mounted keypad to open the door to the property viewing room. On one of the two tables in it was a portable easel with the painting resting on it.

"There ya go," Hooper said with a weary wave of his hand. "Put these on first."

She took a pair of plastic throwaway gloves from the box he was holding out to her and, heart thumping, took her first good look at what she had come to New Mexico to see.

It was a medium-sized landscape of an ethereally pale cliff face split by deep vertical canyons, in a stark, bright setting of sand and sky. In the dimly lit bottom of one of the clefts, barely noticeable, just a few sure strokes of the brush, was the small, shadowed figure of a man—well, perhaps a woman—in profile, facing to the right. Around the picture was a simple, unadorned steel frame—the perfect framing for it, she thought. The metal frame had turned out to be useful too; she doubted that the picture would have so nicely survived its flight into the bristly miniature pines without it.

"Beautiful, isn't it?" she said.

Hooper shrugged and unsuccessfully tried to stifle a yawn. "I guess so. Not really my kind of thing. So, is it the one you got out of the bush?"

"Yes, no question."

"Okay, great. You're good to go, Miss London." He started to take the painting off the easel. "We appreciate the help."

"No, wait," Alix said quickly. "I'd like to take some more time to look it over. Would that be all right?"

He paused, his hands on the frame. "What for?"

"One of the things that Christine LeMay hired me to do is to evaluate its authenticity. It's her painting, after all, unless she decides not to take it. Anyway, I'd think the police would be interested in that side of it too."

"Didn't know there was a question." Another covered yawn. "'Scuse me."

"There's always a question," she said. "Especially when it comes to something as expensive as this."

"So how expensive is it?" he asked without much interest.

"Almost three million dollars."

"You're shitting me!" he blurted, then apologized again, almost before the words were out of his mouth. Well, at least she'd finally gotten a rise out of him.

He moved back from the painting and offered it with a gesture for her inspection. "Go ahead, look away." Then, under his breath she heard him muttering: "Three million bucks. Unbeliev-able."

She had barely started when a telephone on the other table buzzed. Hooper went to it and picked it up. "Sure, yeah, Lieuten-ant, I'll let him in."

To her amazement, it was Roland de Beauvais who was wait-ing on the other side of the door. Even before he uttered a word, she could see that he was back in character—not only the gor-geous cashmere sport coat that he had slipped on, but the con-descending, aristocratic lift of the eyebrows, the incipient, self-confident smirk that made you want to smack him in the face, even the languid, irritating grace of his posture—the man was a consummate actor, she had to give him that much.

No, wait, she thought, not as consummate as all that. He spoke like a Brahmin, he acted like a Brahmin, but he most definitely didn't dress like a Brahmin. Real Brahmins—the Whipple-Pruitts, for example—might have million-dollar paintings on the walls of their living rooms, and half-million-dollar Louis XVI furniture sets in their dining rooms, but that was at home, where there was no one to see them but their own kind. They most assuredly did not saunter around with thousand-dollar cashmere coats on their backs. *Inconspicuous* consumption was their hallmark. They wore holey sweaters and beat-up deck shoes, not designer jackets and Gucci loafers.

A fake through and through is what he was.

"Why, Ms. London, what a nice surprise to find you here," he said. And yes, that grating nasal drawl was back too.

She managed to work up something like a smile. "And what brings you here?" she asked. Damn, she had wanted some time alone with the painting. With this preening slimeball hanging around she wasn't going to get anything done.

"Oh, they've asked me in to see if I can verify that the painting is the one that was in poor Ms. Coane's office yesterday. Awful about what happened." He glanced at the picture. "Yes, that's it, all right, wouldn't you agree?"

"Yes, I would." *Excellent. And now, if you would kindly turn around and leave—*

But the mental message she was sending wasn't received. He continued to look at the painting, showing no inclination to go. "From late in her Ghost Ranch period, obviously," he said.

Alix was surprised. Unsavory he might be, but he knew his stuff.

"Yes," she agreed, "1961, 1962—maybe as late as 1963. Somewhere in there."

"Well, no," he said with a patronizing smile, "I think perhaps just the least little bit later." He studied it a moment longer. "I'd say...1964. Yes, 1964, probably the early part of the year, though. So you weren't very far off."

And I'd say you're full of it, she thought. *Nobody's got that good an eye.*

"Do you recognize the setting?" he asked.

"Not for sure, no, but I'm thinking it's one of her renditions of the Ghost Ranch area itself. What do you think?"

"Oh, it's Ghost Ranch, all right. Quite obviously. What I meant was, specifically."

Why, he's turned this into a contest, she realized. *Everything he's said has been to one-up me and prove he's smarter than I am. Creep.* He reminded her more of the unlamented Paynton Whipple-Pruitt every minute.

"Not really, no," she said, grinding her teeth.

"Tell me, Ms. London, what's your opinion of the painting as a painting?"

"I don't know what you mean."

"I mean, do you think it's a good one? Are you going to advise your friend to buy it? How would you rate this within the O'Keeffe oeuvre?" He waited, smiling, for her answer.

In the first place, Alix hadn't yet had a chance to study it enough to come to a conclusion. In the second place, she wasn't about to offer a tentative opinion, only to have him put her down again. "I haven't decided. Tell me, how would *you* rate it?"

A small shadow—of concern? doubt?—passed over his face, the first honest emotion she'd seen on it. She'd surprised him, caught him unprepared. Maybe he really wasn't the expert she'd taken him for. This was starting to be enjoyable after all.

He studied the picture, his chin cradled in his right hand, his right elbow cradled in his left hand. He cleared his throat. "I think it's quite marvelous. As always, I find myself simply stunned, don't you know, by her treatment of whiteness as a representation of rationality and order, and by how she emphasizes not only its symbolic implications but its formal-structural aspects as well." He finished by clearing his throat again.

What a total load of baloney, Alix thought, smiling at him. Was that really the best he could do? He knew it too, and he knew she knew it as well. She could tell that from the hint of embarrassment, or maybe even humor (was it possible that he was laughing at himself?) that was visible in his returning smile. To her surprise, she had a sudden glimpse of him in a different light. Drop the overwrought speech mannerisms and the too-too blasé demeanor, show a little in the way of honest feelings, and he could actually be a fairly attractive man. Those clear, piercing blue eyes, the square-cut jaw, the—

Whoa, she thought, *that's enough of that.* This was not a road she was dumb enough to let herself start down. She had always been good at focusing her concentration, and now she made use of that ability to turn it away from de Beauvais and direct it to the picture. Time to start doing what Chris was paying her to do. First question: was it the real thing or was it a fake?

To many people, even people within the art world, the idea of anyone's having a "connoisseur's eye" was laughable; a carnival act, pure hokum—at best, self-deception. The way one evaluated a painting's authenticity, so the conventional wisdom went, was to scrupulously apply the tools of science and meticulous scholarship, not to put one's credence in some gauzy, impossible-to-pin-down first impression.

Alix knew differently. Sure, she went with her first impressions, her gut reactions, and yes, they were hard to pin down, but she knew that they were solidly based on scholarship, experience, and training—plus that rare, all-important, inborn faculty that condensed it all into a single, overarching, seemingly instinctive judgment. It didn't work with all artists—she could look at a Duccio or a Cimabue from now till Christmas and nothing would emerge. It didn't mean she didn't like or appreciate them, it simply meant she didn't "connect." But with Georgia O'Keeffe she did, and now, having gazed at the painting for a minute or so, she closed her eyes and let her impressions coalesce on their own. The colors were right...the subject matter was certainly right...the treatment in general looked right...there wasn't any signature, but even that was right; O'Keeffe didn't sign her works, except once in a while on the back (and even then it was more likely than not to be only her scrawled initials, "OK"); she felt that her style was signature enough.

Apparently, de Beauvais was also considering the subject of authenticity. "At any rate, I'd say it's certainly genuine," he said, almost reluctantly. "There really isn't any doubt there either."

"And I'd say it's a fake," Alix declared, surprising herself. The words had popped out before she'd even realized she'd reached a conclusion.

The Boston dealer swiveled around and stared at her, seemingly astonished, or possibly offended. "On what grounds?" he demanded.

Well, that was the nub of the matter, all right. The flashing intuition of *real, fake, good, bad* always came before the understanding of what was behind it. "I'm not sure exactly, yet. Maybe it's that it's too beautiful, too pretty. There's a kind of indefinable edge that you expect from O'Keeffe, and this doesn't have it. And there's something else that's bothering me, something missing. I can't quite put my finger on it…it's hard to say…"

Pretty lame, she thought, but it was the best she could do right now. She expected a sneer from de Beauvais, but he kept a straight face. "I see," he said archly. "How interesting."

Creep, she thought again. Well, it would come to her eventually, she knew that. She took a metric tape measure from her purse and quickly measured the canvas in two deft movements: width, ninety-one centimeters, height, seventy-six centimeters— thirty by thirty-six inches, probably a little larger, depending on whether some of it was hidden by the frame.

"Why bother to measure it?" De Beauvais wanted to know. "If you're so certain it's inauthentic."

"It's what we do," she snapped, jumping at the chance to put the supercilious snot in his place. *I'm a professional*, she was telling him. *You're out of your depth here, mister.* "And I didn't say I was certain. It's an opinion…an educated opinion," she added pointedly.

"No offense, Ms. London, and I'm sure your opinion is invaluable—" he was being equally disagreeable, "—but if the police ask

my opinion I will suggest they not depend upon opinions at all, but rather submit the picture to a forensic laboratory for examination. With the aid of chemical and spectrographic pigment analysis, for example—"

God, the man was windy too, along with his many other faults. "If this was supposed to be an eighteenth-century painting," she said crisply, "scientific analysis would be helpful. The pigments in use three hundred years ago were quite different from the ones available today, as were the canvases, which would have been handwoven at that time—"

"Yes, I'm aware of all that, but—"

"There would be *craquelure* to be analyzed for authenticity, as well as dust and grime. But in this case, the painting is supposedly only forty-some years old. The pigments in use then were the same ones available today. The same is true for brushes, canvases, stretchers, and the rest. There is no *craquelure* to be analyzed, no grime to be aged. Moreover, unless the person who painted this is completely incompetent, which he obviously is not, he will have used the very same materials and techniques that O'Keeffe would have used. He would have—"

Hey, you can be pretty windy yourself, she thought, and stopped. In any case, de Beauvais looked very satisfactorily snowed.

"Okay if I turn it around?" she asked Hooper, who was seated off to the side, silently observing. "Sure. Just don't drop it. Three million bucks. Whew."

She turned it with care and set it back on the easel, making sure that it was the frame and not the canvas that came in contact with the support. The backing, like the backings of most paintings that have been around for a while and have changed hands, had a few stuck-on labels, yellowed and curling, and various indecipherable stamps and scrawls. One of the ink scrawls was the anticipated "signature," a simple *OK* in a loose, five-pointed star. That proved nothing one way or the other. In fact, the *lack* of a signature would have been a better indication of authenticity. Not only were O'Keeffe's initials the easiest thing in the world to fake, but whereas a good many famous artists didn't sign all their work, no *forger* of famous artists would think of leaving one of his fakes unsigned.

One instance in particular came unbidden to her mind and made her smile. A small but elite European museum had been in the process of acquiring an elaborate, sinuous El Greco painting that bore a strikingly bold "El Greco" signature in the lower right-hand corner. Until, that is, someone had pointed out that El Greco himself—"the Greek"—naturally enough signed his pictures with his actual name, Domeniko Theotokopoulos—in Greek.

Her smile brought quizzical looks from the two men, and she quickly sobered her expression and concentrated on her examination. The stamps were mostly illegible, but one of the two labels was from an art gallery: *Galerie Xanadu, 1421 Central Avenue NE, Albuquerque, NM.* So it had a history after all; at some point in the past, it had passed through a dealership or auction house called Galerie Xanadu. That was interesting and worth following up. She borrowed a pen and notepad from the detective and jotted it down.

The other label was right smack in the center of the back: *The Cliffs at Ghost Ranch, Georgia O'Keeffe, 1964.* She thought about that for a moment and then spun toward de Beauvais. "You've already seen this label, haven't you? That's why you were so sure about the *1964* and the rest of it. You saw it when you were in Liz's office yesterday, didn't you?"

He blinked back at her, all aggrieved innocence. "I should say not. I assure you I have never set eyes on this label before."

"Okay, then she told you the name of it."

"She most certainly did not, and I must say, I resent your implication. I mean, really...!"

She ignored him, making it as pointed as she could. To Hooper she said, "I may be wrong about its being a fake, but I don't think so. But give me a couple of days and I should be able to give you something more definitive. If it's all right with you, I'd like to leave now."

"Fine with me," Hooper said. "We'd appreciate it if you could stay in the area for a few days. We might want to talk to you again."

"I will. And Lieutenant Mendoza has my cell phone number."

Hooper rose to let her out, and at the steel-barred door, out of de Beauvais' hearing, she said, "If I were you, Detective, I wouldn't let that man out of my sight in there."

Hooper nodded solemnly. Behind him she saw de Beauvais still staring at the painting with an unreadable frown on his face.

CHAPTER 10

The unreadable frown was still there twenty minutes later as Ted sat in El Canon, the coffee shop at the Hilton hotel. In front of him was a grande cappuccino, untouched and cooling. Beside it his fingers drummed quietly on the table as he tried to reassess the convictions that only an hour ago had seemed like certainties.

The session in the property room had upended everything. He had guessed from the beginning that the painting was a fake, and his hunch had turned into a lead-pipe cinch the minute he learned that the London woman was involved with it. His brief look at the picture in Liz's office the previous afternoon had done nothing to change his mind, but then, this morning, with his chance to examine it at length, those certainties started getting fuzzy around the edges. It was a finer piece than he'd thought at first: arresting and evocative, and done with the unmistakable painterly flair that a previous case had taught him was Georgia O'Keeffe's and Georgia O'Keeffe's alone.

Could it be genuine, after all? He was inclined now, despite London's assertion to the contrary, to believe that's just what it

was. Something funny was going on with it—that certainty still remained—but whatever nefarious doings Liz had been up to, this painting, he thought with growing conviction—this one, at least—was the real thing. The come-on for a scam? A kind of loss-leader to snare other buyers of "yet-to-be-discovered" O'Keeffes? One authentic one to sell ten fakes? Could be; it was an old enough scam.

Absently, he stirred the frothed-milk topping through the cappuccino, took his first long sip, and sighed. The London woman—she was troubling him too. Jamie's call this morning telling him that Alix's reprobate father was involved, albeit behind the scenes, had confirmed that there was some kind of con going on, all right, and Alix was in it up to her eyebrows.

But.

If she was in on a con, wouldn't she have declared the painting to be authentic? What possible percentage could there be in her saying it was a forgery? And yet that was exactly what she'd done in there. Was he wrong about her too? Could she be on the level? And if she was on the level, could it be that she was right about the painting? That it *was* a fake?

He shook his head. "Jeez," he murmured aloud.

And then, what about that weird business of the exploding casita? According to Mendoza, she believed Liz was behind it. Well, whoever was behind it—assuming anybody was behind it—what was that all about?

Another swallow of coffee, followed by another shake of the head. For a reasonably cut-and-dried fraud investigation, this case was turning out to have quite a set of legs.

He could well say the same about Alix London, he thought with a smile that was at once turned into a recriminatory scowl.

Let's not go there.

— • —

Three blocks from where Ted Ellesworth was staring at his cappuccino and trying to make sense of things at the Hilton, Alix London was staring at her coffee and trying to make sense of things in La Plazuela, one of the restaurants in La Fonda, the stately, eighty-year-old grande dame of the city's hotels. Originally, it had been the hotel's courtyard but now, roofed over by a skylit ceiling, it was a handsome, sun-dappled dining room that wouldn't have looked out of place in Granada: red flagstone floor, rustic, hand-carved wooden tables and chairs, a couple of potted, full-grown ficus trees, a gently gurgling tiled fountain in the center—none of which registered in Alix's perception. She was, if anything, more perplexed than Ted was.

It was unbelievable. In the last twenty-four hours—no, fewer than twenty-four; she hadn't even arrived in Santa Fe until yesterday afternoon—she'd come within a hair of being blown through the roof of her casita; she'd been trampled by an escaping thief and murderer; along with Chris, she'd discovered the body of his victim; she'd been grilled by the police; and—here was the ironic twist to it all—a few minutes ago she'd concluded, tentatively anyway, that the painting that was surely at the root of it all was nothing but a lousy fake. Well, no, not a lousy fake, a good fake, but a fake, nonetheless.

There were so many questions to be answered: Had Liz known the picture was a forgery or had she been tricked herself? Had the explosion really been an attempt to kill Alix? (*Yes!* something inside her declared.) And if so, had it really been Liz's doing? (Another resounding *Yes!*) But if Liz had tried to kill *her*, who had killed Liz? Or could the two events be unrelated? Were there two unconnected scenarios being played out?

That seemed to be Lieutenant Mendoza's theory—that Liz had been killed only because she'd had the bad luck to catch the guy in the act of stealing the painting; a wrong-time, wrong-place kind of murder. That, or the killer was one of Liz's dumped artist-lovers or wronged colleagues and the theft of the picture either had nothing to do with it or was an attempt to throw them off. As to the propane explosion, he hadn't expressed an opinion, but it was clear that he didn't take very seriously the idea that it was a botched attempt at murder.

Alix couldn't have disagreed more. She believed in unrelated coincidences, yes, but not on this scale. The explosion, Liz's murder, the theft of the painting, the fact—if it was a fact—of its being a forgery—they were all connected, and the appearance of the double-dealing slimeball Roland de Beauvais in the middle of it all was no accident either. And at the heart of it all, she was more certain than ever, was the O'Keeffe itself. It was the one element that linked everything.

The painting. The damn painting. *Was* it really a fake? She wasn't quite as positive as she'd been at the police station, and it wasn't the picture itself that had her wondering, it was the back— that Galerie Xanadu stamp. It apparently showed that it had passed through and probably been sold by a (presumably) legitimate Albuquerque gallery. Surely it must have been subjected to authentication at the time, and seemingly it had passed muster. That made her think twice. Could that trusty old connoisseur's eye of hers have blown it this time?

On the other hand, being handled by a reputable gallery was no guarantee of authenticity, especially in Georgia O'Keeffe's case. Not long ago, twenty-four of twenty-eight "newly discovered" O'Keeffe watercolors had been sold for five million dollars to R. Crosby Kemper, a Kansas City philanthropist, by a well-known and highly regarded dealer. Kemper then donated them to the Kemper Museum of Contemporary Art, where they hung for several years. Before then, they had been scientifically authenticated by a variety of experts, and had even been on prominent display for two years at the National Gallery, enthroned as the *Canyon Suite*. Nonetheless, in the end they turned out to be fakes, every last one. It had all been a scam.

In a way, this kind of thing had been the artist's own fault. She'd been a notoriously secretive woman. No one had been allowed to visit her studio or see her at work. Consequently, no one knew how many pieces she might have created—if any—that she had privately stowed away without ever revealing. The number in her studio, it turned out after her death, had been staggering: well over a thousand. That is, over a thousand previously unsuspected works that we now knew about—and what about the ones we *didn't* know about? The ones she might have given to relatives or friends (not that she had too many of either) or sold privately? No one could say how many of those there might be or where they were, waiting to be "newly discovered."

As a result, go-getting forgers had a fertile field to plow. And experts, including one Alix London, had to keep a very open mind when looking at a previously unrecorded O'Keeffe. Maybe snap judgments weren't the best idea in the world.

But it wasn't any of this that was the reason for the dull ache at her temples, the hollow feeling in her chest. It was, of all things, her so-called career that had her so befuddled and anxious. How had this wonderful godsend of a job offer turned into such a nightmare? She had thought it would be a first step toward crawling out from under the baggage of her last name. Instead, here she was, entangled in a murder case—the murder of a major art gallery owner, no less—that was sure to create a sensation in the art world, if not the national news. And as if murder wasn't bad enough, now it seemed she had a forged O'Keeffe to contend with. How long would it be before everybody in the know, from San Francisco to New York, began exchanging raised-eyebrow glances and saying, "Well, I can't say I'm surprised. You do know who her father is, don't you…?"

And once that happened, the gossips and rumormongers would take over and do what gossips and rumormongers do: embroider, embellish, and insinuate. Good-bye, fledgling career. No one would touch her once they'd done their work. *After all,* people would say, *where there's smoke…*

She closed her eyes and massaged her temples in slow circles. It didn't do much good. The tongues, she thought, were probably already wagging away.

Well, let them wag. There was nothing she could do about it. She supposed the police would get to the bottom of it all eventually, but "eventually" was going to be a long time if they had to work through their dumped-lover and aggrieved-colleague hypotheses first.

She sighed. The headache was getting worse, close to where she'd want to take something, but otherwise it was good to be sitting in the warm, light-filled space, especially after the last few days of gloomy Seattle gray. Had she really still been in Seattle yesterday at this time, innocent and excited and happy? It seemed impossible. She closed her eyes to better hear the soft music of the fountain…

And sat up with a start. Wait a minute, what had she been thinking? Who said there was nothing she could do about it? What kind of defeatist attitude was that? Leaving it to the police wasn't merely *not* her only option, it was a lousy option. For one thing, they had blinders on. For another, what did they know about researching a painting? Zilch, that's what, and they obviously couldn't care less about it anyway. But she did know, and did care, and she had skills that could be put into play. If the painting was at the root of it all, who better than Alix London to dig into it?

And where better to start than right here in Santa Fe, this very morning, in the archives of the Southwest Museum of Twentieth-Century American Art, not three blocks from where she was sitting? According to Clyde Moody, the archivist they'd met last night at the reception, the archives retained exhibition catalogs from important galleries throughout the state. If the Galerie Xanadu had handled an O'Keeffe it was an important gallery practically by definition, wasn't it, and wasn't there a high likelihood that the picture had appeared in one of their catalogs? And if it was in a catalog there'd be some background information on it, and the more background information she had, the more focused and trustworthy those intuitive skills of hers would be. The question was, how far back did the archives ago, and just when did the Xanadu have the painting? It couldn't have been before 1964, of course, because that was the supposed date of its creation. On the other hand, if it was—

She jerked her head impatiently. Why sit here asking herself questions when the horse's mouth was available a telephone call away? Leaving her barely touched coffee on the table, she went back into the lobby, looked up the museum's number, dialed it on her cell phone, and asked to be put through to the archives.

Moody himself answered. "Archives." He sounded preoccupied, annoyed at being interrupted at some daunting archival task.

"Mr. Moody, this is Alix London. We met briefly at the Blue Coyote last night?"

She paused for him to say "Oh, yes, of course, how are you?" or something like it, but he remained mute. She could hear the scratching of a pencil or ballpoint pen. Whatever it was he was doing, he hadn't stopped for the phone call.

"I'm an art consultant," she said (the first time she'd ever uttered that sentence and probably the last), "and I'd like to stop by the archives today, if that's all right. I'm working with Ms. LeMay, whom you also met last night, advising her on a Georgia O'Keeffe painting that Liz Coane had for sale. I'm calling because I thought it would be best to inquire first whether… Mr. Moody, are you there?"

"I'm here, yes." There was an exasperated sigh, and then a rattle as he threw down the pen. "Ms. London, what is it exactly that I can do for you?"

Alix held in her own irritation. She'd run into other people like the irascible Mr. Moody, museum archivists or art librarians who treated the materials in their custody as if they were their private property and got thoroughly ticked off when researchers (for whose use the collections were presumably created) had the nerve to interrupt their fussy, fastidious, mundane little chores and ask to actually *use* the archives.

Some people, she thought. "I'm interested," she said pleasantly, "in anything you might have on an Albuquerque gallery, the Galerie Xanadu—"

"I'm thoroughly familiar with all the Albuquerque galleries. There is no Galerie Xanadu."

"It may not exist anymore—"

"It *does* not exist anymore. If it ever existed at all."

"—but I was hoping the archives might go back far enough to include it."

"The archives go back to 1932." Pause. "I myself do not, however."

Humor? Was he being funny? She tried a tentative chuckle.

Indeed, that seemed to make him a bit more affable. "Well, let me check the index files," he said more kindly. "Galerie Xanadu? Spelled in the French manner?"

"I'm afraid I don't know how the French spell *Xanadu*," she offered, thinking a small joke of her own might ease things still more, and indeed, there was an arid sound that might be his version of a chuckle. Or not. "Yes," she added quickly, "*galerie* with an *ie*."

Silence for a minute and then: "As a matter of fact, we do have some material from them." He sounded surprised. "Apparently they were in business in the fifties and sixties. We have four... five...six exhibition catalogs."

"That's great!" Alix exclaimed, her excitement rising. "Can I come in this morning and look through them? At eleven, say?"

"Eleven fifteen would be better. I should be free then."

"Eleven fifteen it is. Thank you so much. I'll see you then."

"Yes, I'll have them out for you. Ms. London? Did I understand you to say you were a friend of Elizabeth's? I'd like to offer my condolences on last night's events. Just horrible."

"Actually, no, we weren't friends. I only met her yesterday."

"Oh. Well, my condolences in any case."

CHAPTER 11

Returning to La Plazuela, Alix sat down thoughtfully at her table, on which her coffee still sat, now cold. Before she could do much cogitating, though, the chair across from her was pulled out and Chris's six-foot-two frame flopped into it. She had slipped a note under Alix's door sometime during the night suggesting that they meet at the restaurant for an early lunch, so Alix had been expecting her.

"Morning, Chris, how are—"

"Coffee," Chris croaked. "I am in need of coffee. Urgently."

"Here, have mine. I haven't touched it yet. Going to be cold, though."

"Doesn't matter." Chris grabbed for the cup with both hands the way someone who's been in a lifeboat at sea might grab for the first mug of fresh water she's seen in three days, downed most of it in a series of greedy gulps, and let out a grateful sigh. "There, that's better. Life as we know it. Well, well, good morning to you too," she said a little more brightly.

Obviously, Chris had not had a restful night, but as far as her clothes went, she looked, as always, totally pulled together, nouveau Southwest-style: a trendy, raw-silk Navajo-tailored blouse, a silver and turquoise Navajo lotus-blossom necklace, matching earrings, a couple of silver ring bracelets, jeans, and high-heeled boots. But when she lifted her designer wraparound sunglasses to her forehead, leaving the earpieces stuck in her hair, her bloodshot, tired eyes gave her away.

She shook her head. "Whew, what a night."

"What time did the police finally let you go?"

"One o'clock. What about you?"

"One! I was back here by ten thirty."

"Well, Liz and I go back a long way. There was a lot they wanted to know."

"Did you—" Alix hesitated. "Did you tell them about the thing, you know, with Craig?"

Chris played with her bracelets and chewed on her lip for a moment, then shrugged. "Yep."

"The whole story?"

"Yep." She finished the coffee. "I felt rotten about dragging him into it—obviously, he couldn't possibly have anything to do with it—but the police really do need to know that kind of thing."

Alix nodded. "I suppose they do. Besides, if they found out about it later—"

"Which they would have."

"—they'd have started wondering why you hadn't happened to mention it."

"Exactly. Still, I feel bad, you know? I bet they've already called him in for an interrogation. I just hope he doesn't hold it against me."

"He won't hold it against you. You did the right thing, Chris." She wasn't quite as sure of that as she made it sound, but Chris could obviously use the support. And Alix could use a painkiller. "Chris, you wouldn't happen to have any aspirin on you, would you? I have a bit of a headache."

Chris shook her head. "Not on me. There's a gift shop here, though. Do you want to—"

"No, it can wait; it's not that bad. Let's have something to eat."

They ordered more coffee, huevos rancheros for Alix, and steak and shrimp fajitas plus a Caesar salad for Chris. While they waited, Alix filled her in on this morning's visit to the police station to look at the painting. When she came to de Beauvais's being there, and about overhearing his temporary shedding of the la-di-dah accent, Chris's interest perked up, but what really got her attention was telling her that the O'Keeffe was looking like a fake.

"A fake? A *forgery*? Liz was trying to…to swindle me?"

"Well, we don't know that she was in on it, Chris. It's a well-done piece of work, and she may have been fooled too."

"Yeah, right."

"Well, it's possible. And remember, at this point I'm not a hundred percent certain that it *is* a fake. I've been wrong before." She smiled. "Not often, of course."

Chris sipped the newly poured coffee and reflected. "So what's your advice?"

"Tell me," Alix responded, "what exactly is your situation with the painting? Is the arrangement you made with Liz still good now that…well, now that she's dead?"

"Sure, it's good. It's a bona fide, signed contract. The estate will have to live up to it. And so will I."

The waitress came back and set their orders on the table. Neither of them made a move to eat. "And what the contract says,"

Alix said, "is that it's yours if you decide to take it, but you can still decline, is that right?"

"Not exactly. It becomes mine *unless* I decide, by the thirteenth—Wednesday—*not* to take it."

"So you have three days."

"Right. So what *do* you advise? Hey, the food's getting cold; let's eat."

Alix had thought she wasn't hungry, but the smell of the eggs, cheese, and green chiles had gotten her salivary glands going, and for a few minutes she and Chris dug into their meals with gusto. About halfway through, Alix returned to the subject at hand. "What do I advise," she said, pondering. "Well, I have to say that I feel it to be my moral duty to advise you to get out of it. There are too many ifs, too many issues. There'll be other O'Keeffes available; why mess with this one? Too much weirdness here, Chris. Go back to Seattle. Save your money for something else. That's my advice—my moral-duty advice."

Chris swallowed a chunk of rolled-up tortilla stuffed with steak, onions, and green pepper, washing it down with more coffee. "And I respectfully decline to accept it. I'm in this up to my neck already, and I'm not about to walk away from it as if none of it ever happened. Not while we still have three days. I've formed an attachment to that painting, and I would like to *know* whether it's real or not before I throw in the towel. So tell me, what's plan B? Screw your moral responsibility."

Good for you, Alix thought with a surge of feeling. "My feelings exactly. Well, plan B would start with my going over to the museum archives to see what I can learn about the painting's history. And then use the rest of those three days to see if we can determine for *sure* whether it's real or not. After that—follow wherever it leads us."

"And you can do that—determine for sure if it's authentic—in three days?"

Alix shrugged. "Won't know till I've tried. But I think so, yes."

"But how? I thought it took weeks to get back the lab results on...on...I don't know, materials, pigments, whatever..."

"Oh, sure, but I wouldn't be fooling around with things like that," she said, treating Chris to an abbreviated version of the lecture she'd given de Beauvais in the evidence room. "So I'd be depending more on—"

"The old connoisseur's eye thing?"

"That's it."

Chris had finished her meal. She accepted yet more coffee from the waitress and looked seriously at Alix. "The connoisseur's eye," she repeated. "You started to explain it to me once and I said to save it for another time. I think maybe it's time. What is it, exactly?"

"Exactly? That's not so easy to explain." Alix finished off the last few bites of her own breakfast while she gathered her thoughts. "Basically, it stems from an ability to get inside an artist's head, to see what he or she saw, to understand what they were trying to say, to see the way they said it—the colors, the composition, the way the paint was laid down—and whether they all truly fit the artist involved."

Chris was frowning. "But why is that anything special? Isn't that what any art expert would do?"

"Yes, but if you have the eye, it's pretty much instinctive, or at least it feels that way. You don't have to go back to the books or compare the painting with the artist's other works, or anything. You just know."

Chris's frown was now a dubious scowl. "Alix, no offense, and I trust you and all, but...well, that has a little bit of a sleight-of-hand sound to it. Like some kind of hocus-pocus. I mean, 'You just *know*'? That's not exactly confidence-inspiring."

"You're not the only one that feels that way," Alix said, laughing, "and very few people do have the ability. It's not something you can learn, although you need the learning to make it work. In my case, it's something I apparently inherited from my father."

"Yes, but, honestly, 'You just know'?" She shook her head. "It just doesn't—"

"Look, let me ask you a question. If I showed you two handwriting samples, one of which was yours and one that wasn't, you'd be able to pick your own out with no trouble, wouldn't you?"

"Sure, anybody would."

"True. But how—*exactly*—would you know that it was yours?"

"Well, let's see…" Chris pulled out a ballpoint, scrawled a few words on a napkin, and studied them. Okay," she said, looking at what she'd written. "There are certain things that distinguish my handwriting. I loop the bottom of my *g*'s but not my *y*'s; I think that's unusual. And I dot most of my *i*'s, but not all, with a little circle, and—"

Alix snatched the napkin away. "So without something like this—a sample to compare—you wouldn't be able recognize your own handwriting?"

"No, of course I'd be able to. I'd recognize it in a flash. I was just trying to explain to you—"

"*How* would you recognize it in a flash?"

"I don't know how, Alix, I just would."

"Bingo," declared Alix, "you've just described a connoisseur's eye. When it comes to your own handwriting, you have it, everybody has it. There are a hundred reasons you recognize it—looped *g*'s, unlooped *y*'s—but you don't have to consciously sort through them one by one and see if they match. It happens by itself, and it happens instantaneously. You take one look…and *you just know*."

Chris's frown had melted away. "I see. And you can really do that with paintings?"

"Not every artist, no, but a fair number, and O'Keeffe is one of the ones whose aesthetic sensibilities I seem to be attuned to."

"I won't even ask what that means."

"Good, because I'm not sure I know either. I've got it, I know that, but I wouldn't want to try to explain it—or analyze it too closely. It's sort of like having a goose that lays these golden eggs for you. Not a smart idea to dissect it to see how it works."

Chris nodded slowly, finishing her coffee and absorbing what she'd heard. "Okay, I get it more or less, but, well, you've already looked at the painting. You've come to your conclusion: it's a fake. What more is there to do for the next three days?"

"See if I can verify it," Alix said promptly. "I told you I couldn't be a hundred percent sure—" she smiled, "—only about ninety-seven percent—and what I need to do now is actually step into O'Keeffe's world as deeply as I can. I need to see it through her eyes, to feel it. The picture is of Ghost Ranch, which is way the hell in the boonies, two or three hours north of here. She fell in love with the place and bought this isolated little shack and plot of land up there, at the foot of the cliffs, away from everything— miles from any of the ranch buildings—and lived and worked there for fifty years—from her forties into her nineties. I'd like to go there and see the area for myself."

"She was still painting when she was in her nineties?"

"And only stopped then because she went blind."

"Yeah, I guess that would throw a small crimp in things."

"And even then she became a potter and did that right up until she died—a few months short of her ninety-ninth birthday."

"Some lady," Chris said.

"You don't know the half of it." Alix was very glad now that she'd boned up on O'Keeffe after she'd gotten Chris's call. "Anyway, Ghost Ranch is now a conference center—has been for more than fifty years—and if they have rooms they're not using, you can book them for the night, which is what I want to do."

"So you intend to drive up there, or what?"

"I do, yes. But on the way I also want to stop at Taos. Taos was the first place she spent time up here. Did you ever hear of Mabel Dodge Luhan?"

Chris frowned. "Vaguely...rich, colorful, avant-garde...the big kahuna of the Taos arts scene back in the twenties and thirties, is that who you mean? Knew everybody—D. H. Lawrence, Ansel Adams, Martha Graham..."

"...*and* Georgia Totto O'Keeffe," Alix said. "Right, Luhan was a famous hostess, a big party-giver, and no cultural pooh-bah passing through Taos could escape spending a few nights at her house. Well, O'Keeffe was one of them, and it was the very first place she stayed in New Mexico. Stayed more than once, in fact, and did quite a few paintings of scenes right on the property, and it's obviously where New Mexico got into her blood. I'm sure I read somewhere that the house is still standing, and I'm hoping that whoever owns it now will let me wander around the place a little and get the feel of it. I need to try to see it through her eyes, to see if I can get some understanding of what it was that made her decide to pull up stakes and leave her very comfy, very successful life in New York."

"Well, that's all very interesting, but I repeat—can you do all that in three days?"

"I can sure try—three days, two places, and the furthest is only a few hours from here. Seems doable," she said confidently, then hesitated. "One problem, though."

"Namely?"

"I'm afraid I'll need at least a partial payment on my fee. Rental car, two overnight stays—"

"Sure, you can have it, but it's not necessary. You're working on my behalf; I'm not going to let you pick up the tab."

"That's not entirely true, Chris. I'm working on my behalf too. Probably more on mine than yours."

"No, I don't see it that way. This is still basically my affair, and I have a lot of dogs in this fight. Somebody's maybe tried to stick me with a forgery, somebody's killed one of my oldest friends, and somebody's tried to kill one of my newest friends. I want to find out what's going on. So it's my nickel. End of discussion. I'm also going with you, by the way, just in case you were thinking otherwise."

Alix had indeed been thinking otherwise. "I don't know, Chris," she said slowly. "One person's already been killed over this, and I'm still alive only by the skin of my teeth. Who knows what's coming next? I wouldn't feel right about getting you involved—"

"Getting me involved? Are you kidding? I'm the one that got *you* involved, and I am not about to let you go gallivanting around up there in the boondocks on your own. And there's something else too." Her jaw firmed. "I need to find out if I was nothing but an easy mark for Liz to sucker into paying three million bucks for a fake. I guess I've come around to thinking you're probably right about what happened between Liz and Craig, which would make this the second time she's suckered me. But I want to *know*. I *need* to know. So I'm tagging along whether you feel right about it or not. It's not your choice."

Alix smiled and let herself relax. "I'm glad. It'll be nice to have company," she said sincerely, then added, "Even if it does tend to get a little bossy from time to time."

"I'll pretend I didn't hear that. Well, then." With the flat of her hand Chris slapped the table and stood up. "Come on, expert, time's a-wasting. Let's get you those aspirin, and then we probably ought to get going, head for Taos. We're burning daylight here. It's nearly eleven."

Alix got up as well. "Fine, but I need a little time at the museum archives first. I found out this morning that the painting passed through someplace called the Galerie Xanadu in Albuquerque at some point, and according to Mr. Moody, they have some of their catalogs. I'm hoping there might be some information."

"Mr. Moody? Who's Mr. Moody?"

"We met him last night at the reception. The museum archivist; bow tie, bald—"

"Oh, yeah, squirrely little guy," Chris said, nodding. "Yeah, I remember him. Well, if it's all the same to you, I think I'll pass on the pleasure of further acquaintance with the gentleman and spend the time getting us a rental car and booking rooms for us at Taos and Ghost Ranch."

"Good idea."

"What you said a minute ago about doing this more on your own behalf than mine," Chris said as they walked through the lobby toward the gift shop, "what did you mean?"

She listened uneasily as Alix explained about the effects this all might have on her career. "Oh God, I was so busy thinking about me that I didn't give a thought to what it might mean for you. But look, maybe the reports won't mention our names. We just found her body, that's all."

Alix chuckled humorlessly. "They'll mention mine once they learn who my father is."

"But how would they find out?"

"Oh, they'll find out. They probably already have."

"Have you looked at this morning's Santa Fe paper to see what it says?"

Alix shook her head. "I didn't want to know."

"Well, I do." While Alix bought her aspirin, Chris plunked half a dollar down on the counter for the morning's *Santa Fe New Mexican*. "Whoa, Liz made page one: 'Police hunt for killer of Canyon Road gallery owner,'" she read aloud, then skimmed down the column, opened it to the continuation on an inside page, and spread it out on the counter. She read silently for a few moments longer, then sighed. "I'm afraid you're right. They mention us both as having found Liz's body, and then they say: 'This newspaper has learned that London is the daughter of Geoffrey London, the notorious New York restorer convicted nine years ago in a celebrated art fraud case. Ms. London is still believed to be in Santa Fe, but her whereabouts are unknown. Messages left on her Seattle answering machine have gone unanswered. Calls to her father, who has operated an art importing business in Seattle since leaving prison earlier this year, have also been unsuccessful in reaching him.'"

"They've been calling *Geoff*?" Alix said, wincing. "So he knows what's happened. He must be worried sick about me."

"But it says they haven't been able to reach him."

"Chris, my father is the last person in the world to turn down an opportunity to talk to the media. If he's unreachable now, it's because some other reporter did get to him first, and he knows what the rest of them are calling him about. I bet he's left a dozen messages on my answering machine."

"But if he couldn't get you there, wouldn't he have tried your cell phone?"

"Well..." Alix felt the warmth of a flush rising into her cheeks. "Actually, I've, um, never given him the number."

"Your own father doesn't have your...?" She caught herself. "Sorry. Not my business. Come on, let's head back to the Hacienda."

"It's just that—"

"Alix, there is absolutely no need to explain. It's none of my business," she said again.

Alix sighed and offered a pale smile. "It'd probably take too long to explain anyway."

The Hacienda Encantada was two blocks from La Fonda, and they made it in a couple of minutes. As they entered the main building, Alix looked at her watch. "Okay, I should be finished up at the museum by twelve thirty or so. We can take off for Taos then."

"Great. I'll have the car here, ready and waiting by then."

"But first," Alix said, "I have to call my father."

CHAPTER 12

But first I have to call my father.

What a simple, unremarkable statement that was. What could be more natural? Thousands of people said it every day. But when was the last time it had come from Alix's mouth? A decade? At least.

She tossed her purse onto the bed, opened the French doors to the slate-floored patio, brushed a litter of golden, newly fallen leaves from one of the rattan chairs, opened her cell phone, got the number of her father's business from Information, and accepted the offer to be put right through. Best to get it done right away, even before taking those aspirin. If she gave herself time to think about it, she'd probably do what she'd done last night: change her mind and snap the phone closed, putting it off for another time.

In fact, that might be a good idea. She realized that her throat was dry. What harm would there be in—

"Venezia Trading Company. Can I help you?" Slow, labored, like a kid reciting something he'd worked hard to memorize.

Tiny.

"Hello, Tiny, this is Alix."

The voice came cautiously alive. "Alix? No kidding? Hey, *mia cucciolina*, how're you doing?"

Mia cucciolina. My little puppy. It was what he used to call her a million years ago when he was Uncle Beniamino and she loved to sit on his lap and blabber away up at that big, dumb, good-natured face. So suddenly she never saw them coming, tears were running down her cheeks. Only with an effort did she manage to get a few words through a painfully tight throat.

"I'm fine, Tiny, how're you? It's been a long time."

"Hey, you know me, I'm always fine."

She laughed. "I know. Tiny, is my father there? Can I talk to him?"

"Sure, you can talk to him. Lemme put him on. As soon as I figure out which button to…"

"Oh, and Tiny? You know, I'm working with someone who wants to buy a Georgia O'Keeffe."

"Yeah, I heard. Good for you." Not a trace of resentment there, even though she knew she'd hurt his feelings when she'd told Geoff she didn't want his help. What a thoroughly nice, decent guy he was. Well, if you didn't mind the part about his being a master forger. Or rather having *been* a master forger, assuming you bought the current story.

"Well, you know, I have a few questions I'd really like your opinion on. Can I call you about them in a couple of days?"

She could practically hear him purr. "Anything for you, *piccolina*."

Piccolina. Little girl. Tiny had been born on Jerome Avenue in the Bronx and generally spoke with an accent that showed it, but he loved to sprinkle his speech with the terms of his ancestral

Sicily. Sometimes, with a glass or two of Chianti in him, she could swear he developed an Italian accent.

"Thanks, Tiny, I appreciate it." She jotted down a mental note: she was going to have to make up some questions for him.

A moment later, her father's voice came on. "Alix? I'm glad you called. I was concerned." And in fact, she could hear the strain in his voice. *I'm glad I called too*, she thought but couldn't quite bring herself to say it. "Reporters have been calling me all morning. What in the world have you gotten yourself into out there? Are you all right?"

"Yes, I'm perfectly fine, Geoff."

She spent a few minutes answering his questions, mostly simply to reassure him, since it turned out he knew almost as much about the previous day's events as she did. She considered telling him that she now thought the painting was a fake, but some part of her pulled back, knowing that he would be eager to get involved—to help—and she wasn't up to dealing with that yet.

"What about the explosion in your—what did they call it—casita?" he asked. "You don't think that was an attempt to…to…?" He was worried about her, all right. Geoffrey London did not very often find himself unable to complete a sentence.

"The police seem pretty sure it was just an accident, Dad. A faulty pipe."

Dad? Had she just called him "Dad"? Where had that come from? She'd been calling him "Geoff" since she was twelve; she'd just started one day on her own, in a fit of self-assertion, and he hadn't expressed any objection. She prayed that he wouldn't notice the switch.

Apparently, he didn't. "I don't give a fig about what the police think. What do *you* think?"

Time for a white lie. "Oh, they're probably right…Geoff." She threw the last word in just to try and wipe that "Dad" out of both of their minds. "I can't think of any reason for anyone to do me harm."

"All the same, I don't like the sound of it," he said. "Not one little bit. Not at all. I can't tell you how sorry I am for getting you into this, my dear."

"Getting me into this? You didn't get me into this."

"Oh, I did, I did. Well, perhaps not directly, but in a way, a very real way, it *is* all my fault. That is, I mean, ah, not directly, of course, but…in a way. If you take my meaning."

No, she didn't take his meaning, and it wasn't like him to repeat himself or to natter on like that. A shivery chill crawled up her spine and settled, tingling, at the base of her neck. "Geoff," she said hesitantly, "you haven't…you and Tiny haven't been faking any Georgia O'Keeffes lately, have you?" She tried to make it sound like a joke, but her voice went higher and higher until it practically squeaked at the end.

His bark of sudden, surprised laughter was genuine enough to set her mind at ease. "Good heavens, no! What an idea! My dear woman, I am now the very model of a modern model citizen. So is Tiny. So are we all."

"What did you mean then? How is it your fault?"

"I was referring to—I'm not sure what I was referring to. The entire course of your life, I suppose. If not for my questionable influence, you wouldn't be in the art world at all; you'd have found yourself some respectable profession in which to engage. Worse, if not for my misdeeds, you'd still be married to that charming fellow, what's-his-name, and be planning society luncheons on Beacon Hill, rather than working at all. And you'd have a *très élégant* hyphen in your last name."

The playful twinkle was back in his voice, and it made her smile and play along. "You mean Paynton Whipple-Pruitt? As I recall, you called him a pompous, overbearing, self-absorbed ass."

"I did no such thing."

"You most certainly did."

"I most certainly did not. I called him a *puerile*, overbearing, self-absorbed ass."

"Sorry, I stand corrected," Alix said, laughing.

"Alix, what will you do now? Are you returning to Seattle?"

"No, I have a few, uh, doubts about the painting, actually. I think it would help to see the O'Keeffe country for myself, and I'm going to drive up a little later today."

"That's an excellent idea, but by yourself, off alone in the desert? Given what's occurred? You know, I have a little free time. Would you like me to—"

"Chris LeMay is going with me," she said, heading him off. She was feeling nearer to him than she had in a long time, but she wasn't ready for three solid days of close company yet. "In fact, I've got to go get ready to leave."

"I'm glad you called."

"I'll call again soon."

"Yes, do that, my dear. Good-bye. Bless you."

Thoughtfully, she closed the phone. Wouldn't any other parent who hadn't received a call from a daughter in ten years or so have called attention to it and jabbed in the needle just a little? Not Geoff. He was just plain happy to have finally heard from her and to let it go at that.

New leaves had drifted down onto her shoulders and lap. She brushed them off and went inside to pack so that she'd be ready to leave as soon as she was finished at the archives.

Strangely, her headache had disappeared.

— • —

Gaining access to the archives of the Southwest Museum of Twentieth-Century American Art was only marginally easier than getting into NORAD Central Command. The room was located behind a locked door at the back of the museum library, and before Alix would be permitted to enter she had to present herself at the reference desk. There, after showing her driver's license to prove she really was who she purported to be, she was required to fill out a two-page form starting with "home address" and ending with "purpose of archival perusal," to sign another document indicating her agreement to abide by various proscriptions (no scissors or pens could be taken into the sacred chamber, no archival materials taken from it), and to leave the license and her purse with the librarian for security.

Only then was Mr. Moody paged. He appeared moments later. The bow tie and dark, old-fashioned suit were not only for social occasions such as art receptions, she saw; they were his work outfit too. A small, unexpected touch of whimsy was supplied by the bow tie, on which tiny images of Wile E. Coyote chased Road Runner up and down desert mesas and buttes. There was no whimsy in his manner, however. He greeted her with a perfunctory nod. (Did he or didn't he remember meeting her the previous day? Impossible to tell.) Then he led her to the door of the locked room, where he punched the opening combination into a keypad, first making sure with a scowl that she was not surreptitiously recording the numbers. To please him, Alix turned completely away, as if entranced by the library shelves behind them.

Inside the room, there was a metal desk and chair at one end, a single library table with a legal pad and a few blunt pencils on it, and six rolling steel bookshelf cabinets along one wall. Moody motioned her to a chair at the table, went to the desk, and returned with a cardboard magazine file in which there were a few catalogs. "I've pulled these for you to save you the effort of having to go through the files yourself."

"Thank you," Alix said, although she was fairly sure he'd done it because he couldn't stand the idea of intruders like her prowling freely through the shelves of his domain on their own and doing who knew what dastardly deeds in there: writing on things with pens, maybe.

"I also called an old friend, a long-time art dealer in Albuquerque, to find out what I could for you about the gallery. It was, according to her, quite well thought of, opening in 1962 or 1963 and closing in about 1975. The owner was a man named Henry Merriam, something of an authority on Southwest graphic artists, I understand. I hope that's helpful?"

That she did appreciate. "Thank you," she said again, with more conviction this time. Since he continued to stand there, she said, "Well, I guess I'll—"

"Yes, I have more work to do myself," he said, went to his desk, sat down, and began shuffling papers.

He had been somewhere else when he'd been called, so she assumed he was now remaining in this room to keep an eye on her. From the desk he could unobtrusively watch his visitors, just in case they should sinisterly produce a pair of gleaming scissors or try and stuff something into their shirts. Ah, well, who was she to frown on attention to one's responsibilities? She put his sidewise glances out of her mind and got on with her own work, searching for some mention of *Cliffs at Ghost Ranch* in the catalogs. There were six issues altogether, and they were not so much catalogs as glossy, expensively produced color newsletters—*Xanadu*

Doings—that included occasional informal columns from Merriam—"Meanderings (and Maunderings) of a Dilettante"—along with information on the gallery's exhibitions, sales, and openings.

She had been through the first two without success when the phone on Moody's desk chirped, and after a second he called to her. "It's for you." He pointed to another telephone at the far end of her table. "You may take it there." Both tone and gesture made it clear that the idea her receiving a telephone call in the archives was highly irregular and was not to be repeated. She responded with a "thank you" and an apologetic shrug.

"Alix, hi," Chris said when she picked up the phone. "Slight change of plans and I wanted to check with you before I booked the rooms. Does it make any difference if we do it backwards? First Ghost Ranch and then Taos? Ghost Ranch has some new courses starting tomorrow and they'll be all filled up, but they have rooms tonight. And then we can go back down to Taos tomorrow instead. Would that be okay?"

"Sure, no problem."

"Wonderful. And now I have a surprise for you. I checked on hotels and things in Taos and the Internet turned up an interesting fact. You know that Mabel Dodge Luhan house you were hoping was still around? Well, it is, and the owners run it as a retreat center and a bed-and-breakfast."

"Great!" Alix exclaimed. "Wonderful!"

"However, starting tomorrow there's a conference in town, at the Taos Convention Center—who knew Taos had a convention center?—and all the Luhan rooms have been booked for weeks."

Alix sagged. "Oh. Not so great. Still, at least we'll be able to—"

"The conference is called New Directions 2010: The Emerging Art Market in the New Economy," Chris said, talking over her. "It's the third annual New Directions conference—"

"Wait, that rings a bell. Didn't you tell me Liz was the power behind that?"

"That's right."

"But how can they…I mean, Liz has just been…and they're holding it anyway?"

"Yes, they thought about canceling, but it would have been impossible to reach everyone in time, and then there are the flight reservations, the hotel reservations, the income to the city—it would have been a calamity, so they're putting it on as a kind of memorial to Liz."

"Interesting."

"Yes, but I haven't gotten to the real surprise. It turns out that the Luhan House has had to cancel one of the reservations after all, and it happens to be for the best room in the house, Mabel's very own bedroom. More like a suite, they say. More than enough space for two—and I've booked it. You can wander around the place to your heart's content."

The news perked Alix up again. "Chris, that's terrific! I wonder whose room it…oh. Liz's?"

"Liz's," Chris confirmed. "There's some kind of poetic justice at work there, wouldn't you say? Or maybe I mean poetic symmetry, or poetic—"

Alix could feel Moody's irritated glare boring into the back of her neck. Time to get off the phone. "I better get back to work, Chris. I should be done within the hour and we can head right up to Ghost Ranch. Then tomorrow we can take off for Taos in the morning. I think that should give us enough time in each place."

"Good. I'll make the reservations and register us for the conference. Oh, and wait till you see the car I've rented for us. That'll be another surprise. Bye, now."

Another apologetic face-shrug for Moody and back to work. She found what she was looking for in the fourth newsletter she searched, the November 1971 issue. The monthly sale was called *Masters of the Desert*, and in pride of place on the left-hand center page was a large color print of the picture. It would have been impossible to miss it, even without the extensive printed entry below, which began with:

> Georgia O'Keeffe (b. 1887)
> *Cliffs at Ghost Ranch*, 1964
> Inscribed 'OK' within star (on backing)
> Oil on canvas
> 36 x 30 in. (91.4 x 76.2 cm.)

Bingo. She made a little fist-pumping gesture of triumph. She'd found it! This was it, all right. Eagerly, she read on.

> <u>Provenance</u>
> Private Collection, 1964–1971 (Gift of the artist)
> <u>Guarantee of authenticity</u>
> Painting has been submitted to two recognized O'Keeffe experts and has been authenticated as genuine. These notarized evaluations will be provided to buyer.

That brought a small puff of frustration, of disappointment. Damn, there was exactly nothing to go on here. The picture had been in a private collection, but whose? It had been certified by "recognized experts," but who were they? And who, if anybody, had bought it in 1971? She scanned the rest of the page, but it was all padding: "In this striking painting the artist depicts the craggy cliffs near her home with a subtle range of ochres, Naples yellow, orange, purples, and…Tonal variations are infused with the bold yet delicate contrasts that are the hallmark of her…The awe-inspiring vastness of the landscape has been transformed into something comprehensible on the canvas by the…" Blah, blah, blah.

Nothing. The trail both began and ended here. All the same, she scanned the remaining three newsletters in hopes of learning more, but there was no further mention of the painting. But two things in Merriam's "Meanderings" caught her eye. First, his smiling photograph appeared at the head of the columns, and he looked to be relatively young, in his early forties, perhaps. For some reason she had automatically assumed he'd be older, in his sixties, which would have meant that by now he probably would have gone to meet his maker. After all, the gallery had closed thirty-five years before. But if he'd been in his forties back then, he'd be in his seventies or eighties now, no spring chicken, but likely to be still around. The trick would be to find him.

And that's where the second thing came in. The final paragraph of his July 1972 Meanderings said: "As usual, the Galerie Xanadu will be shuttered and dark in August while Ruthie and I make our annual pilgrimage to Ghost Ranch for a month of education and 're-creation' (in its literal and original sense). We will reopen the first week in September, however, and we will open with a bang. From September 3 to…"

Ghost Ranch. Why, she would be at Ghost Ranch herself before the day was out. Merriam had written about an "annual pilgrimage." That meant he went regularly, right? Well then, wasn't it possible, even probable, that his address or telephone number—or some other lead to getting hold of him—resided in some file there?

"Are you finding what you're looking for?" Moody asked from his desk. "Is there anything else you need?"

"Thank you, no," she began, but changed her mind. "Mr. Moody," she said with what she hoped was an appealing smile, "this friend you have in Albuquerque—do you suppose she might know what happened to Henry Merriam after he closed up shop? Where he went?"

"Oh, I don't believe he went anywhere. It seems he had a massive heart attack. That's why the gallery closed, you see. My friend didn't know him all that well—this was some thirty-five years ago, long before she opened her own gallery—but she's fairly sure he died soon after. In any case, he certainly never returned to the art scene. I'm sorry."

"Oh, that's okay, Mr. Moody," she said, replacing the newsletters in the file box. "Thank you very much for your help."

Another dead end, she thought with a sigh. It looked as if she wasn't going to get any help at all from secondary sources. She was going to have to rely one hundred percent on that elusive, enigmatic intuition of hers.

It was, in other words, back to square one.

CHAPTER 13

"Whoa," said Tommy, the Indiana-farm-boy bellman, gawking. "A Ferrari!" He had carried out their bags to load into the rental car, but once having seen it he just stood there bug-eyed, a bag in each hand.

"A Lamborghini, actually," Chris said casually. "Nice, isn't it?"

"I'll say," Tommy breathed, "it looks like a frigging Batmobile."

Alix watched, amused. It *did* remind one of a Batmobile, she thought: a sinister matte black, sleek, and low, with flat planes rather than curves, and altogether strangely, seductively beautiful. With the vertical passenger doors flung up and open like a couple of wings, though, a stealth bomber might have made an even better comparison.

Once the bags were loaded and the two of them had climbed in—the car was so close to the ground it was more crawl than climb—Chris patted the steering wheel and grinned at her. "So what do you think?"

"It's gorgeous," Alix said truthfully, "but why in the world would you rent a Lamborghini just to drive up to Ghost Ranch?"

"Why not? It'll be fun."

"But it must cost a fortune."

"It does."

"And isn't it a little, um, conspicuous for these parts?"

"Well, of course it's conspicuous. Don't be dense, that's the point. I'm a member of the nouveau riche now, you know. Certain things are expected of me. I have to act the part."

Alix smiled to herself. How much Chris was like her father, himself an ex-member of the nouveau riche—easygoing, flamboyant, bigger than life. And, she thought, not for the first time, how much she herself was like her mother, Rachel, born into old money; low-keyed, reserved, traditional…almost stuffy. Not like her in the larger aspects of her life, which were anything but traditional, but in the little things, the refinements. To this day Alix would have been instinctively uncomfortable wearing serious jewelry (if she had any) before five p.m. or being seen in public in white after Labor Day. And as for those jangly bracelets and colorful shawls and flowing, silky, eye-catching slacks that Chris wore—well, they looked fine on Chris, but they weren't for Alix.

Her mother, though, had been traditional in all things, the big as well as the little. Falling in love with Geoffrey London had been the one wild thing Rachel had ever done, and it had cost her dearly. Not in money, for she had her own inheritance, but in her family's affections. From the first they had refused to accept this roguish, jolly Britisher of hers as one of their own, so it was no surprise that only a single uncle had come to her mother's funeral, and he was the sole other black sheep of the family: in the 1950s Uncle Julian had divorced his first wife and entered into an extremely short (and extremely expensive) Las Vegas marriage to a leggy dancer at the Flamingo. Afterward, much chastened, he had come humbly back to wife number one, but the damage had been done. Rachel's family, the Van Hoogerens, were not big on forgiving and forgetting.

So it was certainly no surprise to Alix that after her father's arrest, not one offer of help, not one expression of commiseration, had come from that side of the family. She was not likely ever to forgive them for that. Or to forget.

"Well, here we go," Chris said, those silver and turquoise bracelets jingling softly as she turned carefully onto St. Francis Drive, heading north. She drove prudently in the right lane, checking the mirrors every few seconds and keeping well away from the vehicles around them.

Alix was amazed. If she'd had to predict what kind of driving problems Chris might have, overcautiousness would have been the last one she'd have come up with. On the sidewalks, people stopped to goggle at the car. Alix would have preferred a bit less conspicuousness herself, considering that there might well be a would-be killer on her trail, and it would have been nice not to stand out quite like that. But Chris was obviously loving it, so she kept her peace.

Even when St. Francis Drive morphed into Highway 84, Chris continued to creep along in the right lane, at a painfully slow forty-five miles an hour, her body as tense as a piano wire stretched to its absolute limit. Clawed fingers squeezed the black-suede-covered steering wheel as if it might get away from her if she loosened her grip.

"Chris," Alix said suspiciously, "you've never driven one of these before, have you?"

Chris made a point of looking offended. "Sure I have, what do you think?"

"When?"

"Today," she said. "I drove from the rental place on Cerrillos Road all the way to the Hacienda, almost four miles. But I'm doing okay, aren't I?"

"Okay for a Toyota Camry with a 'Baby on Board' sign maybe, but not so great for a Lamborghini Gallardo LP 560."

"You even know the model?" Chris said, surprised.

"Yes, I do. I've actually driven one—an earlier version."

"No kidding. Where?"

"In Italy, as a matter of fact. In July and August Fabrizio used to drag me up to his family's summer place in Ravello most weekends. He thought I was getting to be too much of a hermit, which I was, and I needed to spend more time relaxing with people, which I did. I loved it too; the Santullos were marvelous and Ravello is something else. Well, his son Gian-Carlo had been an amateur race car driver and he had a collection of *six* sports cars, including two of these. He took me out for a few days of instruction, said I was welcome to treat one of them as my own when I was in Ravello, and I took him at his word. I spent quite a few Saturday mornings cruising down the Amalfi Coast. It was grand— gorgeous mountains on one side, the Mediterranean, blue and sparkling, on the other...beaches, villas..."

"Cruising down the Amalfi Coast," Chris repeated dreamily, "in a Lamborghini LP whatever. Sounds like a dream." She threw an arch glance Alix's way. "And were you alone while doing this cruising, or was this fascinating Gian-Carlo chap with you?"

"This fascinating Gian-Carlo chap was forty-nine, bald, five-foot-five, and two hundred pounds. And married. With five children."

"Oh," Chris said. Then, after a pause: "Not that that makes him a bad person, of course." And they both laughed.

"Alix, am I doing something wrong?" she asked uneasily a few moments later. "I'm getting these funny looks from passing drivers."

"No, you're not doing anything wrong. It's only that they've never passed a Lamborghini before. Lamborghinis aren't supposed to be passed, they're supposed to do the passing. They've probably never seen one in the right lane either." Neither had Alix.

Chris laughed, but it was through clenched teeth. "Well, the truth is, this thing scares me a little. Correction, a lot. The guy at the rental agency? He wanted to take me out in it, show me the ropes, but it ticked me off. Like what, I can't drive this thing because I'm a poor, helpless female? So I said no thanks, I can handle it."

"And?"

She shrugged. "And I couldn't handle it. Not for the first fifty yards, anyway. I barely *touched* the accelerator and it took off like a rocket. I almost had an accident before I got out of the lot. So, since then, I've been driving, um, somewhat on the slow side. You know, till I get the knack. Paying attention to the speed limit."

"Sure, Chris. Naturally." *But twenty-five miles* under *the speed limit?* This was a Lamborghini, after all, capable of doing two hundred miles an hour, capable (as Chris now knew) of going from zero to sixty in four seconds. It was practically a sacrilege to hobble it like this. Well, she thought with a sigh, let her drive it this way for a while, build up her confidence in the car's wonderfully smooth city driving capabilities.

"That's the right idea, Chris. You're doing fine." She smiled at her friend and settled into her soft, deep, enveloping seat to enjoy the scenery as best she could. Maybe after Chris had had her fill of driving, if you could call this driving, she'd let Alix take the wheel for a while. She could feel it under her fingertips now, imagine the thrilling way the car seemed to respond instantly to your thoughts, the way a well-trained thoroughbred responded to the slightest pressure of its rider's knees.

They continued their excruciating crawl past the Pueblo villages of Pojaque and Nambe, and into the gritty sprawl of Española ("Lowrider Capital of the World," the welcoming sign proclaimed), where they stopped for lunch at a Taco Bell. Word of the Lamborghini traveled fast; in the few minutes it took them to eat, six or seven low-slung, flamboyantly painted cars and trucks arrived in the parking area, spilling a dozen young Hispanic men out to stand in a murmuring, admiring circle around it.

When Chris and Alix came out of the restaurant still carrying their drinks, most of the young men withdrew respectfully, never taking their avid, adoring eyes from the Lamborghini. The one exception was a thin, dead-eyed kid of twenty or twenty-one, in a T-shirt and tight, dirty jeans, who stood leaning arrogantly against his truck, an unlit cigarillo stuck in his mouth. The truck was one of the less garish ones; the only paintwork they could see, aside from a few wreathlike odds and ends, was of a sweet-faced girl in a string bikini (you had to look twice to find the strings), surrounded by the usual orange-and-blue flames. "Bimbi," the flowing pennant beneath said.

"Nice," he said, looking at the car. "You wanna take me for a ride?"

They ignored him, of course, to which he responded with a studiedly insolent grin that turned into a laugh as they got into the car. "I don't know about this," Chris said to Alix as they snapped on their seat belts. "I'm not sure I like having a car that's sexier than I am."

North of Española the countryside grew more bleakly beautiful, with bare, rocky, mauve and rose-colored mountain ranges rising in the distance. There were fewer and fewer other drivers. Alix had the map out and was doing the navigating and color commentary. "Those are the San Juans on our right, Jemez Mountains on the left."

"I don't want to know about right and left. I'm having enough trouble concentrating on the road." They were at the edge of an escarpment now, and the road had turned curvy, following the contours of a winding river that ran along the foot of the cliff, about a hundred feet below. Chris was now driving at about twenty miles an hour and sitting tensely upright, alert and focused, like the one meerkat in the group that's been stuck with the watchdog assignment.

"Chris, if you're getting a little tired," Alix offered hopefully, "I'll be glad to take over for a while."

"Maybe later if you want to, but right now I'm not tired at all. I'm really enjoying this."

"Yeah, I can tell. The white knuckles are a dead giveaway."

Chris laughed tightly. "Well, yes, I suppose this thing still scares me a bit. It's so…responsive. I feel like it's a part of my body. It's as if it knows what I want to do—"

"Before you do," Alix finished for her with a sigh. "I know the feeling." Obviously, it was going to be a while before Chris let her have a go at driving it, if she ever did. "Oh, hey," she said, consulting the map again, "the river down there—that's the Chama!"

"The Chama? Is there something special about it?"

"Yes, it means we're in genuine O'Keeffe country now. She painted it several times. Pretty much this very view in at least one of them. She must have been standing right along the roadside here."

"Oh, really?"

But it was clear that Chris wasn't listening. It was the road that held her complete attention, and that was fine with Alix. With all its twists, and the sheer drop-off on the left, and the cliff face pushing in on them on the right, this tricky, dangerous section of Highway 84 demanded one's concentration. Had Alix been at the wheel, she wouldn't have been driving that much faster herself. Not having any choice, she left it to Chris, sat back, and began to do what it was she was coming up here to do: to "connect" with this clear, bright, high-desert atmosphere. She had been other places where the light was famous for being conducive to works of art: the golden lowland light of the seventeenth-century Dutch and Flemish masters, the watery marine light of J. W. Turner, the vivid orange-green hues of Van Gogh and Cézanne in the south of France.

This was different. Not rich or vivid at all, but thin and pale— pastel skies, pastel mountains. As it happened, she knew the atmospheric reasons for this. As in all deserts, the rainfall here was minimal, so there were virtually no light-distorting droplets of moisture in the air. Unlike most other deserts, however, this one was at an elevation of nearly eight thousand feet, so the air had less than a quarter of its sea-level density. The result was a remarkable clarity, a transparency Alix hadn't run into before. According to her map, the surrounding mountains were twenty-five miles away. They looked as if they were five. And like everything else in sight—the river, the mesas, the buttes—their shapes were crisper and cleaner than they had any right to be, as if a Botticelli or a Breughel had outlined them in pen and ink. She began to get her first inkling of what O'Keeffe—

"Hey, stop, we're here!" she said.

Startled, Chris brought the car to a sudden halt that had them both straining against their seat belts. She lifted her eyes from the long ribbon of asphalt in front of them to take in the arid, empty landscape on either side. "Where?" she asked blankly.

"Ghost Ranch. We just passed the turnoff. You were driving so fast you never saw it."

Chris didn't get the joke. "I sure didn't," she said, working at levering the car laboriously back and forth until she could get it turned around. Alix cringed at every grinding of the gears. They drove back to the turnoff, where a dirt road led toward a range of cliffs, no buildings in sight. Over the road was one of those wooden entrance "arches" made of two vertical wooden poles and one horizontal one across the top—the kind of thing that should have said "Bar-X Ranch." In this case the incised wooden sign said "Ghost Ranch." The open gate below, made of metal piping, had a triangle in the center the size of a highway Yield sign, but this one was ornamented with the Ghost Ranch logo: a stark white steer skull, very much à la Georgia O'Keeffe, on a black background. Self-styled marksmen had obviously found it attractive. It was well-peppered with dings and dents.

"Chris, I never did thank you for working out the logistics. Getting us in here, and then Mabel Dodge Luhan's bedroom, wow! You did a great job digging it up and hooking it for us. So thank you!"

"Hey, I'm the one who should be thanking you," Chris said as they turned onto the primitive dirt road. "You've done me a hell of a favor."

"You're more than welcome, but I wouldn't exactly call it a favor. You're paying me pretty well."

"Oh, I'm not talking about the stupid painting, I'm talking about what you did for me with Craig. I got up my nerve and had it out with him while you were in the archives. I laid my cards on the table. I asked—"

"Chris, did I miss something here? I don't know what you're talking about."

"I'm talking about what you said yesterday about my maybe jumping to conclusions and getting the wrong impression of what really went on between Craig and Liz."

"And you talked to him about it? This morning?"

"That I did. After you left for the museum. I caught him coming back from his interrogation with Mendoza and we went for coffee." Her face reddened slightly. "Everything you said was true—not only about him and Liz, but about *him*. Gallant, that's what you called him, and gallant is what he is. I had to pump him to get him to say anything at all, but I finally dug it out of him. Liz had been coming on to him—she was very attractive back then, remember—and he eventually succumbed. No excuses, even now. A moment of weakness; just what you said. That's what he told me, and I'm convinced it's true."

"I'm glad."

"I'll tell you the truth, it's lucky for Liz she's already dead, because if she wasn't I'd kill her myself."

"If you have any further conversations with the police, I think it might not be a very good idea to convey that thought to them."

"Don't worry," Chris said, laughing. "And let me tell you what kind of a guy he is. You know, Mendoza asked him to stick around for a few days—"

It suddenly occurred to Alix that he had asked *them* to stick around for a few days too. She hoped that Ghost Ranch was considered "sticking around." What the hell, he had their cell phone numbers. They could be back in Santa Fe in not much more than a couple of hours without him ever knowing they'd been gone.

"—and so I said that of course I'd pay the rates on the plane while he was here and also pick up his expenses. Well, he kind of flared up at that. If I wanted to pay the company for the plane, that was my business, but he damn well wasn't going to let me pay for his food and lodging. And he meant it." She smiled. "He can be very masterful too."

Alix detected a sort of proprietary pride in Chris's voice as she talked about him, and a new liveliness that was good to hear. "So what happens now?" she asked.

Chris practically beamed. "When I get back to Santa Fe, we're going to get together and have dinner. And I have the feeling we might get a second chance…nothing that he specifically said, but, you know, a feeling. A woman can tell, you know that."

I wouldn't know, it's been too long, Alix almost said, but she was too happy for Chris to spoil things with her own sorry story. "That would be wonderful," she said sincerely, and it would. It'd mean that at least something good came out of this consulting job from hell.

— • —

"So where is this place already?" Chris asked. "Did we miss a side road or something? There's not a sign of civilization in sight."

They'd driven a mile from the turnoff, and, indeed, they were still in open, empty country: a wide desert plateau with whitish cliffs on either side, with no sign of development other than the primitive road they were on.

"We haven't missed anything," Alix said. "We're there; we're just not at the conference center yet. Ghost Ranch is huge, over twenty thousand acres. The conference center is just a tiny part of it…oh, hey, look, there's a sign of civilization for you right there."

She was pointing to a derelict rough-hewn log cabin a few yards from the road, and Chris laughed. "Civilization circa 1870 or so, I'd say."

"No, wait!" Alix said with sudden urgency. "Stop! I want to show you something."

"But it's just an old—"

"I'm not talking about the cabin now. Just stop the car, will you?"

"There aren't any pull-offs. Where am I supposed—"

"There also aren't any cars, if you haven't noticed. Will you just stop the car, already?"

Chris complied, and a veil of the road dust they'd created drifted back over them. "Okay, what's up?"

Alix got out of the car, to be followed by Chris, who came to stand beside her. "Now look over there," Alix instructed, pointing at a wall of cliffs two or three miles away.

Chris peered in the indicated direction. "Okay, I'm looking…"

"You don't see anything interesting?"

Puzzled, Chris shook her head. "See what?"

"Those photos of the painting that Liz sent you—do you have them with you?"

"Yes, in my bag."

"Let's see 'em."

Chris shrugged, retrieved her bag from the car, and handed over a few postcard-sized photographs of the O'Keeffe. Alix selected one that showed the entire painting and held it up at arm's length. "Now. Look at the picture, and then look at the cliffs. See the two main fissures? Look at the one on the right and imagine you can see—barely see—what looks like the figure of a man half hidden in the shadows at the bottom. Do you—"

"My God, that's my painting!" Chris exclaimed, obviously thrilled. "Those are my cliffs!" She looked from cliffs to postcard and back again, and then, more subdued, said, "Alix, I know this sounds crazy, but even if it does turn out to be a fake, I'd kind of like to have it. It *is* beautiful, and somehow it makes the cliffs themselves more…more *real.*"

"That's true; that's what art does. And I agree, it's a very fine painting, a wonderful evocation of those cliffs. And *very* Georgia O'Keeffish. But you've agreed to pay almost three million dollars if you decide to take it, and I don't think you want to do that if it's not genuine."

"You're right, of course," Chris said with a sigh. She put the pictures back in her bag. "But O'Keeffe really did do pictures of this area, didn't she?"

"Many."

"Then, assuming it turns out to be a forgery, your next job is to find a real one for me. Would that be all right?"

"More than all right. It'd be a pleasure."

"Excellent," Chris said crisply. "Consider it a done deal. Now let's go find this supposed conference center and check into our rooms."

— • —

A little more driving took them down a dry, shallowly sloping hillside, over a log bridge that crossed a wooded creek, and along a stony ridge. They rounded the ridge, and there in front of them was the conference center. Sheltered by the cliffs and surrounded by multihued, fantastically shaped buttes, the one-story buildings circled a broad, grassy plaza. With groups of people strolling deep in conversation, and others sitting clustered in the lacy shade of cottonwood trees, it looked like a small college campus miraculously sprouted in the middle of the desert.

"Your rooms are ready for you," the receptionist told them once they'd found the administration building. "They're in the Coyote block. It's up the hill on the mesa. Just follow the road on the left up and around. Good view. Make sure you sit out and enjoy the sunset. I'm Barb. Just ask me if you have any questions."

"Barb, have you worked here long?" Alix asked.

"Going on twenty years."

"Do you happen to remember a man named Henry Merriam? He used to take courses here pretty regularly. He owned an art gallery in Albuquerque—Galerie Xanadu."

Clyde Moody's contact in Albuquerque had said that she thought he'd been dead for over twenty years—"fairly certain" was the phrase she'd heard Moody repeat on the telephone—but that left some room for doubt. Not much, of course, but here she was at Ghost Ranch, so why not ask?

"Of course, I remember him," Barb said. "He was here just a few months ago. Sweetest old man in the world."

Alix was stunned. "A few months ago…?"

Barb nodded. "August," Barb assured her. "Two months ago, almost to the day. He was standing right where you are."

This was almost too much to hope for. "Would you happen to know where I can get hold of him?"

"Not in this world, I'm sorry to say. He passed away. Nice old guy, too."

Alix sighed. Too much to hope for, all right. But to learn that he'd still been alive, been available, only two months ago, that really stung. "When exactly did he die?" she asked, more out of politeness than anything else.

"It was the very next day." She nodded to herself, thinking back. "That's right. See, he owned that art gallery years and years ago, and there was some kind of mix-up about whether he did or didn't sell some kind of painting or something...I don't know, something like that. So he was driving down to Santa Fe to straighten it out—I *think* it was Santa Fe; maybe it was Albuquerque. Well, he had a bad heart, you know? And he picked the wrong place to have a heart attack—right in that curvy section on 84, up in the cliffs where it runs along the Chama River. You probably drove over it yourselves to get here."

"We sure did," Chris said. "I damn near had a heart attack myself."

"Yeah, I hate driving it too. Anyway, whether he had a heart attack because he went over the edge, or he went over the edge because he had a heart attack, they say he was dead before the car hit the bottom. It was a blessing, in a way. He'd been pretty miserable since his wife got Alzheimer's and he had to put her in a, you know, facility." She smiled pensively. "It was pretty weird, really. You know the last words he said to me?"

"No," Alex said. "What did he say?"

"Well, it wasn't exactly to me, it was on the phone, and it wasn't exactly his very last words, but pretty close. He said, 'I assure you, I am not dead.'"

Chris wrinkled her nose. "'I assure you, I am not dead.' That *is* strange."

"I'll say. 'I assure you, I am not dead.' And then, not even twenty-four hours later—he *was*, just like that. Fate, I guess." A matter-of-fact clearing of her throat and she was back to business. "Your rate includes meals. Dinner is from five thirty to six fifteen. Not haute cuisine, but good and healthy and plenty to eat. You have private baths, but there aren't any TVs, radios, or telephones in the rooms."

"What about cell phone reception?" Alix asked. She found she wanted to check in with Geoff.

"Just about nonexistent. Afraid you're in the boonies here." At Alix's frown of concern, she added, "You're welcome to use the pay phone there on the wall, though. Takes cards."

Alix looked at it. "Um, well…"

Barb gave her a sympathetic smile. "Not real private, is it, honey? Well, if you don't mind driving back out a little way, there's a spot with just about the best cell phone reception in the world. It's the only building you'll see between here and the highway, a log cabin on your left that's got its own mini-cell-phone tower or whatever they call it built right into it—"

"Are you serious?" Alix asked. "That place must be a hundred years old. Why would—"

"It's not even twenty years old," Barbara said, laughing. "You remember *City Slickers*?"

"*City Slickers*?"

"The movie."

"The movie?"

"She doesn't get out much," Chris quietly interceded.

"Oh. Well, see, they filmed the movie here, and that cabin's just a prop they built. Anyway, here comes this huge Hollywood crew out here, and you can imagine how freaked out they get when they can't make all their super-urgent phone calls. So, being Hollywood, they just spent whatever it took to have the cabin wired up as their phone reception area. And when they left, they left it in place. Works great. The only place in twenty miles you can get decent reception. Sometimes when I drive by I see five, six people standing around talking on their phones. I keep telling my boss we ought to put in a Starbucks."

Chris glanced at her watch as they went back down the steps toward the car. "We've got time before dinner if you want to make your call, but would you mind driving yourself? You could drop me off at the room and I could put my feet up. I'm bushed. Driving that thing takes it out of you! If I ever get one I'll make sure it has automatic transmission."

"If you do, all your fellow Lamborghini owners will ostracize you."

"Oh, that really worries me." She handed over the keys. "Drive slow, will you? I don't think I was supposed to take the thing on dirt roads at all. And this isn't the Amalfi Coast."

Life's little ironies, Alix thought after she'd dropped Chris off. She finally gets another chance to get behind the wheel of one of these beauties, and it's on a burro trail on which she wouldn't dare drive faster than fifteen miles an hour even without Chris's warning. Not that it wasn't a pleasure anyway, she thought, moving the chrome gearshift lever smoothly from first to second. There were six gears on the LP 560, and Chris had never gone higher than fourth. Alix itched to drive all the way to the highway and give all six a workout just for the hell of it, but that didn't seem right, not without getting Chris's okay.

She pulled up at the faux log cabin and sat looking at it for a few moments. The set-builders had done a terrific job. Even from a few yards away there was nothing to suggest that it was anything but a moldering, rough-hewn old homestead from pioneer days. When she opened the door to have a peek inside, however, there wasn't any inside. That is, there was a three-foot-wide platform on the other side of the door—just enough to let them film somebody going in or coming out—and then a two-foot drop-off to rocky, sandy desert soil. No floor at all. Hollywood magic in action.

She went back outside to a shady corner of the splintery porch, sat carefully down on the edge, and dialed Geoff's business number.

"Venezia Trading Company. Can I help you?" Slow, dense, unmistakable. Apparently, Tiny now served as Venezia's telephone receptionist.

"Hi, Tiny, this is—"

"Hey, *la mia nipotina!*" he exclaimed happily. *My little niece.*

"Yes, it's me again, *Zio Beniamino.*" Uncle Beniamino. Well, what the hell.

"You wanna talk to your father? I'll—"

"No, wait a minute, Tiny, it's you I'm actually calling. I'll talk with him later."

That pleased him. "About that O'Keeffe?" he said with interest. She could hear a leather chair groan in protest as he settled his great bulk into it.

"Yes, I'd really appreciate your opinion on a couple of things." It was true, too. Making up questions hadn't been necessary after all.

"Okay, shoot."

"Well, the thing is, I'm working with this woman who's thinking about buying it, but I have my doubts, very strong doubts, that it's authentic. That is, I'm almost certain it's not—there's something missing, something that ought to be there but isn't, only I can't quite put my finger on it, if you know what I mean. It's as if—"

"I know what you mean. This is what, one of them flower pictures?"

"No, it's a landscape."

"Yeah? That's interesting." She smiled, remembering that she'd always liked the way Tiny said "interesting." He was the only person she knew who gave it its full four syllables, equally stressed: *in-ter-est-ing.* Somehow it made whatever they were talking about sound more…in-ter-est-ing. "Mostly they fake the flower pictures. Beats the hell out of me why; the landscapes are a whole lot easier. I guess it's because most of the marks—excuse me, the potential, you know, customers—are, like, more familiar with the flowers."

"You're probably right. But as to this one—"

"You got a picture you could e-mail me?"

"Yes, I do. Shall I do that?"

"Yeah, but for now just go ahead and tell me what it's like. You know, describe it."

"It's a landscape, as I said, a desert scene, a cliff face—"

"Uh-huh."

"—very painterly, almost abstract. The horizontal striations in the rock are shown mostly in oranges and yellows, with some ochres thrown in—"

"Uh-huh."

"There are a couple of vertical clefts—cracks—running down the face—"

"Uh-huh"

"—and at the bottom of one of the clefts, in the shadows, you can barely make out the figure of a man—"

"It's a fake."

"—in profile, apparently looking off to the right…*What did you say*?"

"It's a fake."

"How…wh…?" But even as the question tried to form itself in her mind, the answer was there, waiting for her where it had been all along. "The figure!" she breathed into the phone.

The *figure*, of course, the figure! She'd had it backward: the problem wasn't that there was something *missing* from the painting, some subtle touch that should have been there and wasn't. It was the opposite: something that shouldn't have been there but *was*. And not very subtle, either.

"She didn't put people in her paintings, did she?" she said more calmly.

"Not a one. Never."

"Tiny, are you positive? Not a single one?"

"What kinda question is that? Sure I'm sure. Damn thing's a fake. Okay, you got anything else you need to ask me?" More squeaks as he got out of the chair. "Something else I can do for you?"

"No," she said, laughing, "that takes care of everything quite nicely at present, thank you."

"Okay—for Christ's sake, Geoff, quit pullin' on my elbow—I mean, I'm still—"

There were some scuffling sounds, presumably Geoff wrenching the phone away from Tiny, and then her father's merry voice came on. "Hello, my dear. I gather our resident O'Keeffe authority has been of some use?"

"He sure has, Geoff. I should have spotted the problem myself, but I didn't. The painting has this figure of a man—"

"O'Keeffe didn't have figures in her paintings."

She almost sighed, but laughed instead. "That's the point, all right. I knew something was wrong, but it took Tiny to give me something I could put my finger on. I should have talked to him about it before." She hesitated, then added softly: "Or to you. I was stupid."

"Nonsense. Putting one's finger on it, as you choose to call it, is merely the final step, the icing on the cake. Pah, anyone can do that, given enough time. But recognizing it as inauthentic in the first place, ah, that's the important thing, that's what separates you from the rabble of so-called, self-proclaimed experts. And in that regard," he said with transparent pride, "you came through with flying colors—thanks to the genes you inherited from me, may I modestly point out."

"I'm sure you're right." She leaned against a wooden post, feeling strangely good, not certain whether she was basking in the warmth of the afternoon sun or of her father's approval. "I hereby thank you for passing them along."

"And you're in O'Keeffe country now?" he asked.

"Yes, I am, and it's glorious. Golden sunshine, mesas, buttes, every color of the rainbow…"

"I envy you. Would you like to guess what it's doing in Seattle?"

"Raining?"

"Correct. And how long will you be staying?" After so many years of estrangement, she thought, he was finally making small talk, pleasant everyday talk, with his daughter and he was reluctant to see it end.

So was she. "Just today. I'm with Chris, and we'll be leaving for Taos tomorrow morning sometime—although, come to think of it, she might want to go straight back to Santa Fe instead, once she hears for sure that the painting's not genuine." She paused, frowning. "You know," she said slowly, "there is one angle to this that still troubles me a little."

"Oh, yes?" *Here I am, ready and eager to help,* he was saying.

"Well, the thing is, this painting was shown during O'Keeffe's lifetime—in 1971—in what was a prominent gallery, right here in New Mexico. Now, recluse or not, she kept a very sharp eye on her works—especially on one like this, which she was supposed to have given as a gift. Wouldn't you think she'd have declared it not to be hers at the time?"

"Yes, I would, but how do you know it was shown?"

"Because I saw the exhibition catalog myself."

"What do you mean, you saw it?"

"I mean I *saw* it. It exists. I spent an hour over it this morning."

Geoff laughed happily. "Oh, I'd hardly call that confirmatory."

"What do you mean?"

"My dear child, did it not cross your mind that catalogs can be forged as easily as paintings? Far more easily, I should say."

That stopped Alix cold. No, the truth was, it hadn't occurred to her. A fake *catalog*? "But Geoff, I didn't see this in some sleazy gallery—or even some fancy gallery—this was in the archives, the locked archives, of the Southwest Museum of Twentieth-Century American Art."

"Oh, I *see*," he said archly. "Your point being that anything residing in an art museum must therefore be authentic. By definition, as it were."

"Well, no, of course not, but look, there were a good forty pages in it, each devoted to its own painting, all with photos, and provenances, and technical specs. Are you suggesting they were all fakes?"

"Not necessarily. Just the one you were looking for."

"What? But how could—"

"Did it not occur to you that, while the catalog as a whole may well have been authentic—very likely *was* authentic—the particular page on which this particular painting appeared might not have been?"

A Dangerous Talent

"What?" she said again, weakly. "I don't understand. It was the exact same painting I saw. I was looking at it just this morning. The measurements were exactly the same, the—"

"Of course they were the same. That's because your painting would have been painted first. Then it was photographed. Then it was measured. And only *then* would the false page have been prepared with *that* photo, *those* measurements, an invented provenance of some sort, and a few descriptive remarks. After that, all that remained, and this would have been the only ticklish part, would have been to somehow gain access to the archives, remove a preselected page from the preselected legitimate catalog, and replace it with the altered one."

"But Geoff, the catalog pages have page numbers on them, and they're all formatted the same way, with the same size pictures and the same fonts and all. A new page would stand out, it would be different, and this one wasn't."

"Ah, but you see, that's where the preselection would have come in. The process requires two visits to the archives, the first to choose and surreptitiously photograph a page in the catalog— both sides of the page, of course, or all four sides if it's folded in quarto. That way, the scoundrels would be able to reproduce the pagination, the formatting, the material on the reverse side, on the attached page or pages, and so forth. The second visit would be to remove it and substitute the altered page for it—the page with the 'newly discovered' painting on it. A simple process, really, but clever, wouldn't you say? After all, one might foresee a dodge of some sort involving things being taken *from* a museum. But things being put *into* one? Hardly likely to be anticipated."

She absorbed this for a few seconds. It was no wonder that archivists like Clyde Moody were so vigilant and so protective of their catalogs if they had to worry about people sneaking in to "alter" them. Though how on earth could such a thing have been accomplished under Moody's eagle eye? Very clever indeed.

"You sound as if you're pretty familiar with this 'process,' Geoff," she said wryly.

"I've heard talk of it," was his bland response.

"All the same, I have to say it sounds pretty improbable to me. Too complicated."

"If it weren't improbable, it wouldn't be very likely to succeed, would it? Now then. Let me make a few guesses: the gallery is no longer in existence."

"That's true."

"The seller was anonymous."

"Well, yes."

"The provenance is, shall we say, on the scant side."

"Yes, that's certainly true, too."

"The gallery owner has either shuffled off this mortal coil or is otherwise unreachable for verification."

"Well…"

"And given all that," he asked gently, "you didn't think to perform at least a cursory examination of the page? Did it have a watermark? If so, did the watermark differ from the rest of the pages? What about the gloss, the penetration of the inks? The—"

"No, Geoff, I did not think of any of that," she said, exasperated. "Strangely enough, although I may be Geoffrey London's daughter, my mind runs toward establishing authenticity, not fakery. Clearly, I am sadly unschooled in the intricacies of the forger's trade."

He took this, as usual, in good, even high spirits. "How unkind of you," he said with that damnably appealing chuckle, "to throw my failure as a father in my face."

She stiffened. Was *that* what he saw as his failure as a father? In her opinion, he had a few more serious ones than that. He was joking, but he was treading on dangerous ground here all the same.

Still, he was such a charming old bastard that she couldn't help laughing. "Well, look, none of it matters anyway. At this point we know the painting is a fake. So as soon as I've told Chris, which will be a few minutes from now, I will have completed my job."

"Your job, yes, but aren't you curious? Don't you want to know for *certain* about the catalog?"

"Sure I am. When I get back to Santa Fe, I'll see if I can make some time to get over to the museum again and check it out."

"There's more than your curiosity at stake, you know," he said with a touch of severity. "Don't you feel a moral responsibility to inform the museum of this?"

Yeah, right, Mr. Moral Responsibility, she thought sourly. It was amazing the way the man could make her laugh one moment and infuriate her the next. Again, she almost said something but held her tongue.

He clucked his incredulity, then paused. She could tell he was thinking. "Alix, is the name Clara Simons familiar to you?"

"No, should it be?"

"She used to be a curator of documents at the Smithsonian, where she was often called upon by the FBI to evaluate questioned documents. Now, as luck would have it, she's on the art faculty of the College of Santa Fe. We're old friends of a sort, and I thought I might ask her to go and have a look at that catalog and see what she thinks. What's the gallery name and the date? And the name of the painting?"

"Galerie Xanadu, November 1971, *Cliffs at Ghost Ranch*—but don't do it on my account. I'm not *that* interested." This wasn't strictly true, but it felt good to let a little petulance slip through.

He emitted a long, sad sigh. "Where, oh, where," he groaned, "did I go wrong?"

One of these days I'll tell you, she thought. There was a whole lot yet to be gotten off her chest, a truckload of baggage to be put on the table, opened, sorted through, and, dealt with.

But not now. "So long, Geoff, thanks for your help. Take care," she said with more affection than she could have called up even a few days ago. And more than would have seemed even remotely possible a few years ago.

"Drive carefully, my dear," were his final words.

CHAPTER 14

Chris took the news equably enough. "Well, it's not as if it's a big surprise," she said philosophically. "After the way you've been talking, I would have been surprised if it turned out to be the real thing. So I guess you'll just have to find me another one."

She was sitting contentedly in one of the Adirondack deck chairs just outside their room, taking in the view. As promised, it was spectacular. It was still an hour to sunset, but the sky was tinged with rose, and the slanting afternoon light lit the crags with color and brought the canyons into sharp, shadowed relief. The air itself was as clean and crisp and sparkling—but not as cold—as a sunny morning in January with a fresh layer of glittering white snow on the ground.

"It really is beautiful here," Alix murmured, taking it in.

"Mm." Chris pointed to a wooden side table on which was a cold-frosted ice bucket with a bottle of white wine sticking out of it. "Pinot Grigio. Good Italian stuff. I never travel without the essentials. Didn't bring glasses, though. Go get one from your bathroom, help yourself, and have a seat."

Alix did so gratefully, and for a while they both sipped the cool, crisp wine from plastic glasses and took in the view.

"It was quite a ride anyway, wasn't it?" Chris said at length. "Most exciting thing I've been involved in for a long time."

"Me too. People don't try to blow me up all that often. Knock on wood," she added, following through on the arm of her chair.

"Do you still think it was Liz?"

"I do," Alix said after another swallow. "That look, that 'What are *you* doing here?' she gave us when we walked in. That said everything."

"And you think it was because she was afraid you'd recognize the picture for a fake?"

"I do, indeed."

"But there were so many other things she could have done that wouldn't amount to murder. She could have just said she changed her mind about selling it."

"You had a contract."

"Yes, but she would have known I wouldn't fight her on it. For that matter, all she had to do was say she'd concluded it was a fake on her own, and that I shouldn't buy it. There were probably a hundred other things she could have done. But the idea that she'd try to kill you instead…" Chris shook her head. "It's just not rational."

"Well, frankly, she didn't strike me as the most rational person in the world. Certainly not the most sober. I think she just wasn't thinking straight."

"Could be. Makes sense, I guess. It's certainly true she wasn't the Liz I remember."

"Besides, you notice nobody's been trying to kill me since she died. That should tell us something."

"Yeah, almost two whole days now. Reach over to the bottle and pour me a little more, will you? You have some too."

"So the question now is, who killed Liz?" Alix said as she finished pouring.

"And why."

"And why," Alix repeated, musing. "And I don't have a clue to either one, do you?"

Chris shook her head. "Hey, do you think we ought to call Mendoza and let him know you've concluded the picture's a fake? It might be important."

"I already did, as soon as I finished talking to Geoff. I also told him where we were—I just didn't like the idea of pretending we were still in Santa Fe."

"And he said…?"

"Nothing, really. Asked me to come in when we get back there tomorrow."

"Tomorrow? Tomorrow we'll be in Taos."

"You mean you still want to go to Taos? But there isn't any reason to now."

"But aren't you curious to see the place? Check out this Mabel Dodge Luhan House?"

That made twice in the last hour that Alix had been more or less accused of being incurious. "Of course I'm curious," she said testily, "but you're the one who's paying the tab on all this, and I just figured you'd want to skip it now."

"Not a chance. Don't you want to use the only bathroom in the world with windows painted by D. H. Lawrence?"

"The writer?"

"The writer. He used to stay with Mabel, too, like every other visiting *artiste*, and the idea of see-through windows in her upstairs bathroom apparently scandalized him, so one day he got a couple of buckets of paint and covered them over with some kind of weird designs. I'd sure like to see that."

"This is the *Lady Chatterley's Lover* Lawrence? *That* guy was scandalized by a few uncovered bathroom windows?"

"Oddly enough, apparently he was a bit of a prude when it came to his private life. Also maybe a little paranoid, because what he was afraid of was that someone would climb up onto the sunroof outside the bathroom and look in. He tried to get Mabel to quit sunbathing nude on the flat roof upstairs too. No success there, however. Mabel wasn't exactly easy to persuade to stop doing something she wanted to do. She had a steamy affair with this Tewa Indian mystic and let him put up his tepee at the foot of the outdoor steps that led up to her bedroom. This was while she was still married to her third husband, Mr. Sterne—but later she divorced him and married her Indian—that's where the Luhan comes from. But back to the bathroom: that's also where Robinson Jeffers's wife tried to shoot herself over an affair he was—"

"Chris, how do you know all this?"

"Oh, the woman I spoke to when I made the reservation—she was full of information. Couldn't stop talking."

Alix smiled. "Yes, I know somebody else who can be like that. Look, Chris, I would love to spend the night there, so if you really want to, then of course, let's do it. We can leave right after breakfast. There's nothing more we need to do here now."

"Well, to tell the truth, there's another reason too," Chris said a bit hesitantly. "I wouldn't want—"

"—Craig to think you were rushing back to Santa Fe a day early because you couldn't wait to see him," Alix finished for her.

Chris did one of her eye-rolls. "I guess I'm just going to have to get used to hanging around with someone who's a mind reader."

"I'm no mind reader," Alix said, and her smiled widened. "I'm just getting to know you better."

"Now that *really* worries me," Chris said, pushing herself out of her chair. "Come on, I'm starving. Let's go down the hill to the chuck wagon or the campfire or wherever it is you get dinner around here."

– • –

Nobody would call Eddie Sierra the brightest bulb on the block (you didn't get a nickname like Yo-yo for nothing), but he wasn't the dimmest one either, and he'd put a lot of thought into how he was going to handle things the next time around. So when the call eventually came, as he knew it would, he was primed and ready.

"I'm afraid it's gonna cost you more this time," he said when Harry had laid out what he needed done.

"And why would that be?" Harry wanted to know. Eddie didn't know Harry's last name. Probably didn't know his first name either, but who cared as long as he was good for the money? Which he was.

"For one thing, because you want it done tomorrow, man. No planning time, no—"

"Planning! How much planning does it take? Just do it the way you did it last time."

"Yeah, but I got other things on my plate, other things I gotta take care of, all kinds of things I gotta change." He'd have to bring his laundry over to his mother's on Monday instead of tomorrow, for example. "It'll be six thousand this time." He held his breath.

"Okay, six thousand," Harry said.

Shit. He *knew* he hadn't asked for enough. "And another thousand to take care of the damage to my truck from last time," he tacked on. "That cost me twelve hundred bucks." Well, it would have cost twelve hundred if he'd taken it to a legitimate repair shop instead of to Gus's place, where it cost him only a few auto parts he'd picked up here and there. "Take it or leave it."

This time there was hesitation at the other end. Oh, Jesus. Eddie had begun to silently curse himself before Harry spoke again. "All right, seven thousand, but that's it. Don't push your luck. I can find somebody else if I have to."

Seven thousand dollars! Eddie exulted. Of course he'd have to give two thousand to Joey (who thought he was getting half), but even so, five thousand dollars! That was more than he got in six months from Human Services, even when you added in the food stamps.

"This time you're looking for a car with two women in it," Harry said. "They'll be going south, hitting the Chama sometime in the morning. I don't know when, exactly, so you better be up there waiting for them as soon as it's light."

Eddie stifled his instinctive protest at having to get going before dawn. For five grand, he could get up in the dark for once in his life. "So how'm I gonna know it's them?"

"How're you gonna—tell me, Eddie, how many cars go by there? Ten a day? And how many of them have a couple of women in them? Look, this will be the two of them, heading south, both maybe thirty, a good-looking blonde and a fairly good-looking brunette—"

"Wait, the brunette—is she, like, huge?"

"She's tall, maybe six-two."

"I seen them!" Eddie exclaimed. "Yesterday, right here in Española. At the Taco Bell. They were going north on 84."

"That'd be them. They were on their way to Ghost Ranch. Fine, then you know what they look like."

"They're driving a Lambo," Eddie said, suddenly hushed. "Jeez, it's a shame to total something like that."

"They're driving a what?"

"A Lambo. You don't know what a Lambo is, man?"

"Let me guess. A car."

Eddie snickered. "A car, yeah, but calling a Lambo just a car is like calling a, a..." But similes weren't his forte, and his imagination failed him. "Come on, you must have heard of a Lambo. It's short for...I can't remember, Lambogonia, Lamburgeroni, something like that."

"A Lamborghini? That's a sports car, isn't? Don't they do over a hundred miles an hour?"

"Over two hundred, man."

"Oh, Christ."

"What's the problem?"

"What's the problem! Are you—how the hell are you two ding-a-lings in your broken-down wrecks going to catch a car like that? They'll leave you in the dust."

At that, Eddie laughed out loud. "Let me tell you something. I seen the way they drive. You ever seen one of them little old ladies with blue hair, can barely see over the steering wheel, driving her big old Lincoln Continental, like, ten miles an hour and looking like she'd have a heart attack if she went any faster? Well, that's how they drive their Lambo. Trust me, it's a piece of cake, man."

"We'll see," Harry said.

CHAPTER 15

After breakfast the next morning they loaded up the car, got in, and swung closed the winglike doors. Chris inserted the key in the ignition but didn't twist it. She turned to Alix.

"How would you feel about taking the wheel this morning?"

Alix had been stoically preparing herself for the teeth-grindingly slow drive that lay ahead as they made their way ever so cautiously to Taos, wasting all the potential of the powerful and responsive creature at their command. But now, with those words, a dazzling light suddenly flooded her immediate future.

"Um…I wouldn't mind, but why? I thought you were enjoying it."

"So did I, but I got up this morning with a screaming neck ache, and I realized it was from the tension of driving this thing yesterday. You know that Camry with the 'Baby on Board' sign you mentioned? Well, I've come to the reluctant conclusion that that's more my speed than one of these things. This baby is just too much for me, too…I don't know, muscular. I guess when it comes to certain things I'm a weenie at heart."

She laughed just a little ruefully as they climbed back out to exchange seats. "Besides, I woke up a couple of times during the night thinking about that wiggly section where that old guy went over the edge. I'd rather do that part with my eyes closed, if it's all the same to you, and if I did, it would probably work out better for all concerned if I wasn't the one doing the driving at the time. So if you would kindly take all this horsepower off my hands I'd appreciate it. At least I'll know you know what you're doing."

"You think so? Let's see how you feel about it by the time we get to Taos."

Chris began to laugh again but stopped short. "You're kidding, right?"

"I'm kidding," Alix said, settling gratefully behind the wheel. "Believe me, Gian-Carlo put me through some truly intensive training before he ever let me take one of his precious beauties out alone."

For the drive down the dirt access road she restrained herself, maintaining a steady ten or twelve miles an hour. Gravel dings in the flawless, satiny finish would not be looked upon kindly back at the rental agency. So by the time they reached the highway, she was aching to put the car to the test.

She lived with the ache for two or three miles, but when they rounded a curve and a three- or four-mile stretch of ruler-straight road lay ahead, she glanced at Chris. "What would you think about my putting this baby through its paces? It couldn't be safer than right here. There isn't another car in sight."

"Sure," Chris said agreeably, "I'm curious myself, not that I— urk!" Her head jerked back against the headrest as Alix downshifted to build more RPMs and bore down on the gas pedal.

It was as if the car itself reared back, gave a deafening, Hallelujah-I'm-free-at-last whoop, and accelerated like a 767 roaring down the runway. Alix's heart soared right along with it. As a rule she was not a reckless driver, not a reckless person, not even particularly given to temptation, but every rule has its exceptions, and for Alix London the exception came when she got behind the wheel of a truly fine sports car. It was a passion she'd come by relatively late; she'd been twenty-six when Gian-Carlo Santullo had introduced her to the thrill and challenge of his Lamborghinis. As in most things, she was a quick study, and for the rest of her stay in Italy it was those weekends in Ravello with their splendid, solitary drives along the winding, windy Amalfi Coast that she looked forward to most eagerly.

"Whoo," she heard Chris murmur, her foghorn voice a couple of notches lower than usual and uncharacteristically subdued. When Alix turned to look at her she saw that Chris was still sitting rigidly upright, apparently holding her breath, her eyes like saucers, her head still pressed against the headrest.

She slowed at once and pulled over to the side. "Chris, are you okay?"

Chris let out the air she'd been holding in. Her posture relaxed, and her eyes returned to normal size. "I'm okay, yes. It's just that I always feel a little peculiar when the gravitational pressure exceeds five Gs."

"I'm *sorry*," Alix said sincerely, "I didn't—"

"Don't be sorry, it was great! How fast were we going?"

"Not that fast, really. A little under ninety. But it took less than ten seconds to get there. That's what you were feeling." She thought it best not to mention that one of the gauges on the dashboard actually measured G-forces.

"What was all that noise? Is that normal?"

"That noise was four hundred pound-feet of torque, five hundred and twenty horsepower, and seven thousand rpm. And yes, it's normal. It's all part of the Lamborghini experience. Did it scare you? I should have warned you."

"Damn right it scared me." She grinned. "I also absolutely loved it. Come on, let's do it again. Can we do it any faster? What a kick."

"With pleasure. We still have a fair amount of straightaway before the curves, and not another car around. Want me to take it to its limit?"

"You bet, but I'd rather not get airborne, if it's all the same to you."

"I don't think that'll happen, but you never know."

"Oh, hell, I'll chance it." Chris set herself back against her seat again, gripped the raised edges, compressed her lips, and stared straight ahead. "Let 'er rip!"

This time, with Alix having grown re-accustomed to the car's unique electronic gearshift "paddles," they got up to ninety even faster. At twelve seconds they hit a hundred and twenty, and after that she had to stop looking at the gauges and concentrate on the driving. They were just short of a hundred and fifty miles an hour, still going up, when she finally eased up as the road began to climb a ridge and gently curve to their left.

"I never thought I had the fast-driving gene," Chris said, a bit short of breath, "but I have to admit, that was terrific."

Alix nodded happily, more relaxed than she'd been since they'd left Santa Fe the day before. "Maybe we'll get some more open road after we get through the next patch."

The next patch constituted the precarious, swinging, cliff-edge curves that ran above the Chama River, the area where Henry Merriam had died, and Alix instinctively slowed even more. On the left, up against the ridge and just coming into view, was a decrepit rest stop that she hadn't noticed on the way up and wouldn't have noticed now if there hadn't been a truck parked in it and a dark-haired young man leaning nonchalantly back against the hood with a *campesino*'s straw hat down over his eyes. He looked oddly at his ease in this lonely, forlorn spot, with his arms folded and one foot propped comfortably behind him on the bumper. But what caught her attention was how intently he appeared to be watching them—almost as if he were watching *for* them—from under the shadowed brim of his hat, despite the apparently relaxed pose. Something was off here. The skin on the back of her neck crawled.

Chris had her eyes on the rest stop too. "That truck—we've seen it before. Yesterday, in Española." She stared hard. "That's it, all right," she said when they drew close enough to read the name beneath the painting on the passenger door. "Bimbi. Remember?"

"We've seen the guy too," Alix said. "He's the one who wanted a ride."

"He's *looking* at us," Chris said nervously. "What is this about? This can't be a coincidence, can it?"

"I wouldn't think so. What I'm afraid is that he wants to play. That's the downside of a car like this—the idiots in their souped-up junk heaps that want to race you."

"But how could he know we'd be here?"

Alix shook her head. "No idea."

"He's talking on a cell phone," Chris said as they drew abreast. "Why would he be talking on a cell phone? Oh God, look, now he's jumping in the truck. What's going on? He's still looking at us!"

"Chris, I don't have a clue, but I sure don't like it." The crawly sensation had crept halfway down her spine. If they hadn't already been entering the first of the curves she would have turned and headed back the way they'd come. On the straightaway she could leave him in the dust. On the curves, it would be a different proposition altogether, more dependent on nerve and outright craziness than flat-out speed. That was especially true because the narrow road was quickly climbing the ridge. Already there was a sheer, eighty-foot drop-off on their right, with the shallow, gleaming river winding its way through the desert at its base.

In the rearview mirror, she saw the pickup bumping onto the road and turning toward them. He was only a couple of hundred yards back, and she could see that he was gunning the engine. This was not good; damn these stupid macho kids. "Better make sure your seat belt's tight," she told Chris, checking her own.

Chris's face was pale. "Thank God you're driving. I'm having nervous palpitations and all I'm doing is sitting here. Alix, are you going to be able to deal with this?"

"Deal with what? He wants to race, we don't want to race. End of story." So why was her scalp itching like this? Why could she feel the adrenaline practically flowing into her fingertips? No, there was something more than a simple race going on here. He had picked what was probably the most dangerous, isolated stretch of highway between Santa Fe and the Colorado border. Did he want to play chicken, was that it? And if so, would he take no for an answer? And who was on the other end of that cell—

Chris had turned to stare out the back window. "He's crazy!" she screamed. "He's practically on our bumper! What is he *doing*?"

When Alix glanced into the mirror she was shocked. Indeed, the idiot was only a few yards back and closing fast. They were going about thirty miles an hour now, and they were well into the curves; this was really dangerous. Did he actually mean to bump her, was that it? Was this some insane form of counting coup the youths went in for around here?

But just as she was bracing for the impact, he swung left, into the lane for oncoming traffic, and drew level with them. If she hadn't already decided he was genuinely crazy, that would have been enough to convince her right there, because the bends in the road and the jutting red-rock promontories limited his vision to just a few hundred feet. If something doing thirty or thirty-five miles an hour came around that next curve right now he was dead meat. She tried to get a look at his face in hopes of guessing his intentions, but the Lamborghini was too low and instead she found herself looking at the dusty passenger door panel, into the Kewpie-doll face of Bimbi, whose expression gave no clue.

Still, she didn't get truly, deeply scared until Bimbi suddenly swerved directly at her as they rounded an outside curve. Alix jerked the steering wheel to the right, but the front right corner of the pickup still caught them a glancing blow just behind the left front wheel well, provoking a little gasp from Chris. Alix hung on, managing to maintain control, but now she was no longer in any doubt about what was happening to them. This wasn't a joyride by a testosterone-crazed kid; this guy was out to kill them.

And now another vehicle, a lumbering, chugging eighteen-wheeler appeared rounding the bend just ahead, heading for them. *Directly* for them—for Alix and Chris—because the ponderous rig was in the wrong lane. Henry Merriam, the old art dealer, flashed across her mind. Was this what had happened to him?

The pickup on her left was already swerving toward them again, but her mind was working very fast. There was no place to go on the right, that was for sure—no shoulder to speak of and only a two-foot guardrail that didn't look substantial enough to stop them from going over the side if push came to shove. And even if there had been a shoulder and she'd pulled onto it and stopped, what then?

To their left was the better option; even if the pickup was souped up, she had no doubt that with the Lamborghini's fantastic acceleration and ground-hugging ability she could dart into the wrong-way lane ahead of him and quickly leave him behind. But that meant she'd be continuing around the bend in the wrong lane, with zero visibility. If that wasn't worrisome enough, there was the monstrously wide semi itself that she'd have to get by. What would it do? If she played her cards right, it wouldn't be able to switch lanes quickly enough to bring them into a head-on collision (which would probably put no more than a few dents in the semi but would pulverize the Lamborghini), but a simple, properly timed swerve to its right would mash them sidewise into the cliff wall. The question was, did the driver have the time and the reaction speed to bring it off?

Well, she was about to find out. "Hang on," she said through clenched teeth. "Here we go..."

She took in a quick breath, downshifted, and stamped on the gas pedal. In two seconds they were fifty feet ahead of the pickup. She switched back to the right lane, which left them bearing rapidly down on the semi (or rather, vice-versa). They were close enough for her to see that the semi driver's jaw had dropped; he couldn't believe it. A line from *Man of La Mancha* flew into (and out of) her head: "Whether the rock hits the pitcher or the pitcher hits the rock, it's going to be bad for the pitcher."

"Alix..." a frozen, wide-eyed Chris squeaked. "We're... we're..."

Thirty yards before the impending crash, Alix lightly tapped the brake pedal so that she could accelerate into the curve, then swung abruptly left, into the opposite lane, accelerating as much as she dared. The semi driver, startled as he was, managed to haul the steering wheel hard to his right in an effort to crush them. Too late, though. She was already halfway down the forty-foot body of the truck-trailer, so that the cab went scraping along the rock wall five or ten feet behind her. For a fleeting second she exulted, thinking they were home free, but then, as in one of those slow-motion nightmares, the trailer came fishtailing around, straight for them and certain to mash them against the wall. She had no choice but to accelerate even more and shoot for the diminishing, dismayingly small opening between the back end of the truck and the wall of rock.

She almost made it, too, but the weirdly sliding back corner of the trailer caught them hard on the passenger door side. There was a stunningly loud *bang!* as the side air bag next to Chris's head deployed, and now it was the Lamborghini that was fishtailing over the narrow road. Alix knew better than to lean on the brakes, which would have eliminated what little steering control she had. Instead, she tried hard to steer "into" the skid. Unfortunately, "into the skid" meant heading for the edge of the cliff. Fortunately, the guardrail was sturdier than it looked. Also springier. When they ran into it, it bounced them jarringly back onto the road. She caught a dreamlike glimpse of her shoulder bag flying out the open window and into the void. The car was spinning slowly but uncontrollably, and now the rock face loomed ahead. It was the rear of the Lamborghini that would take the hit, she could see that, and there was nothing to do now but hit the brake pedal and pray for the best. As she flinched instinctively, there was another ear-splitting *bang!* and now the front air bag exploded into her face.

CHAPTER 16

She didn't know how long she'd been out—not long, she thought, probably only seconds. What woke her up was an acrid smell as penetrating as ammonia, and when she opened her eyes she saw that the car was full of a powdery gray haze, apparently from the air bags, which were now slowly deflating. Her nose hurt, but when she touched it there was no blood, and no give or wiggle either. Other than that—

In her fog she'd forgotten about Chris. "Chris! Are you all right?"

No answer. Chris's head drooped on her chest. Alix's heart sank. She touched her friend's shoulder. "Chris?"

Chris's head jerked weakly up. "Uh?"

"Chris, are you okay?"

It took a while for her to answer. "Yes…no…I don't think so. My head…"

"Don't move. I'll call for help." But even as she reached around for her cell phone she remembered that it had been in her shoulder bag, which was now probably floating down the Chama on its way to the Rio Grande and eventually the Gulf of Mexico. The thought of the cell phone reminded her suddenly of the guy in the pickup truck, about whom she'd also forgotten. And the eighteen-wheeler. My God, she was really in a daze. She looked anxiously up. The Lamborghini had spun completely around so she was looking back down the road, and there they were, a hundred yards back. The jackknifed truck, its trailer upright, its cab on its side, was more or less wrapped around the pickup, which was also on its side. Dust was still rising from the jumble. Nobody moving. Good. As far as she was concerned, she had no problem with them being dead.

"Alix," Chris mumbled, "I don't...I can't quite..." And then her eyeballs rolled up, her head fell limply back, and she was unconscious again.

Alix was terrified for her. Chris was obviously injured, maybe seriously. She needed to get to a hospital fast. But what was to be done? She felt herself near panicking. They were on a road that might not see another driver for hours. No cell phone, no—

When the calm, reassuring female voice came over the navigation speaker, it was as if Alix were hearing the voice of God.

"This is your Always On-Call service. We have received a signal that your air bags have deployed. Do you need assistance? We have you on Highway 84, four miles northwest of Abiquiu, New Mexico. If you cannot reply—"

By that time Alix had found her voice. "Yes, we need assistance!" she shouted, close to crying with gratitude. "My friend is..."

— • —

"And you honestly think he was trying to *kill* them?" Ted asked, somewhere between astonished and skeptical. "Run them over the cliff?"

"I do, yes," Lieutenant Mendoza said. "Absolutely."

Ted just sat there silently shaking his head. Mendoza had called him twenty minutes ago and asked him to come by his office; something important had happened up above Española. He had just finished giving Ted the details.

"But look, Eduardo," Ted said at last, "why jump to a conclusion like that? They were driving a fancy sports car, they were in open country, lowrider country. Why wouldn't it make more sense to assume the pickup was trying to drag them into a race, or maybe playing a stupid game of chicken, and things just went wrong when the semi came around the bend?"

"Because..." Mendoza turned his Lobos cap backward to underscore the seriousness of the situation and began ticking points off on his fingers. Pinky: "One, the guy in the semi wasn't some innocent lug who just happened to be in the wrong place at the wrong time. He was a thug, an ex-con. The two of them were, and this wasn't the first time they'd worked together." Ring finger: "Two, the story London told made sense."

"Yeah, but—"

"And number three and most important—" his middle finger was bent way back for emphasis, "—we got the Rio Arriba County Sheriff's report. Skid marks and vehicle damage patterns back her up to a T. The pickup and the semi tried to box her in and force her off the road, all right, and damned if she didn't outmaneuver the two of them. She almost got away clean, too, but the semi skidded and the back end fishtailed into them. The Lamborghini totaled, but somehow she managed to keep it on the road and get it stopped without killing the two of them. Let me tell you, not only can that lady handle a car, she's gotta have nerves of steel."

"Sounds as if you're becoming quite a fan," Ted said.

"I'm impressed, yeah." He turned the hat right way around and leaned back in his chair, hands clasped behind his head.

"So are you bringing her in to talk to you about it?"

"About this? No, not officially; it's in Rio Arriba's jurisdiction, Denny Ortiz's baby. But she called me yesterday to let me know that picture's a fake. Absolutely, definitely, categorically. She's coming in to talk about that when she gets back, and I wouldn't be surprised if we get into the Lamborghini thing too."

Absolutely, definitely, categorically, Ted thought. A bit more definite than she was the other day. "I'd appreciate it if you'd fill me in on what she's got to say about it. About the painting, I mean."

"You bet."

"What about the drivers of those trucks?" Ted asked. "Has the sheriff gotten anything from them?"

"From one of them, the semi driver, and it's the clincher. Denny talked to him, and he claims that all he knows is that the other kid, Eddie Sierra, paid him two thousand dollars to do it and he took him up on it, no questions asked, which Denny believes, because this guy is just dumb enough to do it. He also said it was just a practical joke, that they were just trying to scare them, not harm them, which Denny doesn't believe, and neither do I."

"What about Sierra? What's his story?"

"We'll probably never know. He's still unconscious. They don't think he's going to wake up."

Ted nodded. "So what do you think this was all about, Eduardo?"

Mendoza shrugged. "No idea, but I think we can make a couple of starting assumptions. First, this turkey, Sierra, didn't come up with it on his own. Both these guys are losers, as dumb as doorknobs. What's more, where would Sierra get two thousand bucks? No, somebody put him up to it—paid him enough for him to give two thousand dollars to his good buddy."

"Makes sense."

"And then, I think it's safe to assume it was London they were after, not LeMay."

"Why?"

"Well, because of the other attempt on her life."

"Other attempt…?" Ted leaned forward, his hands on the desk. "Wait a minute, you think the casita explosion *wasn't* an accident?"

"I don't think so, I know so. Sorry, Ted, I meant to tell you; guess I forgot."

"No apology necessary. Homicides are your affair; I'm just interested in the art. That was the deal. But as long as you've brought it up…" An inquisitive lift of the eyebrows.

"Well, we figured it was at least worth checking the explosion out, so we did some poking around and we found out that LeMay originally booked a room in the main building for London. Then, according to their records, the day before they showed up she called to change it and put London in that casita instead—that specific casita, as a special surprise."

Ted frowned. "So you think LeMay set her up? But—"

"No, LeMay didn't have anything to do with it."

"But you just said—"

"No, I said their *records* showed it was LeMay. Someone *claiming* to be LeMay. Pay attention."

Ted sighed and sat back. "You're losing me here."

"Ted, just because someone claims to be someone doesn't prove he's who he says he is. As you should be very well aware, Rollie, old pal."

"True enough," Ted agreed with a smile.

"Nope, it was Liz Coane who made that call."

Ted was genuinely startled. "How the hell did you come up with that?"

Mendoza's lips parted in a toothy grin. "Superior policework, my man. See, the hotel's log book shows the call coming in at two thirty-five Thursday, but no telephone number to go with it. So that tells us nothing. But...now switch to our investigation into the Coane homicide. We are there doing the painstaking information-gathering for which we are so justly famous, and of course, one of the things we're examining is the call log in her cell phone—made and received. And lo and behold, we find that on Thursday, September 9, at two thirty-four in the afternoon, she placed a one-minute call to—"

"The Hacienda Encantada," Ted said. "Sonofagun."

"Yup. It was Liz who set her up."

"But how would she have gotten into the casita to rig the propane? And when? Or did she get somebody else to do it?"

Another shrug from Mendoza. "Oh, it probably wasn't that hard. Of course, that particular casita doesn't exist anymore, but we brought in a propane stove guy, and he looked at the way the casitas are hooked up in general, and he says he could have done it easy—that just about anybody could have—from the outside, in back, where the tank feeds in. To make it even simpler, none of the casitas have windows in back."

Ted took this in soberly. "Two attempts to kill London inside of three days," he mused.

"Looks like it. By two different people, too, since Coane wasn't around anymore to arrange the second one." He shook his head. "I sure wish I had some idea of what the hell is going on."

"Well, whatever it is, it proves she's in it up to her ears. I knew she had to be, right from the start. A chip off the old...What?" he asked, aware that Mendoza was staring quizzically at him. "What?"

"Ted, let me get this straight. Here's this girl—this woman— who, by the skin of her teeth and her considerable daring and abilities, manages—barely manages—to escape two attempts to kill her...and your conclusion is *she's* gotta be guilty of something? What am I missing?"

"A lot of things," Ted said warmly. "The fact that her father is who he is; the fact that she followed right after him into the art world; the fact that she got this job with LeMay only through his kind assistance; the fact that—"

"The fact that you've got some kind of a thing about her."

"*I have—?*" But in the midst of taking umbrage he found himself laughing and suddenly relaxing. Even to his own ears his rationale was full of holes. "Yeah," he said, sighing, "you're right, Eduardo. I'm not exactly being objective, am I? Okay, what can I say? I guess there was just something about her that rubbed me the wrong way."

Such as the fact that she had been utterly, supremely unsmitten by his charms? he speculated. But this particular fact he thought it best to leave unreported.

"Well, I wondered about her at first too, but now I've come around to thinking she's straight-arrow. You need to give her a fair chance, Ted."

"You're absolutely right," he said, meaning it, but very much ready to change the subject. "You said they're up in Española now? Neither of them seriously hurt?"

"Right, last I heard. They're keeping LeMay in the hospital for observation at least overnight, though. London, I don't know where she is now. They looked her over and let her go, but she's probably still there at the hospital with LeMay would be my guess. This all happened just a few hours ago."

"Well, would you have any objection if I drove up there to ask her a few things?"

"No objection at all, but you can get there faster than that. LeMay's pilot, her old boyfriend, is worried about her. He's taking their plane up to the Española airport. If you went with him you'd be there in fifteen minutes instead of an hour and a half. Want me to call the airport here in Santa Fe? Maybe he hasn't left yet."

"Yes, please, I'd appreciate that. I've got some questions I need answers to."

— • —

Oh, yeah, like what? he asked himself during the brief drive to the airport a few miles south of the city. *What was so important that he had to fly up there right now, this minute, to see her? Exactly what were these questions that were so urgent they couldn't wait a day or two until she returned to Santa Fe?*

Could Mendoza have inadvertently hit the nail on the head? he wondered uneasily. *Did he have "some kind of a thing" for her?*

CHAPTER 17

She'd been sitting at Chris's bedside for two hours now, chatting with her when Chris wasn't dozing, and simply thinking when she was. There was certainly no shortage of things to think about. She'd wondered for a while if today's bizarre chase meant that she'd been wrong about Liz's having being responsible for the casita explosion. Because, with Liz having been dead for a couple of days, that would mean that someone *else* had tried to kill her this morning. And, surely, it was stretching credulity to imagine that two different people had been trying to murder her, wasn't it? But no, that startled "What are *you* doing here?" remained in her mind, as convincing as ever; the casita had been Liz's doing, all right—or at the very least she'd been party to it.

So who was behind this latest attempt? Not the two dimwits in the trucks, that was for sure. But aside from the now-departed Liz, who else was there? Well, whoever had killed Liz (presumably the big, bearded guy running from Liz's office) was a good bet, but what reason would he have for wanting to kill *her*? It had to do with the painting, she was as sure of that as ever, but what was the *why*? To stop her from deducing and revealing that it was a fake? That was the most obvious thing that came to mind, yes, but where was the rationale for murder? Whoever was trying to unload it could simply pack the thing up whenever the police released it, hold it for a few years, and take it elsewhere—Idaho, Montana, Georgia—someplace far out of the art mainstream, where it could be sold without raising any eyebrows. Inconvenient, yes, but not as inconvenient or risky as murder. Or he could have—

Almost without realizing it, she had gotten up and wandered over to the window, where she stood absently gazing down on the parking lot from the second floor, and now she became aware that she was looking at a medium-sized U-Haul truck that had just pulled into the lot and disgorged two men. She did a double take and looked harder.

"Chris, are you awake?" she asked over her shoulder.

"Awake?" came the drowsy answer. "Mm, I'm not sure, I have to think about it. Why?"

"Because if I were you, what I'd think about is putting on a little lipstick."

"Lipstick? Why?"

"Because you're getting company."

"Company?" She giggled—very un-Chris-like. "I keep repeating you, did you notice? Sorry, I'm still kind of dopey from whatever they gave me. Anyway, what kind of company am I getting?"

"Well, I'm looking at a couple of men who just got out of a U-Haul truck—"

"A—" She stopped herself.

"A U-Haul truck and are heading this way. And one of them is either your pilot or his twin brother."

"My...do you mean, my...you mean CRAIG? Craig is HERE?" Abruptly, the dopiness was gone. She sat bolt-upright. "Where's my mirror?" she asked desperately. "Where's my comb, where's my lipstick, where's—Alix, I don't know what they did with my things. Quick, give me yours, this is an emergency!"

"I wish I could, but my bag is probably twenty miles downstream by now." It reminded her she'd better get on the phone as soon as she could and do something about her driver's license, ATM card, and all the rest. Aside from everything else, what a hassle all that would be. While she spoke, she went to the closet of the private room, and there was Chris's bag on the shelf. "Here we go," she said, tossing it onto the bed.

Chris groped inside, seized a small mirror, and stared at herself, shocked. "Oh my God, *two* black eyes? I look like a raccoon! And look at my nose! It's all, all—"

"Well, you can't do anything about the black eyes, but the nose isn't really that bad—"

"Not that *bad*? It looks like a, like a…rutabaga!"

"Mm, more like a turnip, I'd say," Alix couldn't help saying. "Because of the purple."

"*Alix!*" Chris wailed.

"Look, Chris, really, it isn't all that awful. If you neaten up your hair a little, put on some lipstick…"

Chris was already dabbing on the lipstick. "Oh, and this horrible gown they put me in! *Nobody* could look good in this. Can't you keep him out of here?"

"Chris, if he was concerned enough about you to come all the way here, I doubt if there's much I can do about keeping him out of the room."

"My God, these eyes," Chris groaned. She looked plaintively at Alix. "That'll go away, won't it?"

"I'm sure it will, but I doubt if it'll be before Craig gets here."

"This is no laughing matter," Chris said, laughing in spite of herself. "Oh, what am I doing, it's hopeless." She threw down the mirror and fell back against the pillow. "All I can say is, I hope he likes raccoons. Crank up the bed for me, will you? And if you wouldn't mind giving us some time alone…"

"You bet. I'll leave now," Alix said, having used the remote control to raise the head of the bed so that Chris was sitting up. "And try to look on the bright side."

"And that is?"

"If he's still interested after he sees you today, you'll know he's serious."

"Oh, thanks, that's reassuring. Wait, you said two of them, didn't you? Who's the other one?"

"Never saw him before," Alix said. "Bye, now."

— • —

But even before the door closed behind her, she realized she *had* seen him before. He'd looked vaguely familiar, as if he reminded her of an actor or of someone she'd once known. But now it clicked; it was de Beauvais, Mr. Flimflam himself. It hadn't registered before, probably because she was looking down on him from a new angle, and because the sight of him was so unexpected. What was he doing here at the hospital? And how did he know Craig? And why did he keep showing up every time she turned around—Liz's gallery, the police station, here…

The two men came hurrying down the corridor, Craig a little in front. Seeing Alix standing outside the closed door alarmed him. "Is she all right? Has something gone wrong?"

"No, she's banged up a little, but I'm sure she'll be all right."

"Um—is it okay if I just go in?" he asked.

"Sure. I saw you from the window, so she knows you're coming. She's looking forward to seeing you." She considered telling him about the raccoon eyes (even the emergency-room doctor had called them that) but then decided it was better to let things play out on their own.

He reached for the doorknob, then suddenly turned and surprised her with a bear hug. She hadn't realized how tall he was: six-three, at least; a good fit for Chris. The thought made her smile; she was doing something she hated when others did it for her: matchmaking.

"They tell me you saved her life," he breathed into her ear. "Thank you."

"All I did—" But he was already in the room. She heard him say, "Hello, Chris, I hope I'm not—" before the door closed and she was left alone with de Beauvais, who stood a couple of yards away, smiling his smooth, superior, just-look-how-sexy-I-am smile at her.

"Did you want something?" she asked coldly.

"Yes. First, I want to say I'm glad you're all right. I understand you put on quite a performance on the road this morning."

"Thank you." She waited for the rest.

"And second, I have something to confess."

"I already know what it is. You're a phony."

He looked levelly at her, giving nothing away. "Now why exactly would you think something like that?"

"That overdone Boston Brahmin shtick," she said, which was a lie. It was overdone, all right, but still she'd bought it, right up until the moment she'd overheard him through Mendoza's open door, speaking naturally. "Give me a break. No one's talked like that since—" Since Paynton Whipple-Pruitt, she might have said. "Since I don't know when."

He looked at her a moment longer—sternly, she thought, but then, almost like movie magic, his face transformed itself, relaxing into a grin. A pretty engaging grin, she had to admit, open and direct, with not even a tinge of fakery. His whole body seemed to stand more squarely, and when he smiled, the skin at the corners of those remarkable blue eyes crinkled appealingly. He was a charming bastard, damn him, and it made her uneasy. Whatever his game was, she had no interest in getting interested in him. She already had a charming, ethically challenged old bastard in her life, and the last thing she needed was a charming, ethically challenged young one.

"Ah, but you have to remember, in undercover work it's not veracity we're after," he said, "it's verisimilitude. The idea is to act the way other people *think* you're supposed to act."

He'd dropped the phony accent, but she was so surprised by what he'd said that she'd barely noticed. Undercover work? She stared at him. It was all she could do to keep her jaw from dropping. "You're going to tell me you're some kind of *detective*?"

Silently, he took a leather card case from his hip pocket, opened it, and held it up to her eyes, not snapping it closed after a second they way they do on TV, but leaving it up there for her to read. In the lower compartment was an eagle-topped gold shield that might have been authentic, or might just as likely have been the kind of thing you used to be able to get for two cereal box tops and a buck—"junior secret agent." But the one in the top compartment struck her as the real thing: an ID card with "Department of Investigation FBI Special Agent" printed on it in bold blue letters, along with an imprint of the agency's seal and a small, clear picture of de Beauvais—except that the signature beneath it said "Theodore Ellesworth."

Her reaction, which surprised her as much as it must have surprised him, was to burst out laughing. Whether it was from the tension of the last few days or the intrinsic absurdity of it all, she didn't know, but she had trouble stopping. It had been months, maybe years, since she'd laughed like that. Beauvais—or rather Ellesworth—quietly watched her.

When she'd wiped her eyes and could speak again, she looked at him. "You have to be kidding me. FBI? 'Theodore Ellesworth'?"

He closed the case and slipped it back into his pocket. "That's my name, I'm sorry to say. And I really am with the Bureau. Honest." Smiling, he held up three fingers in the Boy Scout oath sign.

Her attitude toward him was muddled at this point, to put it mildly, but her instincts told her he was telling the truth. "Okay, I believe you. So what is all this about? Tell me why FBI Special Agent Theodore Ellesworth is standing in a hospital corridor in Española, New Mexico, talking to me, instead of doing all sorts of really important FBI things."

"Look, this'll take a little explaining. There's a coffee shop downstairs. Do you suppose we might go and have a cup?"

Alix held back, but only for a second. "Okay, Mr. Ellesworth, lead on."

"That's Ted," he said, starting down the corridor.

– • –

The Española Hospital coffee shop was like any other hospital coffee shop: the aura of anxiety and gloom emanating from its patrons canceled out any efforts at brightness and cheer in its décor. The absence of windows (it was in the basement) didn't help either. The only table with people in good spirits was one that had some nurses at it. The others held people, singly or in pairs, who sat brooding and uncommunicative. Ted and Alix found a table along the wall, well away from the others.

"Let's see," Ted said, settling down with his coffee, "where do I start?"

"How about with what Roland de Beauvais, bent art dealer extraordinaire, was doing in Santa Fe in the first place?"

"Fair enough. I'm on assignment on a string of scams that've been going on for some time: forgeries sold as originals to foreign buyers, mostly in Asia. We have five definite so far, and another four we're pretty sure about. And Blue Coyote Gallery has been the main conduit for them, so we knew Liz was right in the middle of it, either innocently or not so innocently."

"Have you decided which?"

"Yes, the latter. She was in it up to her eyeballs."

"Huh," Alix mused, "I wonder why."

"Wonder why what?"

"Why she'd get involved with something like that. I mean, considering that she was already rolling in money—"

"Where'd you get that idea? She was broke."

"Are you sure? I thought—"

"Nope, she was broke. She was way, way overextended on the gallery thing, and she'd made some terrible investment decisions. She's been one step ahead of defaulting on her loans for years, and recently she's even gotten herself in debt, big-time, to a Phoenix loan shark." He shook his head. "Not a good idea."

"I see," Alix said thoughtfully. "No wonder she was drinking."

"And the drinking had to have affected her judgment. As Mendoza said, why else would she come up with the lamebrain idea that killing you was a good way to solve her problems?"

That really caught Alix by surprise. "Wait, wait, wait. Lieutenant Mendoza thinks she was behind the explosion? But he practically laughed at me when I suggested it."

"That was then. Now he sees it differently." He told her what Mendoza had told him about Liz's phone call to the Hacienda Encantada. "Presumably, she hadn't been expecting Chris to bring along her own art expert—"

"That's true; not until a couple of days before I showed up. I didn't know it myself till then."

"Okay, so she didn't have much time. She must have figured you'd know the painting was a fake, which meant she had to get you out of the picture before you nixed the deal with Chris, and what she came up with was murder. Not a great decision, but then clear thinking wouldn't have been her strong suit at the time."

"No. Okay, that could explain why Liz tried to kill me the day before yesterday, but who tried to kill me this morning? And why?"

"How do you know it wasn't Chris they were trying to kill?"

"Do you really think that?"

"Nah, I think it was you, all right. As to the why…well, we're still working on that." He trailed off.

"I've been giving that some thought myself," Alix said, "and the main thing I keep coming back to is that it just doesn't make any sense."

"Maybe everybody involved with this has been drinking too much," he said with a faint smile.

"Even so. What, they were afraid I'd spot the painting as a fake? So, take it off the market, wait a while, and try again with another buyer somewhere else. Or, if it made them nervous, just burn the thing, forget about it, and get on with the next scam. That's what I'd do—I wouldn't go around murdering people."

"I'm happy to hear that." He was kidding, but she could see that he was taking her seriously.

"And then," she continued, encouraged, "there's Liz. If she was the one behind it all, or one of the ones, why was *she* killed? Given everything else that's happened, it's hard to believe she just had the bad luck to show up when someone was in the act of stealing the painting…and while we're talking about the painting, why was anybody stealing it? I mean, given that it's a fake…whew, this is giving me a headache."

"It's confusing, all right. But I do agree with you on one point for sure. It's all got to have something to do with the forgery— with your identifying it as a fake."

"'With the *forgery*'? Are you saying you think it *is* a forgery now? Boy, things have sure changed in the last day or so."

"Well, Mendoza says you called him yesterday to tell him there's not much doubt about it."

"And you trust my saying so? You didn't yesterday in the evidence room."

"No, no, no," he said, and the smile was back, a playful one this time. "The contemptible Roland de Beauvais didn't trust you. Special Agent Ellesworth trusts you implicitly. In fact, so much so that there's something he'd like to ask your assistance with in his continuing pursuit of justice." The playfulness faded from his face. "I'm serious, Alix. I could use your help with this case in a big way. It would take a couple of days of your time, though."

Watch out now, something inside her warned, and yet she already knew that she was going to do it, whatever it was. Ted wasn't the only one with an interest in the pursuit of justice. Not only had Alix twice barely avoided being murdered, but the career she'd dreamed of was over and done with almost before it had begun, and if there was anything—*anything*—she could do to help Ted and Mendoza find the people responsible, she was game.

And then, of course, there was the little matter of Ted himself. If she didn't take him up on whatever it was, this would probably be the last time she'd ever see him, and that was something she realized that she didn't want. Alix was acutely, uncomfortably aware that she found this open, smiling Ted Ellesworth every bit as attractive as she'd found Rollie de Beauvais repulsive. And that was saying something. It was all too weird for words. An hour ago she had despised this man, found him utterly repellent, and now she felt—well, she wasn't sure what she felt.

"What kind of help?" she asked, her tone painstakingly neutral.

"Well, I know you were on your way to Taos for the New Directions conference. Are you still planning to go?"

"I'm not sure. It's up to Chris, but I know that if we do go, it won't be today. The hospital wants to keep her overnight."

"But they won't. Craig's bound and determined to fly her back to Seattle tonight, and I suspect he'll get his way."

"To Seattle? Why?"

"Because he seems to think that medical care in New Mexico is accomplished by means of rattle-shaking and leeching. He wants her back in civilization. He's already arranged a room for her at the University of Washington Medical Center for tonight."

"Oh." She reflected on this for a moment. "Then I guess I'll be going back with them."

"If you want to, but not necessarily." Ted had a lingering swallow of coffee, making something of a production of it. Alix had the impression he was choosing his words with care. "I'll be driving directly to Taos from here this afternoon. I'm signed up for the conference—as Roland de Beauvais, of course. It's Liz's baby, it's full of the crowd that she dealt with, and I figure that at this point it's my best bet to get more of a handle on the scam. And if I can come up with anything on her murder, Mendoza would like to know that as well."

"That makes sense. Where do I fit in?"

"Well…" He hesitated. "I've got a pretty good background in art myself by now, but I'm obviously not in your league, and I'm worried about getting in over my head and blowing it. So I thought that if I could have somebody with real expertise at the conference with me, somebody I could trust, it could turn out to be invaluable."

Her eyebrows went up. "And that would be me?"

He nodded. "You could drive there with me. You're already registered for the meetings, and you have a room reserved at the Luhan House—"

"How do you know that?"

He grinned. "Ma'am, we're the FBI. We know these things. Anyway, the Luhan House is where the movers and shakers will be, so I tried to get in there myself; I'd like to be in on some of the conversation there's bound to be about Liz, but it's booked up. I'm at the Casa Benavides just down the road."

"So you'd like me to do your eavesdropping for you."

"Yes, that's pretty much it," he said, surprising her; she'd expected him to hem and haw around it.

"Oh." She'd been hoping for something that placed more demands on her expertise than gossip-sifting did, but still—

He mistook her reflection for concern. "If it's your safety you're worried about, I think you can put your mind at ease. Mendoza called the media yesterday to let them know the O'Keeffe's a fake after all and to fill them in on the details. And they loved it; it made a great story. Every one of them ran with it; the five o'clock news last night, the paper this morning. *Three-Million-Dollar Painting in Murder of Prominent Canyon Road Art Dealer a Forgery!* So the word's out, which means nobody has any reason to want you dead anymore, so if that's what's on your mind, you can relax."

It hadn't been on her mind at that moment, as a matter of fact, but it was nice to know all the same. "I'd have to talk to Chris first," she said.

"Of course. You couldn't just walk away and leave her wondering what happened to you."

"Well, there's that, yes, but—" Now it was her turn to hesitate. "But Chris has been picking up the tab for all this, and I can't afford to stay at the Luhan House on my own. I'm going to need to get an advance on my fee from her."

"You're going to—?" With all his skills at duplicity, Ted couldn't hide his surprise, but he recovered fast. "Oh, I thought you understood," he said smoothly. "Naturally, the Bureau will pick up your expenses."

She was puzzled at his reaction. What had he been so shocked about? It took a moment for her to realize what it was: why, he'd imagined she was *rich*. Now that she thought about it, it wasn't so surprising. She *looked* rich, she knew that; a combination of her looks, her bred-in-the-bone bearing, and her way with her carefully chosen but oh-so-limited wardrobe from Le Frock. Besides that, he probably thought Geoff's criminal career had set her up for life.

If he only knew.

"Then there's no problem," she said simply. "Sure, I'll go."

He smiled at her. "Great." He finished his coffee and began to rise. "Well, you'll want to talk to Chris, and I'll—"

"No, wait. I've been cooped up inside ever since the accident, Ted. We have time to take a walk and get some fresh air before we leave, don't we?"

"Sure, it's only fifty miles or so."

"Good, let's walk a little then. There's something I'd like to ask you too."

— • —

There was fresh air aplenty to be found in the area around the hospital, but no place to walk except in and around the huge parking lot. Nevertheless, the day was sunny and breezy, it felt good to be out in it, and they decided to circle the path that ran around the perimeter.

"So," Ted said when they'd walked quietly for a minute or two, "what did you want to ask me?"

Alix almost wished he'd forgotten. Still, it was something she needed to know. She took in a breath, slowly let it out—almost a sigh, but not quite—and began: "I assume you're in the FBI's art unit or whatever it's called."

"That's right, the Art Crime Team—art squad, for short."

"How long have you been with them?"

"Oh, about nine years, more or less."

"With the art squad all that time?"

"Alix, I know what you want to know, and the answer is yes, I know who your father is, and although I wasn't formally in the unit at the time, I did have some part in the investigation."

She almost stopped walking but went on. "You helped in his arrest?"

She wasn't looking at him, but she heard him heave a sigh of his own. He wasn't any more eager to go into this than she was.

"I guess I'd have to say yes, but it was from a distance. I gathered some information on two of the charges. I was in court for one of the trial days too—on the witness list, but they didn't call me, so I got to watch."

"I see. So...well, then, I can't help wondering how you feel about...well, me. I mean, my involvement in all this."

"I don't see what that's got to do with—" he began a bit stuffily, but then his native honesty interceded. "Okay, I admit it. I guess at first, when I heard that you were involved with Liz, I wondered whether...no, I suppose I *assumed* you were part of the scam."

Alix nodded. What reasonable person wouldn't have assumed it?

"And then, when I heard how your father had set you up in so many things, including—*especially* including—this job with Chris LeMay, it just seemed that the two of you must have something—"

It had taken a few seconds for the words to register, and when they did, she stopped him in mid-stride with a hand on his arm. "What are you saying?" She was stunned, hardly able to get the words out. "What do you mean, he got me this job?"

He peered at her. "Are you saying you didn't know?"

"What do you mean, he got me this job?" she demanded again. She could hear the blood throbbing in her ears.

Ted hesitated. "Look, Alix, maybe it'd be better—"

"Ted. Please."

"Okay then." With a shrug, he told her frankly, almost brutally. When Geoff had learned that Alix was in Seattle trying to establish herself, he'd contacted a few of his old friends in the field and asked them to do what they could—

Alix choked out an uneasy laugh. "Am I really supposed to believe this?" But an echo of her last conversation with Geoff was working its way up into her mind. *I can't tell you how sorry I am for getting you into this,* he'd said, then lapsed into incoherence. My God, it was true.

"Alix, believe me, it's so. He asked them to see if they had any work they could send your way, or at least if they could recommend you, and one of them was a curator at the museum in Seattle, I forget his name—Renaissance art, I think."

"Christopher Norgren," Alix said dully, pulling the name from her memory banks. Chris had said Norgren was the person who'd told her about Alix's apprenticeship with Santullo.

"Damn!" she said abruptly, then turned in a frustrated little circle. "Damn!" She was filled with...what? Anger at Geoff for meddling around in her life behind her back? At Ted for being the bearer of unwanted news? Disillusionment at finding out that what small success she'd achieved hadn't been her own doing after all? Embarrassment—

"Does Chris know that my father was involved?" she asked, tight-lipped.

"I don't know. I don't think so."

Alix shook her head speechlessly, replaying what she'd just heard. It was a few moments before she could talk again. "You said he set me up 'in so many things.' What else did he set me up in?"

"Alix, I'm not sure I should be the one to—"

"Just tell me, damn it!"

Another shrug, unwilling but acquiescent. The apprenticeship in Italy had not been the simple lucky break she thought it was; it had come about because her father had called his old friend Santullo and talked him into giving her a one-month trial. Fortunately, she'd passed muster, but the chance would never have come without his input. And as for that condo-sitting job in Seattle—

She held up her hand. "Enough." Her mind was whirling; she could feel all the little spinning wheels starting to go wobbly. All these years she'd thought that she'd been the one secretly helping Geoff to get on his feet—that precious sixty thousand dollars from her college fund. And now she finds out that *he'd* been secretly helping *her* all along, pulling strings and calling in obligations! It was too much to take in. She was going to need time to process it.

"Ted, why do you know so much about me? *How* do you know so much about me?"

"Well, our ops specialist dug it up. I had her look into it for me."

"You had your ops specialist…? Okay, I want the truth now: am I or am I not a suspect in this thing?"

"Listen, Alix—"

"This line you fed me about my coming to Taos to provide you with my 'invaluable' counsel—is that actually on the level, or is it just a way for you to keep me in your sights, see if you can catch me red-handed at, at—"

"Absolutely not, Alix. Do you really think I'm that two-faced—"

She couldn't help laughing. "Pardon me, you were saying what, Mr. de Beauvais?"

He hissed his frustration. "The FBI is not trying to catch you red-handed at anything," he said stiffly. "I assure you, the FBI has no interest in you except as a consultant—"

"A consultant? Oh, then am I receiving a fee for my expertise?"

"If you want to be paid," he said, looking levelly at her with those chilling eyes, "I'm sure something commensurate with your qualifications can be arranged."

"Oh, go to hell, I don't want your stupid money." To her extreme annoyance, she was close to tears.

"You want out then? Is that what you want?"

"Careful, Ellesworth, you're losing your Roland de Beauvais cool."

He stiffened a little more yet. "All right, Miss London, how about if we just forget the whole thing? Thank you very much for your time. I'll see that transportation is arranged—"

"Oh, for God's sake," she said disgustedly, "I didn't say I wanted out. I said I didn't want your money."

He looked uncertain. "So—?"

"I have to say good-bye to Chris and tell her what's going on. Then we'd better get going if we want to get to Taos this afternoon. I'll meet you at your car in twenty minutes."

She turned on her heel and headed back to the hospital, straight across the parking lot. The expression on his face had been impossible to read. Angry/befuddled was about as close as she could come, and it was probably the same one she was wearing. Despite the palpable irritation on both sides, there was something exciting in the air between them, no denying that, a titillating chemistry she hadn't felt in a very long while. But at the same time, this guy had a real knack for irritating the absolute hell out of her. And it was obvious that it worked both ways.

One way or another, the next couple of days in Taos were going to be something.

CHAPTER 18

It had taken a while, but the events of the day—of this surpassingly strange week, for that matter—had finally caught up with her almost the moment she sank into the passenger seat of Ted's rented red-and-white U-Haul.

"Sorry about the plebeian conveyance," he said. "Ordinarily, when I'm being a crooked art dealer I get to drive something a little classier. But Mercedes and Porsche rentals are a little scarce in Española, and this was the best—the only—thing they could come up with in the whole town."

"I'll try and live with it," she said. "I may doze for a while after we get going, anyway." Before he'd turned the key in the ignition, even before she'd gotten her seat belt secured, her eyelids were drooping. She managed to murmur an apology—slurred with fatigue but genuine enough—for losing her temper and Ted did the same. By the time he'd turned north on Highway 68 for the hour-long drive to Taos, she was deeply, deeply asleep, so much so that when she sensed at some level that the car had come to a stop and the engine had been turned off, it wasn't enough to bring her out of it. It took the gentle pressure of Ted's touch on her shoulder and his quiet voice—"Alix, we're here…Alix?"—to get her up from the black, bottomless well into which she'd fallen.

She awoke disoriented, thinking for a few confused moments that she was a little girl again, that she had fallen asleep on the long drive her family made several times each summer between their Manhattan condominium and the summer house in Watch Hill. It had been impossible to completely awaken her then, and among her most treasured memories was the snug, warm, protected feeling of being carried upstairs, her eyelids glued together, still three-quarters asleep, in her father's safe, strong arms, with her head on his shoulder, and then tucked tenderly into bed. The memory was so real and so compelling in her dozy mind that it was all she could do not to ask Ted to carry her upstairs in *his* strong, safe arms and tuck her in. Preferably tenderly.

Was that crazy, or what? Fortunately, she came all the way awake before she gave in to the urge, but it was a near thing and it left her flushed with embarrassment. When he offered to help her with her bag she gruffly refused, leaving him staring at her with an understandably surprised look on his face as she hurried away into the adobe-style building.

There appeared to be a cocktail hour in progress in the main downstairs room, with a dozen or so people sitting in groups or standing around chatting. A few of them she knew. She recognized Gregor Gorzynski, he of the Cheerios, rice noodles, and M&M's, who was wearing the same scuffed leather bomber jacket he'd worn at the reception, and what looked like the same tight, laddered, threadbare jeans. (Did he special-order them that way?) He was in full, rhapsodic flight, performing for a middle-aged, over-mascaraed blonde who followed his every grand gesture. Who was seducing whom was unclear and probably immaterial.

A few feet away in an armchair sat Clyde Moody, the archivist from the museum, looking on with undisguised disdain, while an older couple jabbered in his ear, laughing unrestrainedly at their own stories. Poor Moody looked as if he wished he were anywhere else but couldn't figure out how to get away. Alix offered a tentative wave that he either ignored or failed to see. As she turned to leave a young man she didn't know came up to her with something between a sidle and a swagger. In his hand was a martini on the rocks.

"Well, hello there, pretty lady," he said, breathing gin fumes into her face. "Do I know you?" He wore black Levi's and a form-fitting black T-shirt that showed off a lovingly sculpted torso and muscular arms. The accent was insinuatingly intimate and southern—Mississippi, Alabama, maybe Louisiana. *Do ah know yuh?*

"I'm afraid not." She took a step back.

He took a step forward. "*Will* I know you?"

Another step back. "I doubt it very much." She caught a glimpse of the stick-on name label just below his collarbone— "Hi! I'm Cody Mack Burley." It took a moment to register. Wasn't that the name of Liz's artist protégé, the painter whose works Chris had turned down for display at her bar? She remembered Chris's heartfelt assessment: "weird, twisted women…with their insides showing…yech." Alix stepped back even further.

Cody Mack, unmindful, held up the martini. "So, can I get you a—"

"Maybe another time. Excuse me, I haven't registered yet," she said, turning away, but managing at the last second to manufacture a smile. It could be that she'd want to talk to him after all, given his closeness to Liz. But she'd think about that later, not now. All she wanted to do now was flop into bed and dive deep down into sleep again.

"You're in the big room upstairs, Mabel's old room," Janet, the woman at the reception desk told her.

"That's right," Alix said, although she'd forgotten.

"And will Ms. LeMay be coming later?"

"No, she had to cancel. There was an accident. It's just me."

"Oh, I'm sorry. I hope she's all right."

"She's all right," Alix said. She didn't doubt that Chris, probably being flown back to Seattle by an attentive, concerned Craig at this very moment, was feeling considerably more than all right, raccoon face or no raccoon face.

The stairs to Mabel's second-floor room started behind the reception desk. The unexpectedly low, cramped stairway ran up all four sides of a square stairwell. Heavy-eyed, she hardly paid attention to where she was going, and at the first turn she bumped her head on the underside of the upper staircase. Obviously, she wasn't the first to do it, because it was well-padded for just such an eventuality. Still, it stung. Normally, Alix loved the quirkiness of old buildings, but tonight she had a few choice words for this one. She made it to the top without further incident, though, and once there her impressions ran sleepily together: an old wooden door, a huge, wood-floored room with a massively columned bed, and then nothing but the wonderful smoothness of clean, cool linens and a lovely, enveloping softness as she floated down, and down, and down.

— • —

She didn't surface again until the irresistible aroma of brewing coffee called to her, thin tendrils of fragrance curling up from the kitchen through the cracks between the old floorboards. Was it morning then? Could she have slept all that time? She opened her eyes and saw that indeed she had. It wasn't light yet, but the red numbers on the bedside clock said 6:11 a.m. She'd been solidly asleep for twelve hours. Amazing—she couldn't remember having slept so long before. Of course, she'd never had a day like yesterday before, either. Well, unless it was the one two days before that, when her casita had blown up.

It sure has been one hell of a week, she thought with a long, delicious stretch that would have put a cat to shame. The lure of coffee was powerful, and she was starving—she could smell pancakes now too—but first some serious attention to appearance and hygiene was required. Last night she'd fallen into bed without even taking off her clothes, washing her face, or brushing her teeth. She rolled over and got up, yawning, feeling more like a creature that had slept out in the rain than someone who'd spent the night in what had to be the world's most comfortable bed.

Twenty minutes later, while she was blow-drying her hair, it occurred to her that she hadn't checked her telephone messages in a while. Unzipping the front panel of her overnight bag, she pulled out the cell phone that Chris had thrust at her when they'd parted at the hospital. It took the usual hassle to get to her own voice-mail box, and when she did, she found a dozen calls from people whose names she didn't know—the press, she assumed—which she flicked through and deleted without listening to more than two or three seconds of each.

She did listen to a brief message from her father: Had she accidentally made off with the Galerie Xanadu catalog she'd been looking at at the museum in Santa Fe? It seemed that when Geoff's documents-expert friend went to look at it, it couldn't be found, and Mr. Moody wondered if Alix, who was the last person to have seen it, might inadvertently have carried it away with her.

No, Alix thought a bit huffily, *I did not carry it away with me, inadvertently or otherwise.* Pinching something from under the eagle-eye of Clyde Moody would have been quite a trick. She had left the folder on the table, just as he had asked. It was quite clear in her memory. She would surely run into him here in Taos today and she would set him straight on that.

There were also three messages from Katryn Lombard, the woman for whom she was restoring the paintings in Seattle. Alix's first reaction was worry. Katryn had sent her one postcard and a couple of e-mails from Provence in the months she'd been away, but she had never before telephoned her. And now here were *three* messages, two left yesterday, one today (it was eight hours later in France), each one telling her to call back as soon as she could. Was she being booted out? Did Katryn need her condo back? But on listening to the messages a second time, she realized that the tone suggested otherwise. There was no hint of bad news in it—quite the opposite, in fact. Still, Alix was nervous about it and thought she'd better make a quick call to Provence to set her mind at ease, even before going down for some of that coffee and food.

"Alix, darling, I'm soooo glad you called," Katryn said in her usual bright, emphatic, hurrying voice, as urgent as a doorbell buzzer. "I've been worried sick about you. I read about what happened in Santa Fe, and that you actually *found* the body! How perfectly gruesome." She sounded absolutely thrilled and apparently realized it, quickly adding: "You *are* all right, aren't you?"

Alix sighed. My God, were they even reading about her in Moustiers-Sainte-Marie, France? Her once-bright future as a reputable consultant grew dimmer by the minute. "I'm fine, Katryn," she said. "I appreciate your calling."

"Well, actually, that's not the reason. I mean it's not the only reason. Alix, how long do you think it will take you to complete the work you're doing for me? Could you finish, say, in a month?"

Alix's heart dropped another few inches. So Katryn wanted her out, after all. She could look forward to being homeless as well as jobless. Boy, when it rained... "Well..."

Katryn, who could be perceptive at times, recognized the hesitation for what it was. "Darling, I don't want you to leave the condo. We agreed on a year, and a year it will be. But if you could speed up the process...?"

Whew. "Well, the Signac's finished, Katryn—I think you'll like it—and I'm well into the Utrillo. But the Royle and the Luce—they'll need quite a lot of work. I should be back in Seattle in—"

"Let's say we put the Royle and the Luce aside for the moment. And the Malharro as well. How long would it take you to complete the Utrillo and do the Bonnard?"

Alix shrugged, although there was nobody to see her. "I don't know...two months? No, better make that three to be on the safe side. You see, it's not so much the work itself, it's the drying times involved, and I might have to get some materials from Europe—"

"Three months is just fine!" Katryn said. "Three months is perfect."

"But why the rush, Katryn? What's going on?"

"Because I'm going to put them up for auction," Katryn burbled, "and I want them to look their very best!"

Lee was shocked. The Bonnard and the Utrillo were the gems of the collection and the most valuable as well, worth more than the other four put together. "But why?"

"Because I'm fed up to here with these old Post-Impressionist hacks, aren't you?"

"Well, no, not—"

But the question had been rhetorical. "They've had their day. Nobody cares about them anymore. I mean, they're no longer relevant to today's world, don't you agree?"

Another question for which no answer was expected or desired. Alix waited.

"And so I'm going to be getting rid of them and investing in the *future*, not the past, not old, dead artists, but vibrant, brilliant new ones."

"The future?" Alix asked gingerly. The thought of anybody's getting rid of Bonnard's glowing, sensuous *Woman Bathing* for any reason at all, let alone to replace it with something modern, dismayed her.

"Yes! There's this wonderful new artist, a true visionary—I see him as Picasso's heir, only totally, totally different. Groundbreaking. He's going to change the very concept of what art *is*, and *I'm* going to be his American patron. Isn't that amazing?"

This time an answer was expected. "It certainly is," Alix said, unable to summon up much enthusiasm. "Congratulations."

"He's practically just this minute burst on the scene," Katryn plowed on. "I'm lucky to have discovered him before anybody else has. I'm on his Twitter feed," she said proudly. "And I've spoken with him on the phone—twice. He's a wonderful man with a deep, deep intellect—a genius." Alix heard a snuffly noise that might have been Katryn's version of a girlish giggle. "And talk about hot! I've seen his video on YouTube."

"What's his name?" Alix asked. "Would I have heard of him?" She was getting a funny feeling about this.

"As a matter of fact, I wouldn't be surprised. Maybe you've even met him! That's one of the things I wanted to ask you."

The funny feeling intensified. Surely, it couldn't be, it wouldn't be—

"According to his tweets, he was about to have a show, his very first American exhibition, at the Blue Coyote, right there in Santa Fe, so I couldn't help wondering—"

It couldn't be, but it was. Alix's heart sank. "Gregor Gorzynski," she said dully.

"Gregor *Stanislav* Gorzynski," Katryn corrected coyly. "Stani for short. *Did* you have a chance to meet him? Did you get to see his work? Isn't it fantastic?"

"Katryn," Alix began, but Katryn cut her off, which was a good thing because she didn't know what she was going to say, but whatever it was Katryn wouldn't have appreciated it. "Oh, Alix, I have to go. We'll talk later. *Au revoir, ma cher.* I'm *so* excited!"

Alix stood there staring out the window for a few moments, then limply sat down on the bed. Angrily, she deleted all three of Katryn's messages. Nausea had welled up in her throat. Was this a sick joke someone had gotten Katryn to play on her? Or were there more cosmic forces at work? What goes around comes around? Chickens coming home to roost? History repeating itself? The sins of the father visited on the daughter? The, the... but she'd run out of clichés.

The thing was, this was exactly what had happened to Geoff, what had driven him over the edge, if you believed his story. His forgeries had all been copied from paintings that had been entrusted to him for cleaning or restoring. And the fakes were so beautifully done that he was able to get away with returning them to the owners in place of the originals. Did they somehow seem different—newer, brighter? Well, of course, that was what a skillful cleaning did. He then sold the originals to sometimes gullible, sometimes shady collectors, all at enormous profit to himself.

The evidence against him had been so cut-and-dried that there had been little point in his claiming innocence, and he didn't. He had, however, offered an eloquent saving-Western-civilization defense of his behavior. He had pointed out that every one of the paintings involved, sixteen in all, was being worked on prior to its planned sale to provide the owner with funds to buy something else. And that something else, in each case, was one or more twentieth-century postmodern monstrosities. "Monstrosities" had been his word for them. Sometimes it was Neo-Dada, sometimes Neo-Expressionist, sometimes Deconstructionist, sometimes something without a name. And the idea of selling, say an Ingres nude, in order to replace it with a "statement" made of wires and shellacked animal entrails had outraged his sensibilities. As he saw it, he said with his usual flair, he was rescuing art, taking it from Philistines who didn't care, and who didn't know the difference anyway, and putting it instead in the loving custodianship of those who appreciated its beauty and value.

At the time, all Alix's thoughts had been summed up in five one-syllable words that she remembered muttering aloud while reading about the trial: *What a crock of shit.* He was a crook, and his self-proclaimed objective of saving art from the barbarians had not so incidentally made him a lot of money. (All gone now, of course.)

But that was then. Katryn's call had shaken things up. For the first time she understood something of what Geoff had felt. No, she wasn't about to justify what he'd done, but…sell that exquisitely rendered Utrillo she'd been slaving over so lovingly and replace it with…with…M&M's and rice noodles? Geoff was right, the Philistines were taking over.

The nausea hadn't gone away, and now there was a gripey kind of pain in her abdomen as well. But the source of them wasn't quite as high-minded as she'd assumed, she now realized.

The last time she'd eaten had been at breakfast the day before; she was *hungry*.

Cosmic forces would have to take a back seat to coffee and pancakes.

— • —

When she stepped out into the hall, she found herself looking through a half-open door into an old-fashioned bathroom flooded with a diffuse rainbow of colors. Assuming it had stained-glass windows, she peeked in curiously, only to find that the windows were of ordinary glass, but thickly painted over with primitive images—an Indian headdress, a chicken, another animal (cat? dog? chipmunk?), along with various geometric abstractions—all jumbled together in an eye-searing hodgepodge of reds, yellows, blues, and greens. This, then, was the celebrated bathroom painted by D. H. Lawrence, scandalized by his hostess's practicing her ablutions in full view of any (unlikely) passerby. An inscription in one corner confirmed this: *D. H. Lawrence painted this window.*

Well, she had learned a long time ago that geniuses generally were wise to keep to whatever their specialty was, and it certainly applied here. It was a good thing for Lawrence that he hadn't decided to pursue a career in art. All the same, it was quite something to see, and although the bathroom went with the room down the hall, she promised herself that she would at least brush her teeth there before she left. Just so that she could say she had.

On the way downstairs she remembered bumping her head in time to duck where the stairs turned and there wasn't enough headroom. Bending down brought her face to face with a small painting on the wall that she hadn't noticed yesterday. Mesas, buttes, desert. It was quite well done, and her first thought was that it might even be a Georgia O'Keeffe that the painter had left when she'd stayed with Luhan. But no, on second glance it was O'Keeffelike, all right, but too pretty, too plainly decorative to be the real thing—just an "in-the-style-of" piece intended as an attractive wall decoration. It was a nice rendering, though, deserving of a better display place than a shadowy staircase landing. The picture was modestly signed in blue paint at the lower right: Brandon Teal. The name was unfamiliar.

She had reached the bottom of the steps and turned left, following her nose toward the coffee and pancakes—and now bacon too; *slurp!*—when she stopped stone-still, her mind churning. There was something about...

She dashed back up the stairs to the painting. There was a small picture light attached to the top of the frame. She flicked it on and stared hard. *Yes!* There, at the base of one of the buttes, clothed in shadow, was the barely visible figure of a man in profile. The same figure—the same *exact* figure—that had been on *Cliffs at Ghost Ranch* and marked it as the fake that it was.

She knew the point of the little figure too. Geoff had talked about it when she'd called him from Ghost Ranch. A "just-in-case alibi" was what he'd called it—an unobtrusive but unmistakable element that some prudent forgers added to everything they painted, whether fakes or their own originals (if any). The idea was that it served as a kind of Kilroy-was-here insignia to "prove"—if it ever became necessary—that the forger had had no intent to defraud. No, no, he had painted the thing as a copy, or an homage, or a study. When had he ever claimed it was anything else? Really, if forgery had been in his heart, surely the last thing he would have done would have been to insert something that a) didn't belong, and b) was practically his own personal trademark. Of course, if some later owner, some unscrupulous scoundrel, had taken it upon himself to pass it off as a genuine Whoever, how was the poor, innocent artist to blame for that?

The longer she looked at the painting, the more her certainty grew that Brandon Teal, if that was really his name, had painted Chris's "O'Keeffe" as well. This was absolutely incredible, a terrific development. She considered calling Ted then and there, but it was barely seven o'clock and she was pretty sure Ted Ellesworth was not the early-rising type. Or was she confusing him with Roland de Beauvais? But either way, it could wait. First things first. Pancakes.

The dining room was a spare, somber space that brought to mind the rectory of a monastery with its simple wooden furnishings, floor candelabra, and dull black and red floor tiles. The settings had been laid out, but no one had arrived yet. The big, old-fashioned kitchen opened just off this room, however, and there she found two cooks working away. The smells alone were enough to make her think that maybe, despite the craziness of the last few days, the world at large might still be normal. Add to that the cozy scene in general: two aproned, rosy-cheeked, flour-spattered, middle-aged women cheerfully cutting scone dough into wedge shapes, with a third, younger woman sitting on a high stool beside the tiled work table and quietly kibitzing, coffee cup in hand. This person Alix recognized as Janet, the receptionist who'd checked her in the day before.

She had barely said good morning to the three of them before they saw to it that she had her own cup of coffee, a fresh, warm sweet roll, and her own stool at the table. Heaven. For a while they made small talk: the weather, the fact that this was Alix's first visit, stories about the house. One of the cooks had been working there when the actor Dennis Hopper had owned it for a while in the seventies. Did Alix know that he had refused to sleep in Mabel's bed—the bed Alix had been in—because he'd believed it to be haunted by Mabel's restless and vindictive spirit? No, Alix didn't know (she was also having trouble placing Dennis Hopper, although she kept that to herself), but she could say with certainty that she had been unhaunted by Mabel. She'd slept like a stone.

Janet refilled her own cup. "I'll bet. It's no wonder you were wiped out last night. We heard what happened up near Abiquiu. Your friend—Ms. LeMay—is going to be all right, I hope?"

"She'll be fine. No serious damage done."

"Good. Uh…about Liz…" Janet put on a suitably sober face. "I can imagine how distressing her…her death must be. The two of you were old friends of hers, weren't you?"

"Yes, we were," Alix said smoothly, "although I didn't know her quite as long as Chris did." *Three hours, to be exact*, but she wasn't going to squeeze out any confidences about Liz by telling them that. The only thing that was really distressing her at this point was her own good upbringing, which was preventing her from cramming the entire sweet roll into her mouth at once. She settled for a nibble and a slug of coffee. "Chris was really disappointed not to be able to come to this conference, that's for sure. She was looking forward to meeting some of Liz's other friends. I know I am. It'll be a big help to be able to talk about the good things, share stories." *When did I get to be such a facile liar?* Alix wondered. *One more talent no doubt inherited from good old Dad.*

The three women nodded their sympathy and looked reflective, giving Alix the chance to down a few gobbets of almond-paste-centered pastry, far and away the most delicious thing she'd ever tasted in her life.

"Well," Janet said, standing up, "I guess I'd better get to work."

"Oh, I wanted to ask you something," Alix said. "There's a beautiful little painting in the stairwell, a desert scene—"

"Oh, yes, Brandon did that. He gave it to us. A gift. He's *so* nice."

Brandon? "You *know* him? I mean, personally?"

"Brandon?" she said, resettling on her stool. "Sure, we see him all the time. He lives in Santa Fe. He's signed up for the conference too. I'm sure you'll see him around."

"That'd be great. What does he look like?"

"Oh..." She rolled her eyes upward the way people do when they search for a mental image. "Well, he's pretty hard to miss," she said, smiling. "He's a good six-four and burly besides, and he's got red hair and this beard that looks like orange Brillo—"

Alix blinked. *Big, burly, orange beard...* "Does he...does he smoke a pipe?" she asked, doing her best to tamp down her swelling excitement.

"Like a chimney. Never seen him without one. He says it keeps him calm."

"If that's true," said one of the cooks, "wouldn't you just love to see him when he's nervous?"

"That's true," Janet said, laughing. "Big as he is, poor Brandon's a walking exhibit of raw nerves. He refuses to take his medication. He says it stifles his creativity. The funny thing is, what he doesn't realize is that his problem is that he's *too* creative. His work is all over the map. One year he's a Post-Impressionist, the next year he's a, a surrealist or something. Personally, I think if he could just develop one single style, his own style, you know, a Brandon Teal style..."

She finally noticed the odd look on Alix's face. "Uh-oh, did I say something I shouldn't have? Is he a friend of yours?"

Alix had heard practically nothing since the red hair, the orange beard, and the pipe. *My God!* It was stunning enough to make her forget about the sweet roll, at least for the moment.

"I'm sorry," she said, "did you ask me something?"

"I asked if you knew him."

"I, um, think I ran into him once," Alix said.

CHAPTER 19

She wasn't so excited that it spoiled her appetite, however, so before making the call to Ted she sat down, alone in the big room (technically, breakfast wasn't served until eight o'clock), and did justice to a huge platter of pancakes, maple syrup, and bacon. Two over-easy eggs as well, although they had to go on another plate. And more coffee. And one more of the delicious little almond sweet rolls, or maybe it was two. Then, stuffed and revivified, she lavished sincere gratitude and approbation on the two beaming cooks, got a coffee refill in a cardboard cup, and went out to the cobblestoned front portico of the house. There she stood for a few moments, contentedly digesting, sipping coffee, breathing in the clean scents of what she took to be an approaching desert rain, and—most of all—relishing the amazement and approbation that Ted was about to lavish on *her* when he heard that she had identi-fied the forger of *Cliffs at Ghost Ranch*, who also happened to be the very man she and Chris had encountered in the act of stealing the very same painting from the Blue Coyote after Liz's murder as well. And, to make everything as easy as possible for the FBI,

Mr. Teal was available right there in Taos for a friendly little tête-à-tête at Ted's convenience. Everything was working out just fine.

Why, I'm happy, she realized. It was as if the morning's developments—the call from Katryn, the eye-opening flash of insight into Geoff's motivations, the picture in the stairwell—had combined to shake loose the self-centered mopeyness that had dogged her for so long. The long night's sleep and the great breakfast hadn't hurt either. She felt as if a hundred-pound boulder had been unstrapped from her shoulders, as if she'd unexpectedly emerged from a long, dark tunnel that she'd dug for herself. It was all a question of perspective. The world was endlessly fascinating, if you looked at it right, with twists, and screw-ups, and surprises, delightful and otherwise, at every turn. What was so terrible about that? When things got wacky enough, as they'd certainly been lately, about all you could do was laugh.

She was young, healthy, and talented. She was *alive*. What was her beef? So things weren't working out careerwise. Big deal. She could always go back to Italy, romantic, delightful Italy, and work and learn alongside the great Fabrizio Santullo, couldn't she, and how many twenty-nine-year-olds could say that? He'd practically begged her to stay; he'd be thrilled to have her back.

There was something else that was warming her too, a glow she only now recognized for what it was. She'd had time to process what Ted had told her—how it had been her father who'd orchestrated practically all the good things that had been happening to her—and she saw things differently now. What in the world had there been to be resentful about? There was Geoff, ruined, shunned by everyone (including his only child), watching his remaining years waste away behind bars, and where had his thoughts been? With her, with Alix. He had used up what little professional capital he had left, not for himself, but to scrape up opportunities for her. And he had done it with no thought of gratitude or credit, but only for love. She felt the tears working their way up.

The chirping of her cell phone startled her and headed off any waterworks. She sat herself down on one of the portico's blue wooden benches and flipped it open.

It was Ted, sounding as if he'd been awake every bit as long as she had. "Hi, Alix, I thought we'd better get straight on plans for today. The conference opens—"

"Wait," she said, brimming with excitement, "I have some things to tell you, and I think you're going to like them. There's a small painting here that caught my eye, and when I took a closer look at it..."

It took five minutes to explain, and Ted was gratifyingly impressed, both by her discovery and the rationale for her conclusion, but his reaction to the big news itself wasn't what she'd expected. It was, in fact, pretty lukewarm. Yes, it was nice that we now knew who the forger was, and Ted would most certainly look forward to a "chat" with him, but it wasn't the forger he was after; Teal was very likely a minor figure in this, probably hired for a fixed fee. It was the major players that Ted wanted.

"But isn't it possible that Teal can give you that information?" Alix asked.

"Possible," Ted said doubtfully, "but usually a ring like this, assuming it is a ring, operates on the need-to-know principle. The less the minor players know, the better. I'd guess this guy was probably out of the loop altogether."

"Okay, but what about him killing Liz? Isn't that something you—"

"Teal didn't kill Liz," Ted said.

"What?" She'd started, inadvertently knocking the almost-full cup off the arm of the bench and splattering coffee over the cobblestones. "How can you say that with such certainty? We caught him coming—*running*—out of her office—"

"Yes, but two hours after Liz was killed."

"Two hours?" she echoed. "I thought—"

"The ME's finding at the scene was that she'd been dead two hours or less. Mendoza got the autopsy report yesterday: turns out two hours was just about right."

"All right, but how does that prove he didn't kill her?"

"It doesn't prove it, Alix, but murderers don't stick around after whacking someone. They want to get the hell out of there as soon as they can. Think about it: why would he be hanging around for all that time? It doesn't make any sense. He'd just take the painting and go. No, somebody else killed her. Then Teal came along later, took advantage of the situation, and grabbed the picture."

Alix sighed. Ted was right; they were still a long way from the bottom of things. "That raises something else that doesn't make sense, though," she said thoughtfully. "Why would he steal his own painting?"

"Now *that's* a good question," Ted agreed. "I'll make that topic number one when we have that little chat. Alix, the conference opens with a ten o'clock continental brunch. We'd better be there for that. There's bound to be lots of talk about Liz."

"Okay, I'll see you there."

"Well." He cleared his throat. "That gives us a few hours. Have you had breakfast yet?"

Had she had breakfast yet! More like breakfast, lunch, and dinner put together. "I had a bite, yes," she replied, then realized she'd blown what was going to be an invitation to join him. "But I could meet you for coffee?" she added brightly.

Apparently she'd taken too long to come up with it. "No, that's okay," he said. "I generally don't have much of a breakfast anyway." Pause. "So what are your plans for the morning?"

"I thought I'd get out and see a little of the area. The ladies in the kitchen told me about a nice park just down Morada Lane. I was thinking I might take a stroll there."

Now it was Ted who'd been given his cue—*Oh, really, well, why don't I join you?*—but he dropped the ball as clumsily as she had. "Yes, that'd be Kit Carson State Park. He lived here, you know, Carson did. Died here too, for that matter."

"Oh, really."

This was getting too ridiculous for words. They were circling around each other like a couple of sixteen-year-olds, interested but too ham-fisted to get anything going, and neither one of them could seem to figure out how to make the first move. He knew she was single, of course (he knew everything else about her), and her instincts, always so reliable, told her that he wasn't married either, and that he found her attractive too. Or could it be that those famous intuitive powers of hers were reading him totally wrong? As with D. H. Lawrence, perhaps her aptitudes were better in some areas than in others.

"Well, I'll see you later then?" she said. And there it was, one more opportunity for him to take the ball and run with it if he wanted to.

But apparently he didn't. Or couldn't. "Right," he said, and the phone went dead.

"Fine," she grumped into the mouthpiece although he wasn't there to hear it. "A business relationship is what you want? A business relationship it is. Plenty of other fish in the sea."

She needed a walk in the park now more than she had before the call, but first she thought she'd better change out of her good slacks and relatively new flats and get into sneakers and a pair of jeans in case she did get caught in a shower. Her windbreaker too. No sooner was she back in her room, however, than she started yawning. Impossible as it seemed after all the sleep she'd had, the bed looked wonderfully inviting. Well, why not? There was plenty of time for a nap before that continental brunch. She slipped out of her shoes and slacks, crawled gratefully between the sheets, sighed once, and drifted off again, undisturbed by Mabel's ghost.

– • –

Ted had placed the call to Mendoza about Brandon Teal as soon as he'd finished talking to Alix, and then he went downstairs to breakfast in the Casa Benavides dining room. What he'd told Alix about not eating much in the morning was true—generally just coffee and a bagel or an English muffin—but he liked to take his time with them, reading a newspaper over his second cup of coffee. But this morning, although he had the week's *Taos News* open in front of him, he was merely going through the motions. Why had he been so stiff, so stupidly obtuse with Alix? It wasn't like him; he liked women, enjoyed their company, and there was something about Alix that he liked more than most. What then? Surely not her dubious pedigree? No, he wasn't as hidebound as that; people were themselves, they weren't carbon copies of their parents. Sure, a couple of days ago he'd said to Mendoza that he believed in guilt by association, but it wasn't true; he'd just been rationalizing at the time, looking for a reason for his instinctive dislike of her. (How quickly things could change.)

No, his problem this morning had nothing to do with reasoning. It was strictly gut-level. He'd been tongue-tied because he'd been so anxious not to blow it by seeming too interested in her that he'd blown it by coming across as totally, utterly uninterested. And uninteresting.

The beep of his cell phone was a welcome interruption. On the other end was Mendoza, who wasted no time getting down to business. "Teal's dead, Ted."

"He's *what*?" Ted looked quickly around, biting his tongue. He'd inadvertently slipped out of his Roland de Beauvais persona. Only two words, but two words, heard by the wrong people, and his cover was wrecked. Fortunately, none of the other diners seemed to have noticed. He got up, hurried outside into the courtyard, and stood beside the plashing Moorish fountain.

"I sent a couple of my people out to talk to him," Mendoza went on. "The landlord let them in. They found him in his bathroom—"

"Eduardo, when you say *dead*, do you mean dead as in *killed*?"

"That's exactly what I mean. It was set up to look like an accident, like he slipped coming out of the shower and hit the back of his head on the washstand, but the job was seriously botched. It took the ME about five minutes to come up with homicide."

"Good God," Ted said, "this just keeps going on and on." He shook his head. "I'm assuming the time of death was at least a couple of days ago, would that be right? Saturday or before."

"Why would you think that?"

"Because the news has been out since Saturday night that the painting's a forgery. There's no reason to kill anybody over it anymore."

"Well, I guess there is. Doc says he's been dead over twelve hours, under twenty. He'll give us more details—"

"But...but that means he was killed *yesterday*!"

"Yeah," Mendoza said slowly, "which tells us what, exactly?"

"That somebody's still out there killing people—that getting out the word that we know the O'Keeffe's a forgery didn't put an end to it!"

"Well, yeah, obviously..."

"Which means I was wrong—Alix *isn't* out of danger. Somebody might still be trying...and I've brought her here, where they all are, and let her wander around without any protection. Any one of them could...Jesus, Eduardo, what have I gotten her into? I have to go find her!"

CHAPTER 20

Kit Carson State Park is more playground than park, with tennis courts and baseball diamonds, but there are also groves of trees and sweeping green lawns. That morning, with the low clouds threatening rain at any moment, Alix had the place to herself with the exception of a few kids playing a pickup game on one of the diamonds, a couple of solitary joggers, and one or two other walkers. She was on the circular jogging path, having stopped beside a group of cottonwoods to listen to a sound she didn't remember ever having heard before: the gentle, agreeable clacking of their crisp, yellowing leaves in the breeze.

She waited for a Spandexed jogger to lope by her before starting to walk again; one or two more circuits of the track and she'd head back to the Luhan House to change and then head over to the conference center. She was annoyed at herself for having slept clear through the regular breakfast hours and missing the opportunity to tune in on the chatter, and she intended to make up for it by getting to the conference early.

"Why, it's Miss London, isn't it? Alix?" a dry, familiar voice said, and there was Clyde Moody, looking lost in a voluminous trench coat that would have done Humphrey Bogart proud. On his head was a capacious blue denim Greek fisherman's hat pulled down to his ears. He looked ready for the storm of the century. His usual bow tie (little penguins and mini-icebergs on a field of blue this morning) peeped out from between his lapels.

"Yes, it is, Mr. Moody. How are you this morning? I tried to say hello last night, but you were surrounded by hordes of admirers and didn't notice me."

"Surrounded by admirers? Oh, I doubt that. The last time I was surrounded by hordes of admirers was in my high school physical education class when I knocked myself unconscious trying to use the chin-up bar."

Alix laughed. Apparently Moody was in, what were for him, positively exuberant spirits. "Oh, there was something I wanted to talk to you about," she said. "I understand you weren't able to find the catalogs I was looking at the other day and you thought I might have—"

"Oh, I assure you, I wasn't implying…that is to say, there was no question of your intentionally taking them. I thought only that you might have accidentally left with them."

"No, I left them right there in the middle of the table, in their folder. You don't remember?"

"Actually, I thought I did remember that, but when the folder wasn't in its place afterward, or anyplace nearby, or anyplace that made any logical sense at all—and I searched carefully, believe me—well, I wondered if you might have it. It was just a hope, really." His narrow shoulders lifted in a despairing shrug.

"I'm sorry," she said sympathetically. "I hope you find them."

"Oh, I'm sure we will," he said with a sigh. "These things happen, I suppose." He smiled. "Only they're not supposed to happen to me." They stepped out of the way to allow another runner to jog by. "Well," he said, "it's been nice speaking with you. I'm on my way to pay my respects to Ms. Luhan." He tipped his cap to her, something else you didn't see very much these days.

"Ms. Luhan?" Alix repeated.

"Yes, she's buried here in the park, didn't you know?"

"In the *park*?"

He smiled. "Why, yes. Kit Carson State Park is somewhat unusual, a combination of town commons and town cemetery. Technically, the cemetery part—the Kit Carson *Memorial* Park—is a sub-unit within the larger park. It's that area over there, where you see the fencing and those trees. Mr. Carson's grave is there, as you might expect, but it's Mabel that I go and see. An extraordinary force, a tremendous benefactor of the arts."

"Yes, I know."

"Ah…well…would you care to accompany me?"

Alix considered. "Why, yes, I would, thank you. I'd like to pay my respects to her too." It was the least she could do to thank Mabel for not haunting her.

Moody nodded, pleased. "Come."

The cemetery was like most old small-town cemeteries, cared for but not overly cared for, with worn, sparse grass and weathered, time-tilted gravestones placed not in rows but willy-nilly—all of which contributed a poignant atmosphere of bygone times and vanished ways. They had the place to themselves and stopped briefly at the grave of Kit Carson, where there was a plain headstone with a little decorative carving around the edges and a simple inscription: "Kit Carson, died May 23, 1868, aged 59 years."

Mabel's memorial was even more modest, a rectangular tablet of veined marble, not even knee-high, on a flat base, with an equally terse inscription: "Mabel Dodge Luhan, Feb. 26, 1879, Aug. 13, 1962." Other than the inscription, it was plain as plain could be, with no ornamental carving, no ornamentation of any kind. It sat in a particularly forlorn corner of the cemetery, far from the graves of Carson and the other town notables.

Alix was surprised. Knowing what she knew of Luhan—of Mabel, as everybody here seemed to call her—Alix had expected either something grand or something outrageous. "They kind of put her in the low-rent district, didn't they?" she said.

"Yes, it does seem that way," Moody said as they stood on either side of the stone. He seemed deeply affected—agitated, in fact—to be in Mabel's presence. His hat had been respectfully removed, and now he twisted it in both hands. "I mean, for a woman who did so much for, for…" He clamped his mouth shut and his eyes as well, and just stood there shaking his head.

Oh, brother, Alix thought, *don't let him start crying!* "Still," she said quickly, "it's nice to see that people haven't forgotten her. Look at all the stones." She was referring to the rounded river rocks and pebbles that people had placed on top of the gravestone as remembrances.

Moody jerked his head up and down in agreement. "You know," he said, speaking very fast, even stammering a little, "that custom—leaving stones on graves—originated in ancient Judaic tradition as a way for people to participate, so to speak, in building a memorial to the deceased because at that time, of course, there were no headstones as we know them but rather rock cairns, but in recent times, in recent times, it's become a means of, of, of, of remembrance to, to indicate…" He was practically choking on the torrent of words.

What is all this about? Alix wondered, growing more and more uneasy as he rattled crazily on. *Is he having a breakdown of some kind?* She was suddenly deeply aware of how alone they were, with no one in sight, no one within earshot. She moved back a step. There was something very wrong here—

Crack! She jumped at the sound, and at the same instant something stung her on the outside of her right thigh. She slapped at it with her hand, thinking it was a bee, but when she touched flesh instead of cloth she looked down to see a two-inch rent in her jeans, under which was a shallow, inch-long, greasy-looking furrow in her leg. As she stared uncomprehendingly at it, droplets of blood began welling along its length. *A bullet graze?* She looked up at Moody, who stood there looking more shocked than she was.

"Did you just *shoot* me?"

"I, I..."

But now she saw the hole in the center of the hat he held, the curl of smoke still coming from it. She looked wildly around for a place to run, a tree to hide her, but now he had thrown down the hat and had the pistol pointed squarely at the center of her chest. He was trembling so hard that the gun was jumping up and down as if it were being jerked on a string, but even so there was no way he could miss—not from six feet away. And she recognized the gun as a semiautomatic, which meant that if he did miss, he could pump out another shot, and another, and another, as fast as he could pull the trigger.

Despite knowing how stupid it was, she put her hands up in front of her face. It was all she could think of to do. "Mr. Moody..."

He extended his arms and took aim. "I'm really sorry about this. It's your own doing, really..."

She stared numbly at him, shaking her head "no" as if that were going to stop him. "But...but why...?"

But she already knew why. It had come to her as she asked, a conclusion so simple, so blindingly obvious, that she couldn't believe it had never crossed her mind. The faking of the Galerie Xanadu catalog—Moody hadn't been *victimized* by the fraud, he had *perpetrated* it...along with God knew how many other frauds. And Alix had had the rotten luck to catch him at it.

"I'm sorry," Moody said again. "I have no choice." He clamped his mouth shut.

And so I'm going to die now, she told herself woodenly, not really believing it. How could her life end in Kit Carson's grave-yard, shot to death by a...by a crazed museum archivist? No, it was too absurd, it couldn't...

And didn't. When he pulled the trigger, nothing happened. Alix had instinctively squeezed her eyes shut, but when she heard the little click they popped open. He tried again. Another click. He gave a little cry of frustration and shook the jammed gun the way you'd yank a ketchup bottle to get the contents flowing.

Alix came to life. She grabbed a golf-ball-sized rock from the top of Mabel's stone, flung it at his head, and launched herself at him. Moody managed to duck the rock, but not Alix. Head down, she slammed into him at belt level, wrapping her arms around him and driving with her legs. Alix didn't weigh much less than he did, so the force of her tackle sent him staggering backward, with her attached, limpet-like, her legs churning. Next to Mabel's grave was another memorial stone, a black basalt boulder, and when he stumbled back into it his feet were knocked from under him. Up and over it flew Moody. Up and off to the side flew the gun. Moody landed on his back, crumpled into a triangular space between the boulder and the corner of the fencing, with Alix sprawled on top of him. The gun landed a few feet away, near the fence.

Alix was off him and after it in a flash, leaving him struggling to extricate himself from the corner. In two seconds the gun was in her hand, aimed squarely at the center of his face. He had barely gotten himself turned over.

At first he quailed, shrinking further into the corner and raising his hands in surrender, but then he thought better of it, gave a nervous little giggle, got his legs under him—

"I'm telling you, don't move!"

—and stood all the way up, his hands no longer raised. Strangely, he seemed calmer, more self-assured, without the gun than with it. "What are you going to do?" he asked, taking a step toward her. "It's jammed. You can't shoot me." Another step.

Alix, stubbornly controlling her own trembling, stood her ground. She slammed the heel of her left hand against the butt of the pistol, then quickly yanked back and released the slide. She'd hoped the sinister *snick-snick* of the racking action would be enough to stop him, but it didn't seem to penetrate. He hesitated for only a fraction of a second, then kept coming toward her. She aimed the gun at the sky, offered a wordless little prayer, and pulled the trigger.

Either the prayer or her attempt to clear the gun worked, because it fired. The sharp *crack!* was like music, the jarring recoil a caress.

Moody halted in mid-step, eyes popping. "How did you…it was…"

"TRB," Alix said with all the laid-back élan she could muster. "Tap, rack, and…*bang*. Essential first aid for a jammed semi." She patted the gun with something like affection, showing off like crazy in hopes of convincing him that she was an old, sure hand with these things. In point of fact, she'd taken two hours of training years ago, after the divorce from Paynton, when she'd considered buying a handgun for herself—this same Glock 30, the world's most popular pistol, as it happened. But she'd decided against it, and this was the first time she'd had a gun in her hand since. For some happy reason, it was the instructor's harping on "TRB" that was about the only thing that had stuck with her. Tap, rack, and...*bang*.

"Yes, but you won't shoot me," Moody said, but Alix could see that the balance of power had shifted. He wore a wan, scared look now. He was bluffing.

Alix was quick to take advantage. "The hell I won't," she growled, coming toward him. "Back off, or so help me, I'll kill you." She brandished the gun at him. "Believe me, it'd be a pleasure."

Alix was bluffing too, but after all a bluff with a gun beats a bluff without one. Still, would she really shoot him if she had to? *In a heartbeat*, she told herself and realized she meant it. He'd tried to murder her, hadn't he? Twice, apparently. And probably killed Liz too. She wouldn't hesitate. Moody evidently read her frame of mind in her eyes. He backed prudently away.

She advanced on him, step for step. Her mind continued to work. "You had Mr. Merriam killed too, didn't you?"

"I never heard of any—"

"Oh, yes, you did."

More pieces were falling into place as she spoke. From what Barb had told them at Ghost Ranch, the sequence of events wasn't hard to infer. Merriam had learned from his friend's son that *Cliffs at Ghost Ranch* was being sold at the Blue Coyote in Santa Fe and part of its supposed provenance was an old Galerie Xanadu exhibition catalog now in the archives of the museum.

Merriam knew that he'd never handled any such painting and had called the archives to say so. He'd spoken to Moody, who would have been highly upset to hear that he was not only still alive but ticked off, and was on the verge bringing the entire scam down around their ears. That had been enough to stamp the old man's death warrant right there.

"That was you he was on the phone with that day, wasn't it? That was you he was driving down to see. You killed him right on that same stretch of highway you tried to kill *me* on." She jabbed the gun at him. "*Didn't* you?"

"I—" Moody's hands jumped up in alarm. He leapt backward.

And for the second time in two minutes he caught his heel on the very same basalt boulder, was once again upended, and again wound up wedged into the corner, limbs thrashing, like a beetle on its back.

"Stay still, damn you!" Alix commanded.

Moody kept thrashing and managed to get himself turned over but didn't quite dare to stand up.

"I'm warning you," Alix said, "don't...get...up."

But Moody, never taking his eyes off her, warily gathered his legs under him into a crouch.

"Don't push me," she said, tight-lipped. "I mean it. Get down." When he didn't move, she slowly, purposefully leveled the pistol at his forehead the way her instructor had taught: arms extended but elbows not locked, left hand cradling the heel of the right He didn't sit back down, but he didn't get up either, and for long seconds they just stared at each other. He was working up his nerve, she could see that. Her own adrenaline rush had peaked. It was starting to drain out of her now, and her bravado with it. *What now?* she thought. Was he really going to get up? And then what? Could she really shoot another human being—even a murderer—if it came down to it? *Yes*, she told herself for the second time. She'd try not to kill him—she wanted him around for interrogation by the police and the FBI; there was a lot to be explained—but she'd sure as hell put a bullet in his thigh, or arm, or whatever it took. Yes, but what if one bullet didn't put him down? What if…? No. No *what ifs*. She would do it, all right; whatever she had to do.

Moody thought otherwise. Tentatively, but steadily, he started to straighten up.

"Sit…down," Alix said with quiet force. Her arms had lowered a little from fatigue, and now she lifted them again, carefully aiming at his right shoulder and holding her hands rock-steady. She took one step closer. Her finger began curl around the trigger.

And to her immense relief Moody caved in, throwing up his hands and dropping to the ground. "All right, I'm sitting down! See, I'm down!" He was staring up at her with undisguised dread.

No, not exactly *at* her…

She spun on her heel, and there, to her astonishment, was Ted, ten feet away, slowly, calmly advancing, with his own gun unholstered and in his hand, but pointing at the ground. "That's good, that's fine," he said soothingly to Moody. "Alix, you stay right where you are too. Lower the gun, though."

She did, with a surge of relief. "Am I glad to see you," she breathed when he got to her side. It took willpower to resist the urge to lean gratefully into him for support—her knees had suddenly turned to Jell-O. "I can really use a little help here."

Ted took the gun from her—her fingers had locked on it; he had to pry them up—and looked from the cowering Moody to Alix and back again to Moody.

"I tell you, buddy," he said with the ghost of a smile, "looks to me like you're the one who could use the help."

CHAPTER 21

By noon the next day, the rest of the pieces had dropped into place despite Moody's refusal, on the advice of his lawyers, to answer any questions. Some pieces fit more securely than others, but the overall picture was now clear. The forgery scam had had only two major players, Liz and Moody. Liz found the foreign buyers and did the selling, and Moody saw to it that the faked paintings found their way into the museum's exhibition catalogs, where potential buyers could see for themselves their "authenticity" and "provenance." Brandon Teal—the late Brandon Teal—had forged the paintings, all right, and then one or two other people—hired help, essentially—had been involved in the technical work of faking the catalog pages. Of course, only the catalogs of defunct galleries like the Xanadu were used—real galleries, but long out of business and thus impossible for the potential buyer to contact.

This had all been pretty definitively established when Mendoza got a warrant and sent two of his people to the museum archives, with Ted in attendance. In the catalog of one long-vanished old gallery or another, they had found every single one of the forgeries that Ted had been investigating. In addition, a close examination of Ted's digital copies of the forgeries revealed that Teal's "just-in-case alibi," the little human figure, was there every time, sometimes hard to spot, but definitely there.

Other questions had been answered with the help of a bit of surmise on Ted's and Mendoza's parts and a little less certainty. Why had Teal been trying to steal his own painting? Because (they believed) the arrangement all along was that the fakes would all be sold far away—outside the country—and when Teal learned that *Cliffs at Ghost Ranch* was going to someone from Seattle, someone who'd hired an art consultant to boot, he got cold feet. He went to Liz's office to pull out, found her dead, and took advantage of it to grab the picture. And would have succeeded, too, if Chris and Liz hadn't come along.

As to why Teal had then been murdered, the likely answer had emerged from a check of his telephone records. After four months with not a single call placed to Clyde Moody, Teal had telephoned him Saturday morning, twelve hours after Alix and Chris had collided with him outside Liz's office. So much was solidly established. More surmise filled in the rest. Mendoza's and Ted's hypothesis was that, given his rather memorable appearance—six-four, red-headed, red-bearded—Teal would have known it was only a question of time until the police zeroed in on him as the would-be thief of the painting. Terrified at the idea that he would surely be the prime suspect in Liz's murder (Teal was a famously overwrought man; he turned out to have a medical history of somatization disorder—what used to be called "hysteria"), he had called Moody in a panic: What should he do? Where could he go? Moody would have realized that Teal was a loose cannon who had to be dealt with, and soon. A few hours later, he was dead, the victim of a bathroom "fall."

Clyde Moody, it seemed, was quite sensitive to loose cannons, and the theory was that Liz's being one had been what had gotten her killed as well. This, in fact, had been Alix's contribution, quickly seized upon by Mendoza. During her interviews with him after Moody's arrest, she had told Mendoza about his very evident discomfort at the Blue Coyote when Liz, well into her cups, had been going on and on about "Cul-lyde" and making coyly suggestive allusions to the "amazing things" he could come up with from his "musty old archives."

"And a few hours later, *she* was dead," Mendoza had responded, nodding.

"And obviously, I was a loose cannon too," Alix had said, "but how did he know that? Sure, I went to the archives to look at those Xanadu catalogs, but that's exactly what they were there for—to look at. What made him think I was trouble?"

It wasn't until the next day, when Ted was driving her to the airport for her commuter flight to Albuquerque, from which she would fly home, that she got the answer to that. The Santa Fe police had been reviewing the museum archives' recent visitors' log and had been contacting the people who had spent time with Moody over the last few days. One of them was a woman named Clara Simons from the College of Santa Fe, a questioned-documents expert, and when Moody had asked what her interest in the Xanadu catalogs was, she had no reason not to tell him the truth: that she was following up Alix's visit because Alix had questions about their authenticity. And once again, Moody had wasted no time. The very next day there had been the unsuccessful road chase, and the day after that his frantic, desperate attempt at murder in Kit Carson Memorial Park.

Alix expressed concern that, other than the testimony that she herself could provide about Moody's trying to kill her in the cemetery, everything else that pointed specifically to him was based on inference and extrapolation. Would that hold up in front of a jury in a murder trial? But Ted had set her mind at ease on that as well. Eddie Sierra, the driver of the "Bimbi" pickup, had beat the odds and come out of his coma the previous night. The district attorney had already made him an offer that he couldn't refuse, and Sierra had identified Clyde Moody as the man he knew as "Harry," and Harry as the man who paid him to run Chris and Alix off the road…and to do the same thing (successfully) to Henry Merriam a few months back. So that would be two more counts against Moody: one of attempted premeditated murder, and a second of murder-one. And then, of course, Mendoza had just gotten started on his investigation. There was little doubt that, by the time it was completed, Moody would go away for a long, long time.

— • —

When they got to the airport parking lot, Ted switched off the ignition and turned to face her. "Well, it's certainly been…interesting knowing you, Alix. Not too many dull moments."

"Same here," she said. "Quite stimulating. It's the very first time I've been shot, you know." On its own, her hand crept to her thigh, where, under a gauze pad, the bullet graze throbbed away. She'd had it dressed at the Holy Cross Hospital in Taos, where they'd told her it wasn't much to worry about; it was more singe than flesh wound, and it was probably going to sting for a few days. And they'd certainly been right about that.

"And the last, I hope," Ted said. "Let me ask you something. Did you enjoy it? Not getting shot, of course, but working on the case, the, the—"

"The thrill of the chase? Yes, I suppose I did." It was something that hadn't occurred to her before. "Enjoy" wasn't quite the right word, not with people getting killed all over the place, but close enough.

"Good, I was hoping you'd say that."

She looked quizzically at him. "Why?"

"Well, you know, the art squad occasionally needs to bring on a consultant, someone from the outside, and so we maintain a small pool of qualified experts we turn to when necessary." He smiled at her. "I was wondering whether you'd be interested in being part of that pool."

"Consult for the FBI?" she said, as astonished as she'd ever been in her life.

"Yes. Generally, it involves just a few days' work at a time. Oh, and you'd be paid for your work this time around—" his eyes twinkled, "—whether you want our stupid money or not."

"Well, I…I…sure, why not? I'd love to!" She couldn't help laughing at the sheer unexpectedness of it. "So what do I do now? Do I have to fill out some kind of form?"

"Of course you have to fill out some kind of form. This is the United States government you're dealing with. They'll also want to talk to you. Face to face. Can you come out to DC for a day or so in the next couple of weeks?"

She nodded distractedly, trying to get her mind around this extraordinary development. *Wait till Geoff hears about this!*

"Good. Here's my card. Give me a call when you're ready, and I'll set it up."

"Thanks. And thanks for the ride." She got out of the car, still dazed. *Who could possibly have predicted…*

"Oh, Alix?" Ted said just before she closed the door. "Maybe we could do dinner when you come?"

She hesitated. "Well…"

He smiled. "I'm not married, by the way. Not that you were wondering, of course, but I just thought I'd mention it. So what do you say? Could we? Do dinner?"

"Maybe we could," she said and watched him drive away.

All in all, a highly satisfying lift to the airport.

CHAPTER 22

A *Seattle Weekly* reviewer had described Sangiovese, Chris's wine bar, as *moltissimo rustico,* and so it turned out to be. Sitting in it was like being in a Tuscan farmhouse: rough-plastered, mustard-colored walls; flat, beamed ceilings; floors of unglazed dull pink tiles; and simple, sturdy chairs, stools, and tables of dark wood. The lighting came from upward-directed wall sconces that brought out the texture of the plaster. Sangiovese was between art shows, so the only decorations on the walls were a few hand-painted plates.

It was eleven o'clock in the morning, so except for an employee fussing about behind the bar, arranging bottles and glassware, Chris and Alix, at a table in a rear corner, had the place to themselves. Alix, having arrived back in Seattle the previous evening, had just finished bringing Chris up to date.

"Amazing," Chris said wonderingly, "just amazing. But one thing I still don't understand. If part of their scheme was to sell only to foreign buyers, why was she selling the picture to me? Why the exception?"

"I've been thinking about that too, Chris. Look, Liz had screwed up big-time. She'd blown all that money from Sytex and was in serious financial trouble, right? On the other hand, you got out at the same time, but you made some good choices, conservative investments, and you're doing fine now—better than fine. Would I be wrong in thinking she was the kind of person who'd find that hard to stomach, who'd want to get back at you, take you down a peg, even in her own mind?"

"Oh, I can't believe—"

"Especially considering her…well, her pretty befuddled state these days, what with the drinking and all."

Chris shifted uncomfortably. "Well, yes, maybe so," she admitted. "And then, of course, I'd just rejected her current boyfriend's pictures, Willy Moe Whatever."

"Cody Mack."

"Right, Cody Mack Whatever. Who knows, maybe that was the straw that broke the camel's back." A sigh. "Amazing," she said again. "Well, that's all water under the bridge. Now I have a very important question to ask you." She pulled her chair closer and peered anxiously into Alix's eyes, their faces on a level and only a foot apart. "So how do I look? Tell me the truth."

"Chris, the accident was only three days ago. You can't expect—"

Chris emitted a theatrical groan. "Oh God, you don't have to say it. I look awful, don't I! What do I do? Craig is coming in tomorrow. Maybe I should put him off, come up with some kind of excuse? You know, gangrene or something?"

"Don't be silly. He saw you a few hours after it happened, and it didn't scare him off then, did it? You look much better now. Way better."

Chris was doubtful. "Do I really?"

"Of course you do. Your nose isn't as swollen, and your hair looks great—"

"But I still look like a raccoon."

"Chris, you do *not* look like a raccoon! Trust me, I wouldn't lie."

A tiny flicker of hope. "I don't?"

"No, nothing at all like a raccoon." And then she couldn't stop herself. "Raccoons have black rings around their eyes. Yours have turned green."

Chris scowled at her for a second, and then they both dissolved in laughter.

"They're much more attractive now," Alix managed to get out, and they laughed some more.

"Oh, go away," Chris said, wiping her eyes, still laughing. "I have work to do."

Alix stood up. "See you later then. Six o'clock at the Salmon Cooker?"

"Right. And we can celebrate my new acquisition. You are looking at the proud new owner of *Cliffs at Ghost Ranch*."

Alix flopped back down, astonished. "You *bought* it after all?"

Chris smiled her satisfaction. "Today was the last day to pull out. I called Liz's executor, told him that's just what I was doing, that it wasn't genuine, and that I wouldn't touch it, certainly not for three million bucks. We talked about it for a while, and he finally said, 'Well, what *would* you touch it for?' And I said, 'How about three thousand?' And he said, 'Done!'" She chuckled. "Well, how could anyone resist a 99.99 percent price reduction, especially for something they liked? So now it's all mine once the police release it. A great souvenir."

"Of your near-death experience in the wilds of New Mexico?"

"Of an amazing adventure," she said, her smile widening, "and the beginning of a beautiful friendship."

– • –

Instead of going back to her condo, Alix walked down to First Avenue and got the Number 24 bus to East Marginal Way South, in the heart of Seattle's gritty industrial district, a few miles south of downtown. From there, consulting a Google map she'd printed up, she walked two blocks east, past corrugated metal sheds and old brick warehouses, until she found 51 South Hinds Street, a dingy, brown-brick building much like its neighbors. There was a single street entrance, a pockmarked, painted steel door that might once have been yellow, with "Venezia Trading Company" barely visible in fading letters that might once have been blue.

The door opened onto a short corridor with unpainted concrete walls and floor. Other than a grubby gray runner underfoot, two naked lightbulbs in the ceiling, and a few curling, fly-specked certificates from the building inspection department Scotch-taped to a wall, it was without adornment. The raw concrete emitted a chill, depressing smell that sent a shiver down her back and made her reconsider: after all, it wasn't too late to change her mind and walk away. She stood there undecided for a few seconds, then stiffened her back and pressed on.

At the end of the corridor were two wooden doors with frosted-glass panels that had fresh press-on signs: one said *Showroom,* the other *Offices.* She chose the latter and walked into a bullpen-type area with half a dozen small, glass-partitioned cubicles, and another more spacious one at the back for the boss. The smaller ones were all empty—no surprise, given that it was lunchtime—but lunchtime or no, the boss was in, working with great absorption at his littered wooden desk.

Her heart gave a lurch. He was so *old*! He was seventy now, she'd known that, of course, but his telephone voice, so much like that of the jolly, vigorous Geoff of her childhood, had misled her. The years in prison, she saw now, and the humiliation that went with them, had taken their toll. The plump, pillowy shoulders against which she'd once slept so comfortably on those long rides were bowed, his whole body shrunken and somehow collapsed in on itself. No one would call him "cuddly" now. Nor "ruddy" either. He was pale and haggard; a trim white beard (a *white* beard—on Geoff!) did little to hide the hollows and deep creases in his cheeks. As a middle-aged man in his curatorial years, he'd often been called on to hook a fake white beard over his ears and play Santa Claus at office Christmas parties. Now he had a real white beard, but no one would be likely to ask him to play Santa.

She got within a few feet of the doorless cubicle without attracting his attention.

"Hello, Geoff," she said softly.

He started. She thought she heard a faint intake of breath. He didn't look up, though, not for three or four long seconds, during which she wasn't sure what to think. Maybe this wasn't such a great idea.

At last he put down his fountain pen (he had never approved of ballpoints; at least that hadn't changed) and raised his head.

"Why, hello, my dear," he said, and the familiar, cheery voice did a lot to reassure her. The Geoff she remembered was still in there, alive and kicking. He might not look like Santa Claus anymore, but he still sounded like him—a British version, at any rate.

She came closer and stood in the doorway. "I, uh, happened to be in the neighborhood—"

At that unlikely declaration, an amused sparkle lit his eyes and suddenly there was a sort of shift in her vision; it was if she were looking at the Geoff of old.

"—and I thought maybe we could get some lunch somewhere."

He looked steadily at her. His only sign of emotion was the briefest of quivers in his upper lip, quickly brought under control.

"I believe," he said, "that I might manage to find the time."

The End

ACKNOWLEDGMENTS

The real-life exploits of our good friend Alica Lampert, Lieutenant (Ret.), San Diego Police Department, provided inspiration for some of Alix London's more exciting adventures.

Karen Stewart of CenturyLink gave us expert real-world advice on various happenings in the book.

Our agent, Lisa Erbach Vance of the Aaron Priest Literary Agency, provided active, energetic, and helpful advice and support—services above and beyond the norm—every step of the way. Thank you, Lisa!

Several of the book's scenes are set at Ghost Ranch (Abiquiu, New Mexico) and the Mabel Dodge Luhan House (Taos, New Mexico). These are real places and are described as accurately as we could manage. We owe our thanks to the helpful staffs at both of these historic, wonderful locations.

ABOUT THE AUTHORS

Photograph by Bob Lampert

Charlotte Elkins wrote her first novel while working at the MH de Young Museum in San Francisco. Published under the pseudonym Emily Spenser, it was the first of her five romance novels that have sold in twenty countries. She switched to writing mysteries when she realized how much fun it was to collaborate with her husband, Aaron. Their first novel, *A Wicked Slice*, was published in 1989; since then, they have co-written four more novels starring a golf-pro-turned-sleuth and several short stories, one of which, "Nice Gorilla," won the Agatha Award for Best Short Story of the year.

Aaron Elkins's novels have been published in thirteen languages and made into a major television series. He is the author of sixteen novels featuring forensic anthropologist Gideon Oliver and of three mysteries featuring art museum curator Chris Norgren. He has won an Edgar Award and a Nero Wolfe Award, and he shares an Agatha Award with his wife, Charlotte. Aaron's nonfiction articles have appeared in the *New York Times's* travel magazine, *Smithsonian* magazine, and *Writer's Digest*.